P9-EEJ-044

THE VISITOR IN THE NIGHT

"Jack, is that you?"

"No."

The sound of the voice, suddenly loud and deep and distinct, sent a bolt of ice through her. She clutched the sheets to her like a life jacket.

"Who—" she began, her voice trembling.

"Someone..." the voice said, and now the form took on more edges, moved out of the corner toward her. The pale oval appeared and disappeared again, cut with a slash of red at the bottom: a mouth.

The figure stopped at the foot of the bed. Now the face became wholly visible: a pale oval the color of a dead fish, two empty eyes like cutouts of darkness, a red bright slash of a mouth like a wound. He was enfolded in a black cape that swirled and snapped as if it were in a stiff breeze.

The temperature in the room dropped; dropped again....

HALLOWEENLAND

AL
SARRANTONIO

LEISURE BOOKS NEW YORK CITY

A LEISURE BOOK®

October 2007

Published by

Dorchester Publishing Co., Inc.
200 Madison Avenue
New York, NY 10016

ISBN-10: 0-8439-5927-4
ISBN-13: 978-0-8439-5927-7

Printed in the United States of America.

Visit us on the web at www.dorchesterpub.com.

To
Kate, Richard, and Emma:
Boo for Halloween.

HALLOWEENLAND

PART ONE

ORANGEFIELD

CHAPTER ONE

"I'm asleep, Jack."

Annoyed: his cold hands on her at one in the morning, she could see the illuminated clock face now that her eyes were open, hear his breathing, the catch in it that would make him snore later. Even facing away from him, she could smell the beer on his breath.

"I promised—"

"I don't give a *shit* at this point," she snapped, still curled up in a fetal position, legs pulled up, defensive, half-asleep. "You were supposed to come home five hours ago. We were going to try tonight. But instead you went out beering with your moron friends. Don't deny it, Jack—"

She gasped, not letting him hear it as he slid into the bed behind her, naked she could tell, his hands ice cold but soft as they had always been when he had first caught her eye, this boy of a man with the lock of hair in front that wouldn't stay put, and the violet eyes and the crooked smile. Her heart had melted the first time he looked at her. Melted like the saints and the nuns could not articulate, melted like time stood still and the moon

3

froze solid in the sky and she knew her life was changed forever. His mouth on her later that first time and a kiss unlike any she had dreamed about, two mouths becoming one and then, much later, after fumbling and some laughing, two bodies becoming one. This was nothing like the fairy tales, or the dirty books, or the cable channels only for women where everything was clean and bland with guitar or piano music and then the commercials. This was magic that no one could write or sing or tell you about in the bleachers behind the soccer field when you shared a cigarette with your friends and felt the first chill of autumn blowing up under your Catholic skirt like Marilyn Monroe's in that movie with the sidewalk grating. What the hell were the nuns thinking? Plaid skirts that looked like nothing but delayed sin, in navy knee socks and those black shoes shined to mirrors that made boys look up at your panties—

"Jack, at least let me turn around!" she gasped, surprised at his ardor which was never lacking.

And then turning in the dark to meet his lips and hands and her nightgown pulled up over her head and the panting and the arched back and then three wonderful bit-lip screams while he tasted her nipples and nipped her neck once and then again as he always did, little bites that left pale red marks and she had to wear a turtleneck for two days.

The nuns couldn't change you but they could make you blush at your own body still . . .

And then it was over. He ran his hand through her short hair and whispered, "I promised," and then added, which made her heart flutter, "a baby," and she murmured, sleepy, and then rolled over away from him again, naked, too tired to pull on the flannel, and returned to sleep.

CHAPTER TWO

Then:

Six hours later in the police station in shock, with her sister Janet with the pinched look and Baby Charlie asleep in the stroller behind her.

Detective Grant: he looked old, tobacco stains on his teeth and the index and middle fingers of his right hand. A sot's nose, webwork of tiny broken veins. But the eyes: they were hooded in the shadow of their sockets but wary as a hawk's. He was definitely paying attention.

He had a notebook out and a pencil, and kept looking from the pad to her and back again.

"Mrs. Carlin, let me make sure I have this right." He flipped back a couple of pages and read to himself, lips moving silently. Then the eyes were on her. "You say your husband came home at one o'clock this morning?"

She nodded, and Janet, beside her, shifted in her chair, plastic seated, uncomfortable. "Only tell him what you want to, Marianne."

Detective Grant ignored Janet. Those eyes of his, still waiting . . .

"Yes," Marianne said. "He . . . woke me up when he came in. I was asleep facing the clock. I'm sure it was one."

"And he was gone when the phone woke you up an hour later, at two o'clock?"

"That's right."

Cold. She felt so cold and numb and dead.

The eyes looked down at the notebook, then back at her. "You're *sure* of this?"

She hesitated, looked at the floor. Embarrassed. "We . . . made love when he came home. Then I went back to sleep."

The eyes. But she said: "I'm *sure* it was one o'clock when he came home!"

"Don't say another damn thing, Marianne," Janet snapped. Baby Charlie snuffled in the stroller behind her, then settled back into sleep. "We'll get a lawyer. I'll call Chuck now. He'll know what to do."

She made to get up, huffing her pregnant belly out of the chair, but now Grant turned to her. "Mrs. Larson, I'm just asking your sister some questions. This isn't an interrogation and I'm certainly not charging her with anything. I'm just getting the time line straight in my mind."

Janet glared down at him across the desk. "Then why are we in an interrogation room? I know that's what this is. I watch TV."

Grant leaned back in his chair. "As I told you, I thought it would be more comfortable, especially since they're painting the area where my desk is today. I didn't want you to have to inhale those fumes . . ."

"So you said," Janet said. She was studying the far wall, a mirror, and walked toward it. "There anybody behind there? Like I said, I watch TV—"

"No, there isn't," Grant said, trying to hide his impatience. "Though you're right, it is a two-way mirror."

Before Janet could say it, Grant heaved himself out of his chair. "Let me show you." He walked briskly past Janet to a door beside the mirror and held it open for her. "Have a look."

Janet peered in, noting the short, empty hallway, the view into the room through the visible part of the two-way mirror. "Just like television," she said.

Grant waited for her to have her look, then waited for her to return to her seat before reclaiming his own. As Janet sat down with an "Ooof," she commented: "If this was a real interrogation, you'd offer us a Coke or coffee."

Grant looked up from his notebook. "Would you like something?" he asked.

Janet shook her head. "That's all right. We won't be much longer, will we?"

"We're almost done." The detective studied his notebook and then leaned across the desk to face Marianne again. "You're absolutely positive about the time?"

Marianne nodded. She barely heard him, Jack on the table, under the sheet, the cold room, colder than his hands had been, he was so white, albino white except for the bruises. The side of his chest that looked like it had been crushed, purple, broken, worse than the veins on Detective Grant's nose, almost black. They wouldn't show her anything lower, his legs cocked at an odd angle under the sheet.

Baby Charlie awoke with a squeak, as if thrown out of a dream, and abruptly began to cry. Janet instantly heaved herself back out of the chair and fumbled with a blue bag that hung from the back of the stroller. She produced a half-filled bottle which she thrust at the child without looking at him.

The room was quiet again.

"The reason I ask . . ." Grant began, and then added to the silence in the room.

"You've asked her twelve times," Janet said bluntly.

Grant looked at his notebook and then flipped it closed. "I talked to the driver who hit Mr. Carlin myself. We gave him a Breathalyzer test, which he failed at three o'clock this morning, and a blood test, which he also failed. He's in custody now. He drove home after his car struck your husband, Mrs. Carlin, and he went to bed. We picked him up at his house. He was so drunk he didn't remember the accident. There were two eyewitnesses who saw the accident, both of them friends of your husband, and one of them, Petee Wilkins, gave us a partial license plate number. A couple of pedestrians also saw it from farther away . . ."

Marianne didn't want to hear, she was so tired, so frozen in time, this wasn't happening. His body so white, the black-and-blue on his side and they wouldn't let her see the rest, "I promised," he'd said, "a baby . . ."

". . . everyone we talked to," Detective Grant was saying, "was sure your husband was killed last night in front of Loughran's Bar at just before one o'clock in the morning . . ."

CHAPTER THREE

How many days?

She had no idea. Whatever they had given her worked too well. The wake, the funeral, the burial, all of it had been surrounded in fuzzy light. She felt as if she was packed in cotton candy. Janet, thank God, had acted like a commander in chief, leading her like a zombie, telling her when to sit, to stand, everyone else in the church on their feet and she was immobile, sitting down, staring at anything but the coffin. And then a soft tug, the hissed, "Get up, Marianne, for heaven's sake," and then a push here, a pull there, and then, finally, the empty house and even Janet gone.

Only the pills left.

How many days?

It was sunny out, Indian summer. It had been raining the day of the funeral. At least one day, then. Had the burial been on a Monday or Tuesday? She didn't remember.

She sat up in bed and groaned. As if Jack had never existed, she had already moved to the middle. She was staring at the red numbers of the alarm clock, staring at them, the bottle of pills next to the numbers—

9

With a howl of pain she lashed out with her left hand, knocked the pills and the clock to the floor.

"*Dammit!*"

She sobbed and kept crying, hands balled into fists against her eyes, rolling over onto her side of the bed and curling up against herself as she had that night.

"Jack, Jack . . ."

She opened her eyes and saw the blank face of the broken clock radio staring at her, the red numerals extinguished.

"Oh God, oh God . . ."

After another half hour she crawled like a zombie out of the bed onto the floor. She felt around until her hand closed on the bottle of pills, which had rolled under the bed.

Something gently brushed over the top of her hand, like the tips of trailing fingers, and tried to take the bottle from her.

"No!" she said, out of it, holding the bottle tight. "I want to!"

She ripped the top of the bottle off and quickly shook a mountain of pills into her palm, then into her mouth.

She crawled back into bed and slept again, still clutching the bottle like a precious keepsake.

CHAPTER FOUR

"That's it. Enough is enough," Janet announced.

Marianne forgot that she had given her sister a key to the house. Through a very thick fog, she heard Janet storming around downstairs, then clumping up the stairs.

She tried to feign sleep.

"Get the hell out of bed," her sister ordered.

Marianne felt something in her hand, opened her eyes and stared at the empty pill bottle. Her sister was there, yanking the bottle from her and holding it up for examination.

"How many of these damned things did you take?"

"Lot . . ."

"Goddamned idiot . . ."

Janet threw the bottle down. Marianne heard her sister on the phone, the tap of three buttons before sleep came again . . .

CHAPTER FIVE

A brighter yellow light, sharp edged like the world.

She opened her eyes and smelled starch. The sheets were still white in hospitals. There was a cool autumn breeze smelling faintly of pumpkins and leaves, an open window to her right. To her left was a white panel screen in sections that covered the length of her bed as well as the foot. The sound of a television behind it. A game show, *The Price is Right*. Audience laughter.

She took a deep breath.

As if on cue, the panel at the foot of the bed was folded abruptly aside and her sister was there, glowering.

"About time," Janet said. There was a chair behind her, Baby Charlie asleep in his stroller next to it. Two vases of unattractive flowers were set on a dresser behind the stroller. She could see the edge of the television now, mounted on the wall and swiveled toward her sister's chair.

"Catatonic in the other bed," Janet explained, reading her mind. "So I bogarted the TV. Feel like watching?"

"No."

"You're not going to keep up this gloomy shit, are you? It's getting tiring, and Baby Charlie's been missing his play group."

"How long . . . ?"

"You've been in this rat hole for three days. The candy machines don't even work. But they take Jack's insurance, thank God, and no one's asked me to sign anything." Her eyes dilated for a moment. "Except for Detective Grant."

Memory failed Marianne, then kicked in. "Grant . . . ?"

"The cop. They wanted to swab your business end, so I said go ahead."

She was more awake now, and frowned. "Why?"

"Apparently Detective Grant didn't like what Jack's buddies had to say when he talked to them. Especially that moron Bud Ganley. And since you were so insistent about . . ." She waved her hand, suddenly embarrassed. "You know."

Threads were slowly weaving together, her mind unfogging, a clear picture . . .

"He thinks I was *raped?*"

"Something like that. The detective thinks you may have been mixed up about the time, that ol' Bud paid you a visit after he brought Jack to the hospital. You know Bud, always on the make. And since you and Bud had a history . . ."

She was speechless, and Janet went on.

"He's a weird one, that Detective Grant. Looks haunted, to me. And a lush, too. Remember Chip Prohman? In my class at Orangefield High? He's a desk sergeant, now. I talked to him yesterday. He told me Grant's wife is dead, and he's been involved in some *real* weird stuff the last few years. You remember those Sam Sightings everyone talked about a few years ago? Folks tramping through the woods, looking for Samhain, the Celtic Lord of the Dead? The rumor was Grant was somehow mixed up in that. And all those rumors when the house at Gates' farm burned to the ground—he was in the middle of that, too, according to Chip. But Chip always was an asshole, so who knows . . ."

Janet's voice trailed off. Her unease hadn't left her. She glanced briefly at Baby Charlie for help, but he was snoozing contentedly, head tilted slightly to one side, a river of clear snot flowing from one nostril.

"Look," Janet said, "I didn't think it was a big deal. You were out like a light, and Grant was persuasive. He said they'd be lucky to get a sample after that much time, but apparently they did. A female nurse did it. I was right here, outside the curtain, the whole time. Took two minutes."

"You always hated Bud Ganley."

Janet's unease evaporated. "You bet I've always hated him. What's not to hate? And I wouldn't put it past the prick . . ."

"To come to my house and rape me after my husband had been hit by a car and killed?"

Janet looked at the floor for a moment, then shrugged. "When you put it that way, it sounds pretty damn stupid."

"What did Petee say?"

"You know Petee Wilkins. He'll nod his head like a bobble doll at anything Bud says. He swears Bud was with him the whole time. That they put Jack in Bud's car and drove right to the hospital. Then after they called you they went back to the bar." She snorted. "That part sounds right."

"Bud told me on the phone from the hospital that they couldn't handle what happened, that they had to have a drink. He was almost crying."

"So he and ol' Petee get drunk and leave you alone to

handle it. Like I said, that sounds about right. Well, Detective Grant doesn't believe either of them. He thinks Bud paid you a visit after they left the hospital."

"It was *Jack* who was with me!"

Janet just looked at her.

Baby Charlie came awake with a sudden intake of breath. Before he could start wailing, Janet expertly slid his bottle from its bag and plugged it into his mouth.

"Like I said, Marianne, I'm not going to be able to keep doing this."

"You've already done too much."

"Tell me about it." She locked eyes with Marianne, and her expression grew serious. "You still look a little out of it. You gonna try to kill yourself again? Can I stop worrying about that, at least?"

"Yes. It was stupid. And the weirdest thing is, I think someone was in the room with me."

"Come again?" Janet asked.

"A . . . spirit, trying to keep me from taking those pills. There was a hand . . ."

Janet stared at her as if she had just landed from Pluto. "You think *that* was Jack, too?"

Marianne looked away. "I don't know . . ."

There was a sudden chill in the room—as if clouds had pushed the sun away, and autumn had flipped over into winter. The pumpkin and fallen leaf odor had disappeared, leaving a chill. Marianne shivered, and looked at the window, which darkened for a brief moment, ushering in silence and cold, before snapping back to normal.

Her arms, she saw, were covered with goose bumps.

Her sister was speaking, fussing with Baby Charlie, making sure the straps on his stroller were secure.

"I've gotta go," Janet announced. "Now that you're awake, they'll probably want your bed and release you. I'll talk to the nurse and come back later to bring you home. Your house is clean, most of Jack's things are packed up and in the garage. You can decide what you want to do with them later. You're having dinner at my house tomorrow night. No argument. And you're going to call me before you go to bed tonight, and again when you get up tomorrow morning. And if I hear anything I don't like in your voice, a slur from pills or alcohol, or even cough syrup, I'm going to come over to your house and strangle you. Got it?"

Janet turned away from Baby Charlie to her sister, who was staring out the window blankly. "Earth to Marianne!"

Marianne turned and gave her a weak smile. "I've got it, Janet. Again, thanks for everything."

"You bet." She turned back to Baby Charlie and made a sudden sour face as an odor wafted upward from him. "Whew, little man, we need to make a stop at the changing station on the way out."

CHAPTER SIX

She felt like a visitor in her own house.

She remembered a similar feeling when she came home to her parents' house from college the first time. Janet was already married by then, right out of high school the year before, and the bedroom they had shared, which was still essentially unchanged, looked almost strange, as if someone else lived there. Everything was where it had always been—her bed piled high with stuffed animals, the shelf over the headboard lined with books, the rolltop desk open, a row of knickknacks, figures from *The Wizard of Oz* across the top, the bed tables with the funny-shaded lamps, little gold pom-poms hanging from the shade rims, two of them missing on her lamp, victims of their cat Marvel's hunting ardor. She knew every inch of this space, the messy closet, the red-and-white curtains, the floral wallpaper. She had lived in this room since she was a little girl—and yet, today, it all looked new to her, as if she was visiting herself.

That was how Marianne felt in her house today.

But there was a difference, because she was not coming home to the same house.

Jack's half was . . . gone.

It hit her immediately, when she looked at the hat rack in the front hallway and saw his baseball caps gone. There was only her own gardening cap, on its single peg. Normally it would have been hidden behind one of Jack's hats, which had always annoyed her. There were certain places—the living room closet, stuffed with his golf clubs, baseball glove, bowling ball—where he tended to crowd her out. The garage had been his, the basement his, even though he had been promising her for years to set up her sewing machine down there.

All of *him* was gone, now. The living room closet was nearly empty, three of her coats hanging forlornly. His side of the bedroom closet was bare. Even his muddy shoes and ratty sneakers had disappeared.

Marianne sat on the made bed, folded her hands in her lap, and stared at the open closet door.

Gone.

A movement caught her eye in the corner of the room to her left. The room was dark, the window open a crack, October twilight descending outside. Light washed in from the hallway closet.

"Jack?" she said, tentatively.

The shadow thickened, seemed to take shape, then drew into itself and was gone.

"Jack? Are you there?" She rose, walked to the corner of the room and put her hand out.

Something trailed along the top of her hand like a bare caress, and melted away.

"*Marianne . . .*" the faintest of faraway voices called.

She stood staring at her hand, at the blank corner of the room, listening to the wash of distant traffic outside.

CHAPTER SEVEN

"He was there."

Janet was getting tired of rolling her eyes. Chuck Larson had been truly interested in the beginning, but now that the dessert and coffee was gone he just wanted to escape to his TV room and a baseball playoff game.

"Honey—" he began, trying to rise.

"Shut up and sit down, Chuck. Unless you want to put Baby Charlie to bed."

Chuck sighed, settled back into his dining room chair.

Marianne looked from her sister to her brother-in-law. "I'm sorry, I shouldn't be going on like this."

"What we've got here," Janet said, "is you still trying to deal with your husband's death. My own feeling is that it's time to kick your own ass and move on. But you were never me, Marianne. So in the short run I'd say go with it. If it doesn't stop, we'll get you a shrink."

"I think it was really him."

Chuck, trapped in the sisters' conversation, tried to revive his own interest. "But all you saw was a shadow, and felt something on your hand, and heard someone whisper your name?"

"It sounded like Jack."

"Sounded like? Or was? Is there any of it that could have been something else? The shadow maybe from a passing car in the street? The touch on your hand a breeze from the open window?"

Marianne said, "And the voice?"

Chuck hesitated, shrugged. "In your head? A noise in the house, misinterpreted?"

"It was the same kind of touch as when I took the pills, when the bottle rolled under the bed and I reached for it."

Janet snorted. "That was a dust bunny, kiddo. I cleared them out myself. By the way, don't you ever clean that place of yours?"

Chuck smiled, hoping the evening was over. His grin didn't carry the room, however.

"Honey—" he began again.

"Yes! Please! Leave!" Janet said, exasperated. "Watch your damn game!"

Relieved, her husband raised his bulk out of his chair and headed for the door.

"But put the baby to bed first!" Janet commanded after him.

He physically flinched but kept walking.

Janet turned back to her sister. "How did you sleep last night?"

"Fine."

"Marianne—what the hell is it you aren't telling me?"

"What do you mean?"

Janet gave a grim smile. "You've never been able to hide anything from me. You know that. And you're trying now."

Marianne tried a blank look, then gave up. "I'm glad you let Chuck go. I didn't want to talk with him around."

"So he's not around. Talk."

Marianne took a deep breath. "I think . . . I'm pregnant."

"What!"

"I started throwing up this morning, and, well . . . I just know."

Her sister's face grew florid. "I'll kill Bud Ganley. So help me God, I'll kill him with my bare hands."

Janet suddenly pushed herself away from the table and got up. Somewhere in the depths of the house, Baby Charlie was crying, Chuck's voice trying to soothe him.

"I'm calling Detective Grant right now," Janet said. "He may be weird, but he'll take care of Bud Ganley." She stomped off toward the kitchen and the wall phone.

"Janet, don't!"

Janet stopped and turned around. Her face was flushed with anger. "Why the hell not! You were raped, and now you're pregnant! And I want to watch that son of a bitch Ganley swing by his balls in jail!"

CHAPTER EIGHT

Bud Ganley stretched out and crossed his long legs and wanted more than anything to put his boots up on the desk. But he instinctively knew that wouldn't be a good idea. He had the feeling Grant would kick them off, and there were a half dozen other cops of various ranks in the room who would like to take a poke at him. He'd already gotten rid of his tobacco chaw at Grant's insistence, and knew from the murderous look on the detective's face that if he gave the old man reason enough to pound him, Grant just might do it. And every other cop in the place would surely look the other way.

"Smells like paint in here," Ganley said, stretching his arms over his head and yawning.

"You know something?" Grant asked, tapping his pencil on the desk and staring at Ganley.

"No," Ganley said, looking at the ceiling.

"Well, I'll tell you anyway. The older I get, the more tired I get of guys like you. I've known you since you were, what, seventeen? And you're still the same punk at thirty-four."

Ganley smiled, showing white teeth through his thick handlebar moustache. "Thirty-five next week, Detective. You gonna throw me a party?"

Ganley looked down from the ceiling. For a moment their eyes locked, and Ganley's smile went away.

Man, this guy has weird eyes, Ganley thought. *The rest of him is a complete wreck, but those eyes have seen way too much.*

For a brief moment, a pang of something almost like pity went through the young man. Then that, too, went away.

Ganley grinned. "Can we get to it, please? I've gotta be back at work."

"As long as it takes, Bud," Grant said, lost in his notebook now.

Suddenly Ganley sat up straight and put his hands on the desk. "Look," he said, trying to make his voice sound reasonable, "you know I didn't lay a hand on Marianne—"

"I'm not sure of that, Bud."

The way Grant's voice sounded sent a chill through Ganley. "You're not gonna try to tell me that DNA test—"

Grant was regarding him with a level stare now, then gave a nearly imperceptible nod.

"That's *impossible!* I didn't do anything to her! I swear I didn't! Petee swore up and down I was with him the whole time! The nurses at the hospital—"

"You had time after you left the hospital," Grant said evenly. "And you certainly had motive."

Ganley exploded, standing up. His face grew red. "That was fifteen years ago! And those charges were dropped!"

Grant tapped his pencil against his head. "Not in here they weren't. You tried to rape Marianne when she was in high school."

"I was in love with her! And I got drunk and a little bit

23

out of hand!" Ganley abruptly sat down and put his head in his hands. "Oh, man . . ."

Grant waited patiently. Ganley looked at the floor for a few breaths, then looked up at the detective. "Look," he said earnestly, "straight talk, okay?"

"Fine with me."

"What I did back then . . ." He took a deep breath. "What I did back then was way wrong. I even knew it at the time. I guess they call it date rape now. Or at least attempted date rape. But I was nuts about her, absolutely out of my head. And I knew we were going to break up, and my head was just full of snakes and I was drunk—"

"No excuse. Not now, not back then."

Ganley took another deep breath. "Okay, you're right. And thank God I didn't really do it."

"But you would have, if Jack Carlin hadn't knocked you on your ass."

Ganley nodded. "Yeah."

"I always found it puzzling how you and Jack became such good friends, especially after he and Marianne hooked up after that night."

"It just happened, man! Jack's a great guy—*was* a great guy . . ." He put his head in his hands again and looked at the floor.

"You can leave, Bud," Grant said.

Ganley looked up, puzzled. "But you said about the DNA—"

"I didn't say anything. And like they say in the movies: don't leave town."

Ganley bounced out of his chair, suddenly grinning, his trademark bopping gait evident as he wove his way through the maze of desks in the bull pen. At the front desk he stopped and smiled at the sergeant. "Chip! How's it hangin'!"

Chip Prohman tried to put a dispassionate look on his fat face. "Hope you didn't get yourself in big trouble this time, Bud."

"Nev-ah, my man! Nev-*ah*!"

He was out the door, all eyes on him, except for Grant's, which were set like lasers on his notebook, while he frowned.

CHAPTER NINE

Something in the corner again.

Marianne came awake at a sound like two pieces of soft fabric being drawn one over the other. Reflexively, she looked over at the bedside table, but the clock, set back in place, was blank, broken. It was deep night, the window open a crack, cold breath of breeze barely bothering the curtains, no hint of moonlight in the darkness behind the curtains.

The sound came again, from the corner.

Marianne pulled herself up in the bed and stared into the gloom.

"Jack . . . ?"

The sound increased in volume. Now she heard a louder, more distinct sound, like a cape flapping. The shadow in the corner grew deeper in the soft darkness surrounding it, and a hint of blank white, like an oval, peeked out at her and then was gone.

"Jack, is that you?"

"No."

The sound of the voice, suddenly loud and deep and

distinct, sent a bolt of ice through her. She clutched the sheets to her like a life jacket.

"Who—" she began, her voice trembling.

"Someone . . ." the voice said, and now the form took on more edges, moved out of the corner toward her. The pale oval appeared and disappeared again, cut with a slash of red at the bottom: a mouth.

The figure stopped at the foot of the bed. Now the face became wholly visible: a pale oval the color of dead fish, two empty eyes like cutouts of darkness, a red bright slash of mouth like a wound. He was enfolded in a black cape that swirled and snapped as if it were in a stiff breeze.

The temperature in the room dropped; dropped again. Marianne shivered.

"Where's . . . Jack?" she managed to whisper hoarsely.

The figure tilted its head slightly to one side, but said nothing. Marianne noticed now that there were arms of a sort, also dead fish colored, and hands with unnaturally long fingers, enfolded in the cape.

"I wanted to see you," the thing said. It's voice was deeply neutral, without inflection.

Marianne shivered, hid her eyes as the thing drew up over the bed toward her.

"No!" she gasped.

She clutched the sheet and blanket to her face, felt a wash of cold unlike anything she had ever felt before. It was like being dropped into a vat of ice water. No, it was worse than that—like being instantly locked in a block of ice.

There was a wash of breath over her, colder still—

She opened her eyes, gasped to see that face inches from her own, the empty black cutout eyes regarding her, unblinking.

The mouth opened, showing more blackness still—

"No!"

She covered her face again, and, instantly, she knew the figure was gone.

She lowered the blanket and sheet.

The room was as it had been, the corner a stand of gloom, empty, the cold gone.

A breeze from the open window rustled the curtains, and she drew in her breath.

Something beyond them, in the night, moved past the window, a flat retreating shadow.

CHAPTER TEN

Bill Grant hated his empty house.

It was full of memories, all of them bad the past few years. Even when his wife Rose had been alive the house had not been a happy place, her depression regulating their lives like a broken wristwatch. When they had bought the place on his lousy beat cop's salary twenty years before, it had been filled with nothing but good memories. But when the dark moods began to overtake her, the parties stopped, and then the socializing altogether, and eventually even the amenities with family.

And then, abruptly, she was gone, leaving Grant with only his job, and all that other business—what Grant liked to call *weird shit*—that seemed to happen in Orangefield every Halloween.

And *weird shit* left nothing but more bad memories, which made his empty house feel even emptier.

So he did what he often did now, especially as Halloween approached, which was to sit in his chair in his finished basement with an open bottle of Dewar's scotch, get drunk, watch old movies, and hope to God that *weird shit* wouldn't happen.

Grant poured two fresh fingers of scotch into his favorite glass—what had once been a jelly jar from the sixties encircled with pictures of the cartoon character Yogi Bear (outlined in yellow), his friend Boo Boo (outlined in blue) and Jellystone Park (drawn, originally in a garish green). Over the years and thousands of dish washings, all but the faintest outline of Yogi's fat head was still visible, none of Boo Boo but one of his feet, and some bizarre section of Jellystone Park that may or may not have been a picnic table. Grant no longer remembered.

Grant used the jelly jar because it reminded him of himself: slowly fading away with each new washing of *weird shit . . .*

He downed the two fingers in two neat swallows and refilled the glass with two more fingers of scotch.

He hit the remote change button hard, angry that AMC had started to show commercials with their movies—he liked his westerns as neat and unblemished as his whiskey.

But Turner Classic Movies was showing a period piece, something along the lines of a 1930s version of *Dangerous Liaisons* without sex, so, grumbling, Grant hit the button hard again and put up with the few commercials breaking up the old John Wayne western *Stagecoach* on AMC.

"That's more like it!" Grant toasted the TV as the movie came back on. What a great John Ford flick. The only one he liked better was *The Searchers*. He'd have to buy it on DVD someday to avoid all the breaks.

He was refilling his glass yet again when a tap came on the casement window to his left.

He nearly spit his whiskey back into the glass, remembering the last time that had happened (*weird shit*), but then he went smoothly into cop mode, rose, and drew his 9mm out of the drawer in the side table next to his lounge chair.

The tap came again as he reached the window. Reaching up, he pushed the dirty white curtain abruptly aside.

There was a face there. A young girl . . .

She made a motion, and he recognized her. He nodded and pointed up.

The face retreated and Grant dropped the curtain back into place.

He grabbed the scotch and his glass on the way, thought better of it and put it back.

Leaving the TV on, he went upstairs, hearing his own heavy tread on the creaking stairs.

She was not at the back door, which was closest to the basement window, so Grant went to the front door and snapped on the porch light as he opened it.

"Come in, Marianne," he said, holding the screen door open for her.

"I'm s-s-so sorry—" she began, but he cut her off.

"Nonsense. Come in and sit down. Can I make you some tea or coffee?"

She looked like a scared rabbit. "C-c-coffee would be great."

"Are you all right?"

She nodded but was shivering like a leaf.

Grant moved past her into the kitchen, and she followed, sitting at the kitchen chair he pulled out for her. He fiddled with the coffeemaker, which had already been preprogrammed for tomorrow morning. After a few minutes of trying to fool the computer chip in it, he was able to get it to work. In a few seconds the comforting *blurp* and *drip* sounds commenced.

Grant sat down at the table across from the young woman. She was looking at her hands, locked in a prayerful grip on the top of the table, as if she had never seen them before.

"I haven't seen you in . . . what, two weeks?" Grant said, mustering his soothing cop voice. He knew he was pretty drunk, but was able to overcome it. He tried to lighten his tone and gave a small smile. "What's bothering you? Besides everything, that is?"

The girl continued to stare at her hands on the table. It was obvious she was trying to bring herself to say something, so Grant continued his monologue.

"I know what you're going through, Marianne. I lost my wife a few years ago. That hole still hasn't filled up completely. But it does get better, I can tell you from experience."

She was still fighting with herself.

"I . . . heard about your pregnancy, of course," Grant went on. "As you probably know, the DNA results on Bud Ganley were negative."

This was the spot where, like it or not, he would have to harden his voice a little. "You obviously did have relations with someone that night, Marianne. What I have to ask you is a hard question: who was it?"

Her eyes darted up from her hands, and Grant saw that they were filled with terror. For a moment, darker thoughts than Marianne Carlin's private life assaulted him.

"Detective—"

Her hands were trembling, now, and when he reached over to steady them they were cold as winter.

"Don't say anything yet."

He abruptly got up and went to the coffee machine.

The cycle wasn't finished yet but he yanked the carafe out and poured a cup for her anyway. He pushed the carafe back into its place and noted the spilled coffee hissing on the hot plate beneath it.

He wanted very much to go back to the basement and get his bottle of scotch. But after putting the steaming mug down in front of Marianne and taking a step toward the cellar door, he abruptly turned back and poured himself a cup of coffee.

"Milk or sugar?" he asked the young woman.

Her teeth chattering, she answered, "Milk, p-p-please."

He yanked open the refrigerator door, pulled out a quart of 2 percent milk, let the door close.

He sat down in front of his own black coffee, pushing the milk carton over to Marianne. When she made no move to open it, he did so himself, pouring it into her mug.

"Say when."

She focused on him, not on the coffee.

"Someone in a black cape with a white face was in my bedroom tonight," she said in a rushed, terrorized voice.

It might as well have been shouted through a loudspeaker. Grant dropped the milk carton, which hit the table and began to spill. He stared at it for a moment and then reached out and righted it.

Oh, God. Weird shit.

Marianne's eyes had never left his face.

To take his mind off of what she had said, he grabbed a dish towel from its rack behind him and sopped up the spillage with it. His mind was tightening and loosening like a fist.

Samhain.

When he was finished he tossed the wet towel into the sink and sat back down. She was staring at him with a pleading look in her eyes.

33

"Just tell me what happened," Grant said.

She did, every detail, and Grant's faint hope that she might have been delusional, or worse, faded.

"Detective Grant, what's happening to me?"

He opened his mouth to speak, thinking of a hundred ways to answer her question, but then said nothing. Mustering all of his cop's resources, he forced his lips into the same small smile he had showed her at the beginning of the interview.

"Drink some of your coffee. Believe me, there's nothing to worry about."

Like hell there isn't.

For a brief moment, her face showed relief. "You know what I saw? I'm not crazy?"

With all of his effort, he made his smile widen. "The last thing you are is crazy. I've seen this kind of thing before in Orangefield. For now, I just want you to forget about it."

"Really?" Her voice was filled with something like hope. "I called my sister, and she said it sounded like a Sam Sighting. She was laughing when she said it. But I heard—Janet heard—that you've been involved with this kind of thing before. The trouble at the Gates' farm—"

It took all of his effort not to scream. "Leave it to me, Marianne. I'll look into it for you. If it makes you feel any better, other people in Orangefield have reported the same kind of thing you have."

And almost all of them ended up dead.

Her hands had stopped trembling and were cradling her coffee cup.

His forced smile widened even more. "You'll do what I say?"

She suddenly nodded. "All right. But what was that thing I saw?"

His smile was locked into place, and he let his tired eyes crinkle in what may have looked like merriment. "It may be something, or nothing at all. Let's call it a 'Sam Sighting' for now, if you want."

In all innocence, she said, "What if I keep seeing it?"

"Just . . . don't worry. It won't hurt you."

A lie. You don't know that.

"Do you feel better now?" he asked.

She looked down at her coffee cup, nearly empty, and nodded, then smiled. "Better than I have in . . . a while. Thank you, Detective Grant. I . . . usually end up talking to my sister, and she's . . . well, a bit overbearing."

Grant forced himself to laugh in concurrence.

"Are you seeing a doctor?" he asked.

"Doctor Williams."

Grant nodded. "I know him. That's good, Marianne."

Without realizing it, he had risen and was ushering her out of the house. At the front door he stopped her and gently took her arm.

"If you need me, anytime, night or day, call me." He fished one of his ever-present business cards out of his wallet and gave it to her. "All the numbers are on there, at the station, home and cell. Don't hesitate. I'll . . . protect you, Marianne."

"Protect me?"

He forced a smile back onto his face. "Don't worry. I'll call you to make sure you're all right."

She took the card and suddenly raised herself on her toes and pecked him lightly on the cheek.

"Thank you, Detective."

"I need to ask you one more time, Marianne. Are you absolutely sure it was your husband with you that night?"

Her eyes were unblinking. "Yes."

"All right."

She was out the door and gone into the night.

He closed the door, locked it.

Samhain.

Ignoring the dirty cups in the kitchen, the coffee still warming which would taste bitter in the morning, he stumbled to the basement stairs and forced his feet to descend them. He sat in his lounge chair and, after looking at the curtained casement window, stared at the television. *Stagecoach* on AMC had been replaced by another, inferior western, riddled with commercials he didn't even register.

Weird shit.

Slowly, methodically, he emptied the Dewar's bottle, hammering himself down into sleep, and false peace.

CHAPTER ELEVEN

"Bud?"

The voice was deep, not at all friendly, and Bud Ganley didn't even bother to stick a hand out from underneath the truck and give the finger. After all, he was earning a buck now, and didn't owe anyone anything. This clown could wait. If it was a cop, screw 'im, if it was a customer, screw 'im, too. Whoever it was, he could talk to the boss, Jim Ready. Bud was just the hired help.

"Bud Ganley?"

"Eff off," Bud said from beneath the truck, continuing to work on mounting the rebuilt engine. He'd been sloppy with the chains and the block and tackle, he knew, but if he got it in place soon everything would be fine. If he didn't have this truck finished and ready to go today, Ready would really fire him for sure.

"I'd like to talk to you, Bud."

"I said—" Ganley began to snarl, but suddenly it became very dark around him and he was no longer beneath the truck in Ready's Garage.

"What the—"

"I was polite, and that didn't work. So, now I'm not polite."

It was so dark he thought he was in the middle of the woods somewhere. But it had been broad daylight, eleven-thirty in the morning, almost lunchtime, so this couldn't be . . .

He tentatively reached up and felt the engine block, swinging slightly on its chain cradle, above him.

"Jesus, I'm blind!"

"And dumb, and deaf as well, Bud. I've watched you for a long time, but never been much interested in you until now."

"I can't see!"

"You'll see again. Don't worry about that."

Now there was something in front of him in the darkness, where the engine block should be—a swirling black thing that came closer and then hovered above his face. He saw something rise out of the folds of black—a pasty face with no eyes and a smiling red mouth.

"Let's talk, Bud."

"Who the hell—"

"I'm someone who wants to talk."

"What do you *want?*" Ganley said in a panic.

"I want to know if you planned on seeing Marianne Carlin again." The thin red mouth added with emphasis, "And I want you to tell me the truth."

"Yeah, sure, why not? I mean, her old man's gone now, right? Why shouldn't I see her? Who knows, she may fall for me yet, right?"

"Didn't you try to . . . hurt her once?"

"What are you, some sort of cop trick machine? Is Grant in there behind the costume?"

The thing looked for a moment as if it were going to laugh, then the red lips became straight and grim.

"How would you feel about leaving Orangefield, Bud?"

"What! Eff you! I've lived here all my life! No way!"

"What if I asked you to leave, and never come back and never think about Marianne Carlin again?"

"Christ! Now I *know* Grant's in that costume! Eff you, Detective! You can't tell me what to do and I don't listen to anybody but me!"

"That's what I thought. You've always been that way, and I'm sure you always will be. Thank you for talking, Bud, and thank you for your honesty."

"Eff you!"

The black thing with the white face was gone. Now the blackness dissolved around Ganley, as if someone pulled a blindfold away. He saw the engine above him at the exact moment it slipped its chains and fell toward him.

He got out one puppylike squeal before it hit.

CHAPTER TWELVE

"Thanks for seeing me, Doc."

Williams smiled his crusty old doctor's smile. "Country doctors always like seeing their old patients, Bill. I miss Rose a lot. I remember all those bridge games years ago—"

Grant cut the doctor off before he could go into one of his ten-minute reminiscence sessions.

"Doc, I'm here to talk about Marianne Carlin."

Williams' long, hound dog face formed a frown. He rubbed his chin. "Well, gee, Bill, we might be getting into doctor-patient confidentiality areas there—"

"I already know she's pregnant," Grant said. He wanted to reach for a cigarette but thought better of it here in Williams' office. Out in the hallway a nurse stopped at a doorway directly opposite and slid a form into a plastic holder mounted on the wall. A moment later she ushered a woman and a young, sniffling child into the room and closed the door after them. She gave a quick glance into the office and nodded at Williams.

"I'll be there in a minute, Martha."

The nurse nodded again and walked briskly away.

Williams leaned back in his desk chair and put his hands behind his head. "If you know she's pregnant, then why are we having this conversation?"

Grant said, "I need to know if she's *really* pregnant."

Williams frowned again, then nodded. "You mean an hysterical pregnancy, something like that?"

"Right."

The doctor scratched his cheek, rubbed his chin, looked at the ceiling. "Well, then, once more we enter that gray area, Bill . . ."

"It's important. I think she may have been raped the night her husband was killed. I thought it was Bud Ganley, but a DNA test cleared him."

"Bud Ganley." Williams frowned. "I just got off the phone with the coroner not twenty minutes ago about Bud Ganley."

"What about him?" Grant asked. The hair on the back of his neck began to prickle.

"He's dead, Bill. Surprised you haven't heard about it yet. Truck engine slipped its block and tackle chains while he was mounting it from below, crushed his head like, well, you provide the image. Grape, tomato, whatever. I was on duty at Orangefield General earlier today when they brought him in." He made a sour face. "If it had been yesterday, would have been my friend Gus Bellow instead of me looking at him. Wish it had been."

"Is his body still at Orangefield General?"

"Probably transferred it to the funeral home by now. He'll be in the ground in a few days. Won't be much of a wake, I imagine. I never did like that kid much. He was the kind that would take two lollipops from the jar."

Grant said nothing, which caught the doctor's attention. "You okay, Bill?"

"Just thinking . . ."

The nurse appeared again in the doorway and made a scolding motion at Williams.

"All right, all right," the doctor said, nodding. He pointed to the watch on his wrist. "One more minute, Martha. I promise."

As the nurse retreated Williams turned back to Grant. "They're stacking up out there like planes over an airport. Gotta go."

"Is she really pregnant?"

"Now, Bill—"

"I told you, it's important. She seems to think she is."

Williams asked, "When was the last time you saw her?"

"A week and a half ago. She came to my house. I've talked to her on the phone a few times since then, but haven't seen her."

Williams rose and came around his desk as Grant got out of his chair. The doctor put his arm around the detective's middle, brought it up to his shoulder and squeezed. "You know, if I was your doctor, and I am, I would tell you to cut down on the cigarettes, which I can smell on your breath, and your drinking, since I felt what is probably a pint bottle in your raincoat pocket as I reached around you just now to bring my hand up to your shoulder. You see, I have to be a detective in my work, too." He sighed. "I remember ten years ago, when your Rose and my Gladys, God rest both of them, dragged us to all kinds of things, it seemed every Saturday afternoon . . ."

His extended reminiscence was cut off by Grant's stone face and the reappearance of Martha in the doorway. The doctor nodded to her and then leaned over to whisper into Grant's ear.

"Point is, you're a lousy detective, Bill. She's got a belly on her you can see a mile away."

"Wha—"

Williams whispered, "She's five months pregnant, Bill."

CHAPTER THIRTEEN

"Think of it as a favor, Mort. A big one."

"You got that right. You think I've got nothing else to do than run lab tests on closed cases? That kid Ganley's dead, right?"

Grant spoke evenly into the receiver. "Right."

"And he was your number one, right?"

"Correct."

"And he came up neg, right?"

"Correct again."

"And now you want me to run not the other idiot, what's his name, Petee Wilkins, but—"

"Yes, Mort. That's what I want you to do."

A long pause on the other end, then a snort. "You got it, hojo. Though God knows why I'm doing this."

"Tomorrow, Mort?"

"A.M."

There was a click in Grant's ear.

CHAPTER FOURTEEN

Marianne Carlin didn't answer her phone, so Grant drove to her house. It was chilly and getting chillier, October marching steadfastly away from Indian summer and toward winter. The sky was a stark, cold, deep blue, a shade particular to this season. The elms and oaks were in full riot, bursting with red and yellow, already starting to shed. The road was littered with a beautiful blanket that had not yet become a nuisance and danger, waves and dunes of leaves that filled gutters, washed over curbs and clogged storm drains.

Already, a few pumpkins were out on stoops, uncarved but waiting for nearing Halloween.

Grant avoided the center of Orangefield, where the leftover bunting would still be strung for the Pumpkin Days Festival, which thankfully had ended. A week of drunken teens, greedy locals and a bloat of tourists in the Pumpkin Capital of the World living by the twin unwritten Orangefield codes of "Have A Good Time" and "Make A Buck." Ranier Park had been turned once again into a mecca for commerce, with two huge circus tents erected—one filled with aisles of Halloween wares, the other a haven for lovers of bad live music, with seven days of varied fare: country, rock and roll, jazz and, heaven forbid, rap music. For the first time in ten years Grant had avoided Pumpkin Days duty, taking part of the week off and burying himself in administrative work the rest. It had been a blessing.

Marianne Carlin's house, a tidy ranch, was on a tidy street. The lawn was dotted with leaves not yet in need of raking. There was no pumpkin on the stoop, but a clutch of Indian corn hung from the front door, which was painted red.

As Grant parked his Taurus, Marianne emerged from the side of the house, wearing gardening gloves. Sure enough, now that he looked, she showed a belly, even beneath her painter's overalls.

Grant caught up with her as she entered the yawning opening of the garage next to the house. He found her fumbling around in a wheelbarrow, which was filled with gardening tools.

He cleared his voice and she turned around, startled.

"Oh! Detective Grant!"

Grant smiled. "Sorry."

She smiled, too, and regained her composure, handing Grant the trowel she had plucked from the wheelbarrow. "Would you carry this for me?"

She walked past him, and led him back to the side of the house, where a tangle of dead weeds and still-blooming annuals clogged a small plot.

"It's a mess," she explained, taking the trowel from him. "I pretty much ignored it this year. But I thought going at it might be good for me. For the plants, too."

"Marianne, why didn't you tell me you were five months pregnant?"

She had knelt down to plow at the black loamy soil, and looked up at him. "Because I didn't know. I didn't know until the day after Jack died. I started to feel sick, and then I started to show. And every day I seem to show more."

Grant heard a car door slam. He turned to see Marianne's sister Janet trudging toward them over the lawn. In the backseat of her Buick, Baby Charlie waved his arms from his car seat. His face was red and he looked to be wailing, but the closed car and the distance prevented him from being heard.

Janet stopped and put her hands on her hips, regarding Grant. "You again! Just the man I want to see!" She reached out and grabbed Grant by the elbow, tugging him away. As Marianne began to rise Janet pointed at her. "You stay there. I'll be back in a few minutes and take you to lunch."

Marianne obeyed, and Grant was hauled over the front lawn toward his car, parked in front of Janet's. She had a grip like a bench vise.

She let go of Grant's arm and faced him.

"Actually," Grant said, "you're the one I want to see. Did you know your sister was five months pregnant?"

"Five months my ass." She pointed to her own belly. "*I'm* seven months pregnant, and I've been puking since day one." She jerked a thumb at the Buick. "Same thing happened with Baby Charlie. Puking and feeling like puking for nine months straight, and showing after two. Big as a house. It runs in our family. *Nobody* escapes it. And I'm telling you, Marianne wasn't pregnant five months ago. I would have known. I've got radar. I can sense it. When she started to feel sick after Jack died, *then* I knew she was pregnant. But she wasn't till then. She *couldn't* have been."

"Why?"

"Jack had a vasectomy when they got married. In fact, he had it reversed the day he died. He and Marianne had decided to have a kid. Marianne told me he'd promised to come home early that night, so that they could start trying to get her preggers. But instead he went out celebrating with those two asshole friends of his. Macho manhood and all that crap. Did I mention I'm glad Bud Ganley is dead? One less loser in the world."

"Is there any chance Marianne was having an affair, and got pregnant five months ago?"

"*Ha!* My sister? She was wild crazy in love with Jack Carlin, and he was the same with her. No way in hell."

She put her hands on her hips again. "My turn. You're the guy who knows all about the weird stuff in this town, right?"

"Well—"

Janet didn't let him continue. "Marianne's been acting just plain strange. And getting stranger. She tell you about the guy with the cape?"

"She came to see me right after it happened. I've been calling her on the phone every few days since then to make sure she's all right. Every time I phone her, she says she's fine."

"Oh, you need to catch up, Detective. This cape character's been back just about every night. Now she says he's her friend, and that she's not afraid of him anymore. She even calls him Samhain. I stayed with her one night in her bedroom, but didn't see a damned thing but that dog shit ugly wallpaper of hers. The next night she claimed he was back. Either she's nuts, or there's still something mighty screwy going on."

Grant said nothing.

"It's like she's in a fog. A couple weeks ago, she was just

beginning to show. Now she's bigger than me." Janet took a deep breath. "The thing I want to know is: if she's pregnant, five months or otherwise, how the hell did it happen?"

"I don't know."

"Well, I've said my piece," Janet continued, shaking her head, "and now you know everything I do. I gave you that stuff of Jack's you asked for when I was cleaning out the house, and I'll help any other way I can. I think my sister would have been just fine by now, after Jack's death, if all this other monkey business hadn't started. I'm worried about her, but I don't know what to do. Maybe you can worry about her, too. Between the two of us we can do a lot of worrying."

She turned and shouted to Marianne, "Come on! Let's go eat! I'm starving!"

Marianne threw down her tools and stood up. She looked even more pregnant than she had when Grant arrived.

Janet was shaking his hand. "Thanks for listening, Detective."

She dropped Grant's hand, and trundled over to help her sister into the front of the Buick.

Grant couldn't help but be struck by how much bigger than her sister Marianne looked.

CHAPTER FIFTEEN

"You're sure, Mort?"

"Ninety-nine point nine percent. I'm positive if we did the full test every marker would match. This is the guy, all right."

Grant was silent.

"Just to make sure," Mort said, "I took samples from both the hairbrush and the toothbrush. Same result."

Grant made a sound that was something like, "Thanks."

"And you said this guy was her husband? If he was dead how could he—"

Grant said, "Exactly," and hung up the phone.

CHAPTER SIXTEEN

It always seemed to rain at burials. There was a blue tarp over Bud Ganley's casket, which Grant had no doubt was a cheap one. There were only a handful of mourners: Ganley's mother, his employer, Jim Ready, a couple of like-aged slouchers who looked like pool room buddies, and Petee Wilkins, who stood off by himself. Grant had made his way into the back end of the cemetery, through a small stretch of woods, and stood at the top of a moderate rise looking down at the proceedings below. His raincoat collar was up against the chill, and his cigarette was used up.

He lit a new one and watched as the reverend finished his ministrations and the two slouchers, who turned out to be the grave diggers, began to lower the casket into the ground. They pulled the blue tarp off it then, and Ganley's mother threw a clod of dirt on it and turned away, not looking at Petee Wilkins. The way she walked told Grant that this was the last in a long line of disappointments.

Petee stood watching as the two grave diggers began to shovel the mound of waiting dirt into the hole. Grant ambled down the hill and approached him. Too late to flee, Petee noticed him and stood rooted to the spot, looking at the ground. Grant was struck by how much Wilkins looked like a skinny rat, down to the twitching nose and sniffles. He had always been a follower. Grant had first met him when Wilkins was twelve, and got caught trashing a house on Sagett River Road. The punk he was with got away, but Petee got caught. He was the kind who would always get caught.

"'Lo, Detective," Petee said, running the back of his hand across his continually running nose. He wouldn't look up. Grant was reminded of Baby Charlie.

"I just have one question to ask you, Petee," Grant said.

"Sure. Whatever."

"I want you to tell me the dead-ass truth, and if you do I won't bother you again. That's a promise."

Petee's nose twitched, and his shoulders spasmed up and down with what might have been a form of assent.

"Okay?" Grant asked.

"Sure."

"Just answer me this. Did you and Bud Ganley take Jack Carlin home before you took him to the hospital?"

Petee drew the back of his hand quickly across his running nose. His nose twitched twice. "No, Detective Grant."

"Are you sure? Look at me, Petee."

Wilkins glanced up briefly. Even his dark brown eyes were small and ratlike. "He wanted us to, but we didn't!"

"He was alive after that car hit him?"

Petee was staring at the ground again. Behind them, the two grave diggers went about their work, which lent a susurrus of shoveled dirt to the conversation. "Yeah, but just for a couple of minutes. At first he begged us to take him home. Then he got all glassy eyed and kept calling for Marianne, saying he had to go to her. That he had promised. He started yelling a bunch of stuff." He glanced up at Grant briefly again. "Then he was gone. He died right there in the street before we put him in Bud's car and took him to the hospital."

"Why didn't you tell the police that he was alive after the car hit him?"

Sniffle, wipe. "Bud was afraid we'd get in trouble. And I was afraid."

"Afraid of what?"

Twitch, shrug. "Afraid . . ."

"Tell me, Petee, or we end up down at the station with you in a holding cell."

"Oh, shit." He shuffled his feet, looked back at the grave diggers, who were wiping their hands, stared at the ground again. Grant noticed that his knuckles were white, his hands trembling. "Afraid . . ."

"Petee—"

"I was afraid of what he said, and what happened! I believed Jack, is all! Bud ran to get his car, and Jack was all busted up and dying, and he stared right through me and was yelling, 'I promised you a baby! I promised!' And then . . ."

"And then what?"

"And then he died, and . . ."

Grant was about to prod him again when Petee blurted, with a groan, "And something flew out of his body and away, Detective! Smoke, or fog, or . . . something that looked just like Jack!"

"Petee—" Grant began.

"Aw, shit, Detective," Wilkins said, wiping his nose and then his eyes. He was crying now. "Can't you leave me alone? Can't you just leave me the hell alone? All my friends are dead now, and my life is shit. Can't you just lay off me?"

Grant took a long breath, and said, "Sure, Petee. Like I promised."

Wilkins turned abruptly, almost stumbling into one of the grave diggers, who was loading his shovel into a wheelbarrow, and walked off, hitching sobs and wiping at his face with his hands.

Grant stared after him for a moment, then turned and made his way up the slope, lighting a cigarette. The rain had turned to a chill mist, coating fallen leaves and making their brilliant colors slick. The trees were almost denuded now.

It was two days till Halloween.

CHAPTER SEVENTEEN

Grant had never heard Doc Williams sound flustered, let alone frightened. But frightened was what he sounded on the phone.

"You'll come to see me right now, Bill?"

"Of course. But why don't you just tell me—"

"Not on the phone. And for God's sake not in the office. I'll be in the coffee shop in the strip mall across the street."

"I'm on my way."

Williams was not there when Grant walked into the coffee shop, but he walked out of the men's room a moment later. He was pale as a sheet, and looked unwell.

He motioned Grant to the booth farthest from the counter, in an empty corner of the shop. Grant sat down and the laconic waitress, chewing gum, ambled over and asked him if he wanted anything. "Doc here already ordered coffee for ya, new pot's brewin', be a few. Any pie? Cake? Pumpkin pie's good t'day."

She stared over his head, and Grant told her that just coffee was fine.

"Be back when it's ready."

She turned and shuffled back to the counter, where an open newspaper awaited her.

Grant turned his attention to Williams. "Let me guess before you tell me. Marianne Carlin is more than five months pregnant."

To his surprise, Williams nodded and waved that off. "Yes. Actually, she's almost reached term. I'm not even going to try to explain it." Williams stared straight into Grant's eyes. "I was threatened, Bill."

"By whom?"

"He was . . . very insistent. Told me that if I went near Marianne again he would kill my family, and me. And . . . he told me not to go to the police for help."

Williams glanced nervously past Grant to the front window. At that moment the waitress was shuffling toward them with two mugs of steaming coffee, which she set down ungracefully, managing to spill some onto the table.

"Sure you don't want to try the pumpkin?" she asked, not quite stifling a yawn.

Doc said quickly, "Thanks, May. We're fine."

She turned and shrugged, shuffling back to the counter. "It's real good pie . . ."

"Why did you call me, Doc?"

"Because he said I could tell you, and only you. He said to tell you his name was Sam."

Samhain.

Doc Williams was still talking, and Grant had missed some of it.

". . . on the telephone. I thought it was a prank at first. I was sitting in my office, and picked up the receiver, and

56

my hand up to my elbow went cold, as if it had been plunged into ice water. I thought for a second I was having a stroke. The voice told me what I just told you, and then said to tell you that Marianne Carlin was to be left alone until Halloween was over. He said you would understand. And that was it. When I put down the phone receiver my arm was back to normal, not ice cold anymore."

Williams looked at Grant with a special pleading. "In the afternoon, when I was leaving for my rounds at the hospital, something was waiting for me next to my car in the parking lot behind my office. It was this 'Sam' creature, all black swirling shadows and a white face like a horrid Halloween mask. He repeated what he'd said and told me to call you. He came up close to me and his breath smelled like . . . *nothing*. Like empty space. I thought he was going to kill me on the spot. What the hell is going on, Bill? Would this thing really hurt my family?"

"Yes," Grant said. "I think he would. Do what you were told. Let me worry about Marianne Carlin."

Williams stared at his untouched coffee. "I've never seen anything like this, ever, Bill! I'm a *doctor*! Who the hell is this 'Sam'?"

Grant waited a moment before answering: "He's the thing you fight every day, Doc."

CHAPTER EIGHTEEN

Grant's finger was getting numb from pressing the door-bell at Janet Larson's house. He'd peered through the front windows—everything looked normal, a scatter of toys on the rug, a half-empty bottle on the coffee table in the living room, a changing bag nearby. There was a Buick in the driveway, the same one Grant had seen at Marianne's house. The doors, front and back, were locked. An uncarved pumpkin sat on the porch next to the door, the outline of a to-be-cut face fashioned in magic marker.

"Y' won't find 'em there, mister!" a voice called, and Grant turned to see an old woman staring at him from the property next door. She had stopped precisely at the border between the houses, next to her driveway. She had a face like a lemon, and Grant noticed that there was no pumpkin on her stoop.

"Do you know where Mrs. Larson is?" Grant asked, stepping down from the porch to better talk to her.

"Left early this mornin', the whole bunch of 'em! Piled

into the SUV like Satan was chasin' 'em. Kid squawking like always."

"Do you have any idea where they went?"

The old woman made her face look even more sour, turned around, waved her hand in dismissal. "No idea, 'cept they had a couple bags with 'em. Usually means they're off to New Hampshire, to his brother's in Derby. Only place they ever go." She stopped and turned around, making a sudden fist and shaking it at the house. Her face became very red. "Used t' take in their paper when they went away, but they're ingrates! Not even a thank-you! Young and selfish."

Her face lost its color, and she turned and walked slowly back to her house. "Well, they'll get what they deserve when they don't dish out any candy to the little monsters tomorrow and the house gets egged."

There were three Larsons in Derby, New Hampshire, and the second was the right one. After some negotiation with Chuck, Janet finally got on the phone.

"Make it quick, Detective. Baby Charlie needs a change."

"Why did you leave so quickly?"

There was a long silence on the other end of the phone. "Let's just say I was asked to."

"By whom?"

"He said he knows you. He also said he'd kill Chuck and Baby Charlie if we didn't go."

"Did you—"

"I don't have time for this, Detective. I'm too busy being scared to death. As you've seen, I put on a good bluff, but underneath I'm just a grade-A chickenshit like most people. I believed what I was told."

"When—"

"I stayed at my sister's house again last night, Detective. Most of the night there was nothing to look at in the corner of her bedroom but that ugly wallpaper. And then there was something else. And, well, here I am."

"What if your sister needs you?"

"She's on her own, now. All she did was coo and sing, anyway, when this thing appeared. He seemed pretty fond of her, too. Me, I don't like ghost stories, much less the real thing."

Grant started to ask another question, but the line went dead.

CHAPTER NINETEEN

Riley Gates' farm was, now, one of the saddest places on Earth. In its prime, when Gates, a former police detective and Grant's mentor, had been alive, it was a place Grant always looked forward to visiting. When they had both been married, and before Rose became sick, there had been many parties at Riley's place, and even after Riley divorced and Rose died, Grant had still considered Riley Gates one of the finest men he had ever known.

But now . . .

Driving past the long-closed farm stand on the main road, with its faded sign RILEY'S PICK YOUR OWN PUMPKINS, and then through the broken front gate over the rutted road and up to the blackened, gutted, burned house, Grant felt nothing but hollow. He parked near the barn, its paint peeling, one door off its hinges and the other ajar. He got out of his car and walked toward the rutted field that, in earlier years, would have been filled today with families picking their last minute Halloween pumpkins. This year only a few misshapen rogue fruits had grown, pale-colored, wilting and untended. There was a cool breeze in the late day kicking up dust devils in the fallow plot. The sky was growing blue-purple, and the sun in the west, directly across the field, looked shimmering orange, like a pumpkin hiding behind a veil.

Riley's weigh station—a hand-built square booth that had once held a huge scale, long stolen, with a chair beside it, still miraculously in place—stood forlorn at the edge of the field. Grant went to it and sat down in the chair. He faced the lowering sun, shook out a cigarette from its pack, lit it and waited.

CHAPTER TWENTY

"Hello, Detective Grant."

Grant came awake with a start. For a moment he was disoriented in the darkness, then he remembered where he was. There was something in front of him, moving in and out of vision, a deeper darkness than the night. It had turned colder, and Grant felt a chill. The sky had clouded over, and it felt like it might rain.

Grant sat up, pulled his raincoat closed and shivered. His hand went to his pocket and pulled out the remains of a pint of Dewar's.

"Still imbibing, I see," the shape in front of him said.

"Any reason not to?"

"It's been a while."

"Not long enough for me."

The thing was silent for a moment. Grant felt a deeper chill, catching a glimpse of that white face, that cruel red line of a mouth.

"I hoped I'd never see you again," Grant said.

Samhain's smile widened perceptibly. His surrounding black cloak hung almost lifeless, swirling slightly at the bottom. "I'm sure. But I rather enjoy your company. And it seems we have mutual business—again."

With every ounce of his courage, Grant fought to stay under control in front of this . . . *thing.*

"Oh, come now, you're not afraid of me anymore, are you, Detective?"

"Why shouldn't I be?"

"What is there to fear? You already know who I am, and what I represent. All men face me eventually. Don't you consider it a privilege to . . . shall we say, interact with me now and again, before your time?"

"It's a privilege I could pass up."

Samhain threw back his head and gave something like a laugh. It sounded hollow and cold. "I have been studying your kind for thousands of years, and still you puzzle and interest me."

"What is it you want, Samhain?"

"Ah." The blackness swirled, the Lord of Death came closer. Grant felt the temperature drop, a dry cold that belied the weather.

"I merely want you to leave Marianne Carlin alone."

"Why?"

"Because she has something I'm . . . interested in. Mr. Ganley was going to bother her, so I had to dissuade him."

"I thought so."

Samhain turned back to Grant and came even closer. "I cannot scare you off, Detective, like I did the doctor and the sister. We both know that."

"You tried once before."

"I did. And I failed."

"You'll fail again. I won't let anything happen to Marianne."

"You think I want to *harm* her, Detective? You don't understand at all. That's the last thing I want."

"Then what *do* you want?"

"I'm not ready to tell you, Detective. But I will tell you this. Tomorrow is Halloween. Please leave her alone until the day is over."

"I won't let you near her."

Samhain gave something like a sigh. "We both know that I can only bring direct harm to those who can be influenced. I cannot influence you. You know many of my tricks, but not all of them. I would prefer that we discuss this . . . reasonably."

"I don't think that's possible."

After a pause, the shape said, "I thought we understood each other."

"I doubt it."

The thing swooped up very close, its surrounding black form snapping and moving in the cold breeze. Grant felt the deeper cold of its breath on him, and the white face was very close to his own.

"Don't. Interfere."

Grant held that empty gaze, felt bile rise in the back of his throat, felt a black cold charge run up his back and make his teeth chatter. Samhain reached out a spectral hand, long white vaporous fingers ending in short, sharp silver claws, and held it in check in front of Grant's face.

"Listen to me, Detective."

"I won't let you near her."

The figure receded to its former position. The face was half-hidden again, the shadowy folds of its surrounding darkness part of the night itself.

"We'll see."

All at once the thing was gone, leaving only the cool night and a few stars peeking from behind scattering clouds.

His hand trembling, Grant brought the last of his whiskey up to his mouth and drank it.

CHAPTER TWENTY-ONE

"Wake up, Petee."

Petee Wilkins was having the only good dream he ever had. He had it every once in a while and always enjoyed it. In it he and his best friend Bud were in the house they broke into on Sagett River Road, eating from a huge box of chocolates they had found in the kitchen. Petee had never seen a candy box so big, covered in gold foil and tied with a silky red ribbon. The card had said, "To Bonny, Please, please forgive me! Signed, Paul." They had gotten a good laugh over that.

"Wonder what the old poop did!" Bud laughed, stuffing his face with what turned out to be chocolate-covered cherries. After a moment of bliss he cried, "Ugh!" and spat them out onto the kitchen table, which was huge and marble topped. "I *hate* chocolate-covered cherries!"

Petee laughed and then gagged, spitting out his own mouthful of candy, which he had actually been enjoying.

Bud started laughing, holding his stomach, and then Petee began to laugh, too.

"Funny!" Petee said.

Bud took the box of chocolates and dumped it out on the floor. Then he began to stomp on the candy, making chocolate mud.

After a moment Petee joined in, and then Bud said, "Come on!" and they tramped into the living room, leaving chocolate sneaker prints on the white rug.

There was much more to the dream, trashing the living room, throwing a side chair through the large screen TV—

But now Petee abruptly woke up.

"Oh, no—" he said, looking at the hovering, flapping, black thing above him with the oval white face.

"Now how can you say that, Petee?" Samhain asked.

"I thought you were gone for good," Petee whimpered.

"Didn't I tell you I might need you someday?"

"Sure. But I didn't think . . ."

"That's right, Petee, you didn't think. But you don't have to. I did you that favor back in . . . what was it? Junior high school?"

Petee nodded, wiping the back of his hand across his running nose. He sat up in bed and looked down at the covers, not at the thing.

"That's right," Samhain said, "I kept you from getting into big trouble when you and that idiot Ganley drowned the Manhauser's cat. Oh, your father would have beat you to death if the police had been involved in that one, don't you think?"

Petee would not look up. "Yeah," he said, grudgingly.

"And what did you promise at the time? Didn't you promise to do me a favor if I ever needed one?"

Eyes downcast, Petee nodded.

"Good. And now it's time. Here's what I want you to do, Petee . . ."

CHAPTER TWENTY-TWO

Another Halloween.

The day dawned gray and bloodshot. Grant woke up in his lounge chair in the basement with a sour taste in his mouth. A finger of scotch lay pooled in the bottom of the Dewar's bottle on the table next to the chair. The glass next to it was empty. The television volume was low, the movie on Turner Classic Movies a film noir with too much talking.

Grant got up, walked to the casement window and pushed the partially open short curtain all the way open. A mist of rainwater covered the storm window, and the sky through it was battleship gray–colored and low.

He could just make out a row of pumpkins, already carved into faces, frowns on one end slowly turning into smiles by the other, on the rail of his back neighbor's deck. It was a yearly tradition.

He turned off the television, oddly missing the sound after it was off, and trudged up the stairs to the kitchen. He checked the back door, which was locked and bolted, and then the front.

Back in the kitchen, he made eggs and toast and a pot of coffee, then dialed into work from his cell phone.

"Chip? This is Grant. Captain Farrow knows I'm not coming in today, right? You told him, like I asked?"

The desk sergeant said something, and Grant snapped, "Then tell him now, you dimwit. I won't be in."

Grant pushed the off button on the phone and tossed it onto the kitchen table.

From upstairs there came a sound, and Grant froze in place, listening. Then it came again, bedsprings creaking. The detective relaxed, turning back to his eggs, which were bubbling and snapping in the frying pan now.

After breakfast he cleaned up the kitchen, poured a second cup of coffee and went back down to the basement. A sour rising sun was trying to fight its way through the scudding clouds.

Maybe it would clear after all.

Grant settled himself back in his chair, turned the television back on and watched two westerns back-to-back, muting the sound every once in a while to listen for sounds upstairs.

At eleven A.M. he went back upstairs and pulled a fresh bottle of Dewar's from its bag, which he had placed on the dining room hutch the day before. He brought the bottle downstairs. He emptied the last finger of scotch from the old bottle into the glass, twisted open the new bottle and added another finger.

A sound from upstairs, a moan, and Grant set the bottle of scotch on the TV table, took his glass, and went up to the kitchen.

"Shit."

Another moan followed, and Grant slowly trudged up the stairs to the second floor of the house. There was a short hallway with two bedrooms and a bath off it. He passed the bath and his own bedroom and stood in the doorway of the other, sipping scotch.

Marianne Carlin lay on her back on the guest bed, the covers kicked aside, half-asleep.

Her belly under her nightgown was huge.

As Grant watched, she moved her head from side to side, eyes closed, and moaned again. Grant thought he saw something move in her belly, like a snake under a sheet.

Grant went to the bed, put his glass down on the bedside table and picked up the washcloth that lay folded on the edge of the water bowl there and dipped it into the water. He wrung it out and patted the young woman's forehead with the cloth.

Marianne mumbled something in her sleep, the name, "Jack," then wrenched herself over onto her side away from him and began to softly snore.

Grant rearranged the covers over her, folded the washcloth back on the edge of the bowl, retrieved his alcohol and left.

Another movie brought him to lunchtime—a grilled cheese sandwich—and then two more short old westerns got him to four o'clock in the afternoon. The schools were out by now, and the younger trick-or-treaters would start soon. He went upstairs to check his candy bowl by the front door, and for good measure added another bag to it, which made it overflow. He picked up the fallen Snickers bars and put them in his pocket.

He glanced outside and saw that the sun had lost its all-day fight with the gray clouds and was dropping, a pallid orange ball, toward the western horizon.

A porch light flicked on at the house across the street, which seemed to trigger a relay—two more houses lit up, one of them with tiny pumpkin lights strung across its gutter from end to end, the other with a huge spotlight next to the drive illuminating a motor-driven, wriggling spider in a rope web arranged in the lower branches of a white birch.

Back in the basement, Grant noted that the pumpkins on his back neighbor's deck railing were now lit, flickering frowns to smiles.

He tried to watch another movie, but his palms had begun to sweat.

Upstairs, the doorbell rang. He went up to answer it. Two diminutive sailors, one with a pirate's eye patch, looked up at him and shouted, "Trick or treat!" They thrust their near-empty bags up in a no-nonsense manner, glaring balefully at him.

He gave them each two candy bars, and they turned immediately and fled sideways across his lawn to the next house. Grant was closing the door as a mother, parked watchfully in a Dodge Caravan at the curb, began to shout, "Use the sidewalk, Douglas . . . !"

The van crept up the street, following Douglas and his fellow pirate.

As Grant was stepping back downstairs the doorbell rang again, and soon he was sitting in the living room with the lights out, smoking his second cigarette, waiting for the bell to ring.

It did, again and again: hobos, men from Mars, ballerinas followed by more hobos.

There was a lull, and Grant went into the kitchen, made another grilled cheese sandwich for dinner.

The doorbell rang again.

Abandoning the grilled cheese sandwich, Grant grabbed a handful of candy bars, yanked open the door—

Petee Wilkins was standing there, snuffling, looking at the ground. There was something in his right hand, which he jerked up—

Instinctively, Grant twisted aside as Petee's eyes briefly met his and the gun went off. It sounded very far away and not very loud. But it must have been a better handgun than Grant assumed, because the slug hit him in the side like a hard punch. As Grant kept twisting, falling into the candy basket and to the ground, he heard Petee hitch a sob and cry, "I'm sorry!"

Then Petee was gone.

Grant lay stunned, and waited for pain to follow the burning sensation of the bullet.

It came, but it wasn't as bad as he feared.

As he sat up, a lone trick-or-treater, dressed in some indeterminate costume that may have represented Mr. Moneybags from the board game Monopoly, complete with miniature top hat, stood in the doorway looking down at him. He said the required words and Grant fumbled on the ground around him and threw a handful of candy bars his way.

"Gee, thanks, mister!" Mr. Moneybags said, and ran off.

Grant scooped as much of the candy around him as possible out through the doorway, then stood up with an "Oooof" and, holding his side, kicked the door closed.

He limped into the kitchen and had a look.

There was blood on his hand, which was not a good sign, but there wasn't a lot soaked into his shirt, which was. He pulled his shirt out of his pants, took a deep breath, and studied the wound.

Just under the skin, left side, in and out, looking clean. He knew he would find the slug somewhere in the front hallway.

"Thank you, Petee, you incompetent asshole," he whispered, and cleaned the wound at the kitchen sink as best he could. He tied three clean dish towels together and girded his middle.

The blood flow had nearly stopped already.

The front doorbell rang, but he ignored it.

He called the police dispatcher, whose name was Maggie Pheifer, identified himself, told her to have a patrol car visit Petee Wilkins' father's house, where they would probably find Petee Wilkins hiding under his own bed. "Consider him armed and dangerous, just in case. I'll call back in later."

From upstairs came a moan, louder than the others.

"Shit," Grant said and, taking a deep, painful breath, hobbled to the stairs and limped his way up.

CHAPTER TWENTY-THREE

Marianne Carlin's eyes were wide open. She lay pushed back on the bed, knees apart. She was breathing in short little gasps.

"Hello, Detective," Samhain said calmly from the foot of the bed, where he floated like a wraith. "I see Petee didn't do his job, which is just as well. I really didn't want you dead, only . . . incapacitated."

Grant felt suddenly short of breath, leaned against the doorjamb. He slid down to the floor, staring at Samhain.

"My, my," Samhain said, "Petee seems to have done a fine job at that."

"What do you want, Samhain?" Grant said, gasping. There was a growing pain in his left side, which wasn't going to go away.

Samhain said nothing, staring at Marianne Carlin, who gave a moan and arched her back.

"You want the baby," Grant said.

"Yes," Samhain said simply.

"Why?"

Again the wraith was silent as Marianne threw her head

back in pain. Grant wanted to help her but felt as if his body was filled with lead. He could barely lift his left arm.

"Do you know what ghosts are, Detective?" Samhain said, quietly. "It happens now and then that someone on the way to my realm from yours gets . . . caught in the middle. These are usually very strong personalities. Often, there is something very important that they are leaving behind. Unfinished business, if you will.

"This was very fortuitous for the one I serve. Let us say we have been . . . waiting for this to happen. And let us also say that my master was able to . . . make use of it."

Samhain stood silent vigil at the foot of the bed, staring at Marianne Carlin in a kind of wonder.

Grant said, "The baby is from your world."

"Oh, no, Detective. This child is from someplace far worse than Death. This child *is* something far worse than Death."

Grant gasped, gathered his strength. "What have you done?"

Samhain turned a mild, almost fond, look on Grant. "I serve, nothing more. And after many tries, over many years, the one I serve, the Uncreator, will finally enter this world . . ."

His attention was brought back to Marianne, whose cries were coming more closely together. Her stomach was taut with effort, her legs spread impossibly wide.

"It will not be long now . . ." Samhain said, in wonder. He moved up over the foot of the bed to hover above the birthing woman.

Grant took a deep breath and pushed himself back against the doorjamb. With a supreme effort he stood. For a moment the world went black, but he held his position and when his sight cleared he urged himself forward.

"Don't interfere, Detective," Samhain snapped.

"That thing will destroy the world."

Samhain laughed. "Much more than that, I fear."

Grant took two halting steps forward and then the pain in his left side flared to broiling heat. He stumbled, reaching out to clutch at the side of the bed as he fell to his knees. He pulled himself up, fighting for breath, to see the crown of a baby's head appear between Marianne Carlin's legs.

"Good, Marianne, good!" Samhain urged, as the young woman screamed and arched and pushed.

Grant took a long shuddering breath, put his right hand into his coat pocket, resting it on the butt of his 9mm handgun.

Samhain moved up and closer over the woman, almost alive with excitement.

"Push, Marianne! Push!"

Marianne Carlin screamed. The baby's head appeared, a gray wrinkled thing with closed eyes and a puckered mouth.

It was followed in a rush of blood by the rest of the body, tiny hands and skinny legs and tiny feet.

Samhain moved over the baby, straightened, his head thrown back, his red mouth opened wide.

"*Master!*" he cried.

The thing on the bed kicked, and then its tiny mouth and slitted eyes opened.

It looked up at the thing hovering overhead and wailed, a hollow, long, hoarse shriek of joy.

"How delightful—a girl!" Samhain cried.

Grant tightened his grip on the 9mm.

Marianne Carlin was not moving on the bed. There was a frozen look of abject terror on her face, and there was way too much blood.

Instinctively, Grant knew that she was dead.

The thing on the bed, gray and pale and otherworldly, held its tiny hands out to Samhain, and opened its mouth again.

Samhain turned to Grant. "I told you not to interfere," he hissed.

Grant's grip loosened on the handgun, and he fell to the floor and saw black.

PART TWO

ORANGEFIELD

FIVE YEARS LATER

CHAPTER TWENTY-FOUR

"Hey, Bill, you see this?"

From his desk, where he sat contemplating walking out into the midmorning heat to smoke a cigarette, Grant swiveled his hooded eyes up at Desk Sergeant Chip Prohman, who was standing in front of him and pointing excitedly to the front page of the Orangefield *Herald*. There was a drawing of something that looked like a large Ferris wheel centering the page, and a banner headline with the word "Halloween" in it that Grant could not make out.

"What is it?" Grant asked unenthusiastically.

In answer, Prohman held the front page out straight, and now Grant could read the entire headline: HALLOWEENLAND COMING TO ORANGEFIELD!

"What the hell is Halloweenland?" Grant growled.

In answer, the sergeant lowered the paper to Grant's desk and read, following along with his finger, "'Halloweenland will be the largest Halloween-themed attraction ever mounted in the United States. "It's a modern descendent of the quaint Halloween Hay rides and monster walks," said its principal owner, Mr. Dickens. When asked his first name, Mr. Dickens, who, this writer must admit, looked something along the lines of one of his scary attractions, smiled and said, "Just Dickens will do."'"

Grant grunted. "Just what Orangefield needs, another ghoul."

Prohman went on, still following with his finger. "'According to Mr. Dickens the theme park, to be built on a fallow piece of land just outside town, will employ some of the latest technology, but will mostly remain true to the traditional carnival Halloween scares and attractions that patrons have come to expect. "Some may find it quaint," Dickens said, "but I can promise all will find it enjoyable."

"'Mayor Gergen, when reached for comment, stated that "Halloweenland represents a great leap forward for the Orangefield community. It will put us on the map once and for all as the premiere holiday destination for Halloween."'"

The desk sergeant paused and took a deep breath, as if reading were great exercise for him. He put his finger back on the story. "'It is estimated that Halloweenland will generate, in its first year, upward of $200,000, some of which would benefit the town. Though the mayor would not give specifics, citing confidentiality, it is surmised that Mr. Dickens was given generous tax breaks to bring his attraction to Orangefield.'"

Prohman looked up. "That's it."

Grant pulled the paper toward him and turned it around. There was nothing more, and the picture of the Ferris, he noted, was nothing more than a stock drawing from the Bettman Archive.

He pushed the paper back at Chip Prohman, who took it eagerly and went back to his own desk. Grant would have bet a twenty that the fat desk sergeant was thumbing his way to the comics page at this point, where the reading wasn't such a chore.

Grant turned his eyes back to the classified ads of the *Boston Globe*, one of a pile of current major city papers on his desk. His cigarette break was forgotten; it would wait till later. His computer screen was on, too, set to one of a list of east coast dailies with online presences.

There was nothing in the *Globe*, either in the classifieds in answer to the discreet inquiry he'd been running there for more than four years, or in the news section. He dropped the paper onto the pile next to his desk and picked up the *New York Times*.

He felt eyes on him, and turned to his right to see Captain Farrow's office door open. The captain filled the doorway, glaring at Grant. "See you a minute?"

It wasn't a request.

The door closed in dismissal. Grant got up and crossed to it. He could see the captain settling himself behind his desk through the frosted glass as he opened the door and let himself in.

"Sit down," Farrow ordered.

Grant left the door open and sat in the single chair in front of the captain's desk.

Farrow steepled his fingers and continued to glare at Grant. His head was completely bald, which somehow accentuated his scowl.

Farrow said, "Have you gotten anywhere with the Pallman burglary?"

Grant shook his head no.

"Why not?"

"Nowhere to go. I'm sure it's the same two high school morons who broke into that house on Saver Road two weeks ago. There's only so much—"

"How much time have you logged on it? Mrs. Pallman

called and said you spent a total of four minutes at her house. She says she got the feeling that you had better things to do."

"Your words or hers?"

Farrow's face reddened. "Actually, mine. I repeat: how much time have you logged on it?"

Grant took a deep breath. "Four minutes."

To Grant's surprise, Farrow's face went placid. He almost looked like he was going to smile. He put his hand on a sheet of paper on his desk. "Thank you for being honest," he said. "I have your log for the past few months, and it looks like you haven't been doing much of anything except this"—he waved his hand in dismissal—"five-year-old missing persons case." His beady eyes locked on Grant's. "True?"

Grant nodded. "True."

Before Grant could continue or expand Farrow held his hand up. "I don't want to hear again how important it is. I don't want to hear anything. It's over."

Grant waited for more, and now Farrow was nervously moving the piece of paper in front of him around.

"You're fired, Bill," Farrow said quietly, not looking up. "I cleared this with Mayor Gergen, and with the district attorney. You've been drunk on the job eleven times in the past six months, you've been ignoring your duties, you're a mess, it's done." His voice fell to almost a whisper. "Get your things together and leave."

Now he looked at Grant again, and his eyes were filled with something almost like pity. "Look at yourself, Bill! You need to dry out! You need to stop smoking! You lost your house, you almost lost your car—yes, the finance company called here—you've lost almost everything. You can't be a cop and act like that."

Something in Grant's eyes made Farrow look away again. "Please, Bill, just go. Before it gets embarrassing."

Grant swiveled in his chair to see two burly uniformed cops, Paige and Jenner, standing just outside the doorway.

"We'll help you with your stuff," Paige said quietly, staring at the floor.

"There's just one thing," Grant said, turning back to look at Farrow. There was sudden quiet in the room. Despite all of the feelings running through Grant—sorrow, rage, regret for the badge he would no longer wear—he almost burst out laughing. The moment was just like one of the classic westerns or Dirty Harry movies he had watched.

The silence stretched, and then Grant said, pulling out his shield and pulling his .38 police special from its holster and placing them on Farrow's desk, "I'm still a cop."

CHAPTER TWENTY-FIVE

The boxes of newspapers were under the card table that served as his computer desk. The screen displayed the homepage of the *Providence Journal*. Grant poured himself two fingers of scotch and put the bottle back down on the packing crate that served as his bar. There was an unmade bed against one wall, his television and DVD player on another packing crate next to the single window. Under the window was his only other luxury, a dorm-style refrigerator that hummed all night and sometimes kept him awake, when he was able to sleep at all. It was filled with beer and a single stick of butter. There were no pictures on the walls, no mementoes, knickknacks, keepsakes of any kind. When he had sold the house he had sold it furnished, by choice. Farrow had been wrong about that—he hadn't lost his home. He had needed its sale to finance the search, the private detectives, the newspaper subscriptions, the occasional bribe for information—everything. If his nerve center wasn't much to look at, it was still a nerve center.

And in five years he had found . . . exactly nothing.

Not one shred of evidence that the girl existed, or had ever existed. Grant had no doubt of that, and that was what kept him going. That and the look on Marianne Carlin's face when she had died giving birth to that monster. That monster that he had protected and harbored and allowed to be born . . .

. . . and who was now five years old.

He drank the two fingers of scotch and, without conscious thought, poured another. It occurred to him vaguely that he had been fired and already did not miss his job. It had merely been another nerve center, and the paperwork had finally caught up with him. He had been half expecting it for a couple of years.

Maybe they would promote Chip Prohman to detective, and then they would see what *real* police work was all about.

He downed the drink in his hand and refilled, turning to the computer screen.

When he took his eyes away from the screen it was dark outside and the scotch bottle was nearly empty. Never fear, there was always another. He thought about dinner—a can on the hot plate, or the pizzeria? He decided he didn't want to go out. He decided he wasn't hungry, and that, yes, he was pissed about losing his job after all. He put a cigarette in his mouth and lit it, and emptied the scotch bottle into his glass. There was a cool breeze coming in from the window. At least they let you smoke in the Ranier Hotel. Nice sleeping weather for early October, if only he could sleep. He knew he wouldn't sleep tonight. He had barely slept for five years.

Where was she?

That was the one question that had centered his life since the baby was born. Where? No orphanage had harbored her, Grant was sure of that now. No foster home had taken her in. He would have found out by now. Those eyes, those gray, flat shark's eyes, they couldn't be hidden. Someone would have noticed, someone, some *thing* should have sent up a flag by now.

There should have been some clue by now—and Grant was very good at finding clues.

And yet there was nothing.

As if she had dropped off the face of the earth.

For a while Grant had believed even that—that Samhain had somehow secreted the child away from all humanity, squirreled it away in a cave or bunker or underground warren, like a sick rabbit.

But the child was human, Grant was sure of it, and would have needed human things—food, shelter, warmth, perhaps even human contact, though the thought made Grant's blood cold. Yes, it would need the milk of human kindness, to feed off the very thing, come one Halloween, it would wipe from existence.

Where?

Grant found that the scotch was gone, replaced by a headache. He was getting nowhere again. And tomorrow he would start over, doing the only thing he knew how—to look, to wait for that one clue, that one tiny bit of information that would lead to what he sought.

To the little girl he would murder in cold blood.

CHAPTER TWENTY-SIX

He awoke with the taste of dried scotch in his mouth. He had made it to the bed but had not taken off his shirt or shoes. The headache was still there, just out of reach and waiting to pounce.

His cell phone was ringing.

It was not in his pants pocket or jacket pocket (at least he had hung his jacket on the back of the chair) but it was tangled up in the bedcovers on the floor.

He sat on the bed and pushed the call button. The headache was beginning to make its move.

"Yes?"

"Detective Grant?" a voice he knew but couldn't place said.

"That's right."

"Janet Larson," the no-nonsense voice announced.

He still couldn't place it—then suddenly he could.

"Yes, Mrs. Larson, how are you? How's Baby Charlie?"

"He's no baby anymore. First grade. And Baby Louis is in preschool, thank God. It's almost quiet around here. Too quiet, to tell you the truth."

Grant said nothing. What should he say? That's nice? Sorry your sister died in my house giving birth to a monster? Sorry you had to deal with the Lord of Death?

The silence stretched, and then Janet blurted, "I never thanked you for trying to protect my sister. I heard you got shot."

Grant didn't know what to say, so he said, "It healed nicely. No pangs in wet weather."

"To be frank," Janet went on, "it's taken me five years to make this call. I blamed you for a long time. I should have blamed myself."

"For what?"

"For not knowing. For running away."

"Samhain would have hurt your family."

"That's no excuse."

"Isn't it?"

"No. I always prided myself on being strong, and I wasn't strong. I was weak. It's been a . . . very difficult five years, Detective."

"Samhain hasn't . . ."

"Nothing like that." She laughed nervously. "I just mean . . . personally. Chuck and I divorced about a year ago, and I haven't been as . . . tough as I once was."

"I'm sorry to hear that."

"Believe me, I'm sorry to say it. It's been . . . tough not being tough, if you know what I mean. I've had nightmares about Marianne and that . . . baby. And, well, I haven't been the best mother to Baby Charlie and his brother. The thing is, I wanted to tell you that there was nothing you could have done."

"I'm not so sure of that."

"Absolutely nothing. That Samhain creature had things sewed up from one end to the other. I've thought long and hard about this, and it's true. Either you and I are both to blame or we're not. And I've decided we're not."

Grant was silent.

"That's all I've got to say about it," Janet said with finality. "I was wrong to harbor bad thoughts about you." She paused, and Grant could feel a change in the air. "But that's not the real reason I called you."

A tingle, the slightest breath of hope, brushed along the back of Grant's neck.

"I talked to someone at the police station who said you had just been fired."

"That's right."

"I'm sorry to hear that. I almost told him what I wanted to tell you, but something told me not to. Chip Prohman was a dope in high school and for all I know—"

"Believe me, Janet, he's worse than a dope now."

Grant waited, his anticipation building. He found that he was holding his breath.

"I think I might know where Marianne's baby is. Though she would be, what? Almost as old as Baby Louie."

Grant could not keep his voice steady. "Yes, five."

"I thought you'd want to know."

"Yes, I very much want to know. Where is she?"

"Well, I'm not sure, exactly. This was almost a year ago, last summer, when I was still pissed at you. Chuck and I were going through the last of our problems. We had separated, and he had moved everything he wanted out of the house. I threw all the rest on the front lawn and put out a rummage sale sign one Saturday. This was . . . just after the Fourth of July, whatever Saturday that would be."

Grant waited while she took a breath. His hand was

clutching the phone so tight he could hear the plastic case threatening to break.

Come on, come on . . .

"Anyway," Janet Larson continued, "we were having this rummage sale, and Baby Charlie—who I just call Charlie now, I mean you don't call a six-year-old 'Baby' in front of his friends or nasty things happen—Charlie was helping me and we must have had a hundred cars show up before noon, parked all over the street, in the driveway, up on the curb, you should have seen that pill Mrs. Jakes next door with her sour face, and a mob scene for a while. I guess some of Carl's crap was worth something, because by noon most of it was gone. In the afternoon we had a few more cars, and one in particular caught my eye because it passed the house twice before parking across the street. Big black thing, not a limo exactly but along the lines of a Lincoln Town Car, those big boats. The windows were tinted all around and it just sat there, nobody got out. Some woman was arguing with me over the price of one of Carl's old golf clubs, not the new ones which he took with him, and I was distracted, and when I looked back the window in the backseat of the Town Car had rolled down and a face as white as the moon was staring at me. Just for a second but it was ghastly, pale as a sheet with two dark eyes and hair that hung down in a straight ugly cut. I've never seen a more ghastly looking little girl. Just for a second, because the window was already going up and then the face was gone. But that girl looked at me, the face blank, and I knew who it was. It was Marianne's baby, I'll swear on it. I didn't see that Samhain, the one in the cape, and I didn't feel his presence, but for all I know he was driving the damn Lincoln. It started up then and pulled away from the curb but I went down to the street and I've got good eyes and I took down the license plate number. Maybe that'll help you."

Grant began to breathe. "Yes, it might. Can you give it to me?"

Janet Larson read out numbers and letters. "I hope it helps. That face was so . . . I don't know, dead. Not dead, like that Samhain's face, but something worse. If you can be worse than dead. What will you do when you find her?"

"I don't know," Grant lied.

"Whatever she is, she's half my sister, you know."

"That's true."

"If you find her would you let me know? I'd like to know if she's anything like Marianne, if anything of my sister, my family, is inside her. I don't know. It's just that I thought you had the best chance of finding her."

"Thank you, Mrs. Larson."

"Since Chuck and I divorced, I've been thinking a lot about what family I have. Maybe I'm nuts."

"Anything but, Mrs. Larson."

Janet Larson laughed. "Anyway, I hope you can find her."

"Me, too."

"And I hope you believe me when I say I'm sorry for the way I felt about you. You did what you thought was right."

Grant let her ramble on a little more, spilling out her apologies and regrets, and then he gently got her off the phone after lying again that he would get in touch with her when he found the girl.

He stared at the cell phone and pushed the off button, watching the LCD screen go blank after flashing the word "Good-bye."

"Good-bye, indeed," Grant said out loud, filled with the first hope he'd had in five years.

CHAPTER TWENTY-SEVEN

It took twenty minutes to trace the car, and only that long because he was no longer employed by the Orangefield Police Department, and had to talk one of the uniformed cops—who turned out to be Paige, who had escorted him home yesterday—into running the plate number for him.

It matched up to St. Bartholomew's Church in Newton, Massachusetts. Grant found the phone number of the rectory. After speaking with Mrs. Finch, and then a deacon named Brandywine, he was eventually put through to a priest they thought might be able to help him.

"Father Coughlin?"

There was a cough on the other end, followed by a pronounced throat clearing. Detective Bill Grant expected the voice, when it finally spoke, to be raspy or weak. It was neither—it was strong and clear as a bell.

"Yes?"

Grant identified himself, and briefly stated the reason for his call.

"Do I know you?" the priest asked.

"No, but you will."

The brief silence ended in a snort. "You ended my afternoon nap. We used to call fellows like you wisenheimers. Did you by any chance go to Catholic school?"

"Wrong religion. Episcopalian."

Another snort. "Virtually the same thing, though neither of us likes to admit it."

"Except for the nuns. And we still use the communion rail."

"I wish we did, too. Would you be willing to drive over so we can have a proper talk?"

"That would be fine. Though I'd like to ask you now—"

"A proper talk, like I said. You don't by any chance follow football, do you?"

"No. Baseball fan."

There was something artificial and almost scripted about the way the priest was talking. He sounded like a movie cliché—Barry Fitzgerald in *Going My Way.*

"Good. Then you won't be looking at your watch. We'll have a nice long talk. Say, tomorrow at three in the afternoon?"

"I'm looking forward to it."

"Me, too, Detective Grant. Me, too." Grant expected the priest to chuckle, but there was only silence.

The line went dead before Grant could say good-bye.

CHAPTER TWENTY-EIGHT

It was a beautiful Sunday morning in October, with a high, bright blue cloudless sky, when Grant left early for the drive to Massachussets. On his way out of town to the Northway entrance ramp, before hooking up with Interstate 91 down through Vermont and then eventually over to the hated I-95, he stopped at Riley Gates' fallow farm. The faded sign, RILEY GATES: PUMPKINS FOR SALE, was long gone.

He drove up the rutted long lane and braked the car. The lawn chair was still there, facing the now-empty pumpkin field.

Grant touched the chair, and then turned to look at the gutted skeleton of what had been Riley's house. The things that had happened in that house, and, later, as he had waited in this chair . . .

Something new and sleek cut the sky above the yawning blackened cavity of the roof.

Grant moved ten yards to the right to get a better look. It was a curving structure, the top of a dull gray wheel set high into the sky.

Halloweenland.

Grant remembered the story in the paper. So that was where they were erecting it.

After taking a final look at the fallow pumpkin field, Grant got back into his sedan and drove back to the main road.

Hope things are better where you are, podna, he said to himself, thinking of Riley Gates.

Halloweenland had a better gate, with a bold shiny KEEP OUT sign bolted to it, but it wasn't locked. Grant parked next to it and pushed it open, entering the property. No ruin here; the chain-link was brand new.

There wasn't much to see, but plenty to imagine. Already a huge parking lot had been set up to the right, paved and marked out. To the left what looked like the beginnings of an arcade, with a boardwalk, and a few tents, probably for amusements and skill games, had been erected. And straight ahead was the Ferris, a half-completed monster, with the beginnings of a massive main tent, outlined in steel girders. As Grant got closer he saw that there were plots laid out for more thrill rides, and a trailer marked OFFICE up on blocks. On one the brightly colored cups of a cups-and-saucers ride lay on their sides. They were spanking new, the engraving on one proudly boasting that it was manufactured in Germany. It was painted a deep red, and beside it on the grass lay its saucer, pearly enameled white. They looked like props from some giant monster movie.

He felt the presence of the man behind him before he heard the voice, which was low and toneless.

"Can I help you?"

Grant turned around and blinked. The newspaper

story had labeled Mr. Dickens as scary as one of his attractions, and it hadn't exaggerated. Dickens was bald as an ostrich egg, his eyes impossibly small and dark. Still, they managed to look hooded. He had no eyebrows, and his lashes were short and the lightest ash blond. And yet he wasn't albino, and a dark patch of facial hair, a "soul patch," lay under his lower lip. His body was medium-sized but seemed squat. His large hands looked as if they would feel moist if you shook them. He gave the appearance of something that didn't live on land all the time, an underwater creature, perhaps.

Grant pulled out his auxiliary badge, the one he hadn't turned in.

"You must be Mr. Dickens."

The other didn't look at it. "Just Dickens, if you don't mind."

The toneless voice did not go with the face, the hands, the wool suit, the black shoes. The accent was overly formal.

"Are you here about the permits?" Dickens continued, before Grant could speak. "I told that man in Mayor Gergen's office, what's his name—"

"I'm not here from the mayor. I'm just a curious cop."

Dickens' face went blank, and then, studying Grant closely, he said, "Ahh. Curious about what?"

Grant shrugged, feigning a loss for words.

Dickens' face slowly changed, softening the tiniest bit, but he didn't quite smile.

"You read the newspaper article, and couldn't resist."

Grant nodded. "That's right. After all, I may be . . . assigned to this place, and I just wanted to see what it looks like."

Dickens spread his hands out. "Well, what do you think?"

"It's bigger than I thought. And farther away from town than I thought it would be."

"We want nothing to do with that Ranier Park business," Dickens replied, not hiding his disdain. "I made that very clear to the mayor before we signed the contracts that this is a completely separate attraction." Now self-satisfaction replaced scorn. "I wouldn't doubt that we take quite a lot of business away from the so-called Pumpkin Days Festival."

"That's fine with me," Grant said.

Now the other did smile—but it was an ugly, small gesture, the thin lips hardly parting to reveal what looked like chiseled small teeth.

Grant thought to himself, *My God, more Weird Shit?*

"Don't get me wrong, Mr. Grant," Dickens said, sounding as if he didn't care one way or the other. "That town celebration is all well and good, in a . . . pedestrian sort of way. The people come, they see demonstrations of pumpkin carving, and buy a few trinkets, and see"—here the man sniffed—"demonstrations of commercial products which they are told will enhance their lives. Rug cleaners and such. And they might listen to music of one sort or another"—here again he did not hide his disdain—"and then they go home. All very good for the mayor, for the selling of pumpkins, for the shopkeepers.

"But here we will offer something different." He put out his hands and swept them in an inclusive motion. "There will be rides, yes, and attractions, and gewgaws to win for the pretty girls. But there will be . . . more."

When Dickens didn't offer, Grant said, "Such as?"

Dickens smiled without showing his teeth. "That would be cheating! And I, an impresario, am no cheater!"

Grant said nothing.

"Have you seen quite enough?" Dickens asked, his tone not encouraging Grant to say, "No."

"I suppose so," Grant said, conceding the dismissal. "But let me ask you: will you really be ready for Halloween?"

Dickens threw his head back and barked a laugh. Again the slightest look at those tiny white pointed teeth.

"I should say so! I have excellent help. I hope to see you here then, yes?"

Grant locked eyes with the strange little man for the briefest moment, before nodding.

"Perhaps."

"Good. Until then."

Dickens bowed curtly and then put out his hand, which Grant felt obliged to take. It was moist, as he had feared—like the flipper of a seal.

Dickens removed his hand as abruptly as he had offered it, and turned and walked away, his steps short and precise.

"Auf Wiedersehen, Detective Grant!" Dickens called, without turning around.

Grant thought he heard the tiniest of chuckles.

The door to the trailer opened, closed.

There was the click of a lock.

After a moment, Grant turned and walked back to his car.

His thoughts were not on the moist handshake or the mocking laugh, or even on the bizarre appearance of the carnival impresario.

Grant thought instead: *How did he know my name, if he didn't look at my badge?*

CHAPTER TWENTY-NINE

Three hours and twenty minutes later found Grant in front of the rectory door of St. Bart's Church in Newton, Massachusetts. Behind it he heard the unmistakable sound of a televised football game. As he rang the bell the sound disappeared, and there was the sound of a shuffling gait approaching the door.

It opened, and Grant blinked—the man facing him was much older than he had sounded on the phone.

He was also obviously blind.

"Detective Grant, I presume?" the priest said, putting out his right hand.

Grant shook it. "Thank you for seeing me, Father."

"Was that a blindness pun, Detective?"

For the first time in a long time, Grant found himself momentarily flustered, but his unease was immediately dispelled by the priest's booming artificial laugh. There was definitely something wrong here. "If you can't make fun of a disability, why have it?" Coughlin said. His continued handshake drew Grant into a short hallway past a set of stairs and into a room. "I have some excellent scotch waiting to be done away with," he said.

"How did you know—"

The priest stopped, turned with a cocked eyebrow. "Hmm? Oh, I didn't know you like scotch. But *I* do." He turned and continued to shuffle. "If you like it, too, so much the less for me."

The room was tidy and small, and still managed to make Grant's hotel room look like a closet. And a dirty one, at that. It was well furnished and cozy, warm and inviting. Too warm, in fact. Grant took off his coat.

"Make yourself comfortable, Detective," the priest said. He was easing himself into one of two very comfortable-looking side chairs angled half toward one another and half toward an old nineteen-inch black-and-white television.

"You're staring at the television, no doubt," Coughlin said, reading the silence. "There's no remote, and only those huge dials to change channels, so I'm afraid you'll have to get up to turn down the sound when we get well into it. No color televison for this blind priest, not from this diocese. Not from *any* diocese, these days, I'm afraid. No cable, either, so we'll have to put up with the Patriots and the Jets. You're a Jets fan, I suppose, being from New York?"

Before Grant could speak the priest cut in: "But of course, you said yesterday that you're a baseball fan. Mets?"

"Yankees."

"Would you pour, Detective? I certainly know how, but things will go more quickly this way."

Grant turned his attention to the tray set on an ottoman between them, laid out with a bottle of Johnnie

Walker red and two glasses. He made a slight sour face at seeing the Johnnie red.

"Since you are a scotch man, are you a Johnnie Walker man?" the priest asked brightly.

"Absolutely," Grant fibbed.

"No, Dewar's, I'd say. I could smell it about you when you came in."

Grant laughed shortly. "Got me there, Father."

"It's an old trick from the confession box. Lean in close and smell the breath."

Though everything the priest said was homey and warm, there was still something wrong in the air. Grant's weird-shit detector was firing on all cylinders. It was like the priest was in some sort of trance.

Something's wrong here, he thought.

He poured, handed one glass over to the priest and drank off a bit of his own.

It was warm in his throat, in the warm room, and down into his belly.

"First drink of the day, if you don't mind my asking?" Coughlin asked, chuckling to himself.

"You watch a lot of detective shows on television, Father?"

"Another pun? Watch?"

Grant was getting a little tired of the routine. What seemed just jocularity was instead a man talking a mile a minute so he didn't have to get where he had to. It usually happened with a man who wasn't intrinsically criminal but somehow found himself mixed up, after perhaps a lifetime of straight arrow law abiding, in something nasty and illegal.

No, it wasn't that: it was like looking at a man who was waking up from a nightmare.

The priest was sipping his scotch, his hand shaking ever so slightly.

"What I was telling my housekeeper just the other day—"

Grant reached out and flicked off the television set.

"And it sounded like the Pats were about to score a field goal—" the priest started, almost sadly.

"Time to talk, Father Coughlin. And no bullshit. I came over here because you wanted to talk face-to-face. I take it there was a reason you didn't want to talk on the phone. Correct?"

The priest nodded, and put down his glass. Grant noted that it was empty. He emptied his own and poured more scotch into each.

"Very sad. It was Mrs. Finch, the housekeeper. When she's here she listens in on the extension, nothing I can do about it. That's why I was so coy with you on the phone yesterday. I'm afraid even that was too much, as you will see."

"What does that mean?" Grant asked.

"Please let me tell my story in my own way. I know this is about the girl, Anna."

Grant's pulse quickened. He watched as the priest brought his glass up, hand shaking more noticeably, and drained it in a single swallow. As he lowered it Grant moved to fill it again but the priest shook his head. "No more now. It would cloud my thoughts. Later, perhaps. Oh, yes, much more of it later."

"As you like." Grant topped his own drink and put the bottle aside.

Father Couglin stared hard at something only he could see. His brow furrowed. "This all seems so much clearer to me now that it's over, in a sense. It all happened in a rush, and of course there's Christian charity to account for. I'm sure now that I was chosen because I was blind. She must be truly hideous to behold." The blind eyes turned toward Grant. "Did you know that the blind can often *feel* the way something looks? It's like heat from the sun, or call it intuition.

"She was brought to the rectory five years ago by someone who gave off the opposite of heat, Detective. I don't know how quite to explain this to you, but it was as if winter had stepped into the hallway, and it was the middle of Indian summer. Early November. A beautiful day, too, but even the smell of late blooming flowers, the smell of the warmth itself—all of it went away in an instant, snuffed out and replaced by . . ." he waved an arm ". . . blank, odorless *cold*."

"I know what you mean, Father."

"Do you?" The priest's face showed surprise.

Grant was silent.

The priest fumbled for his glass. "I believe I will have a little more of that scotch, Detective. This is all so strange. Like I'm slowly waking from a dream."

Grant dutifully filled the glass and watched the priest drink.

"Please continue," Grant said.

The priest stared into space again, concentrating. "He didn't stay long, this . . . cold thing. He said his name was Samhain. But he put the child into our care, and extracted a vow that nothing would be said for five years. No one was to know. This puzzled me then, and it puzzles me now, except for the fact that when Mrs. Finch saw the child later she nearly fainted. I still remember her saying, 'Saints in heaven!' and I know she crossed herself because she told me of it later. But she also said that a child is a child and that we would do as I had vowed. I know now that the cold fellow came to the rectory when she was out doing errands because she never would have stood the sight of him, and his plan would have gone awry. He was very clever."

Grant waited while the priest drank again.

"I still don't know how he extracted a vow from me. This is not something a priest would normally do. Paperwork, and the diocese, and so on. Not to mention the state. But once I had made that vow . . ." He shrugged.

"This . . . Samhain was very persuasive."

The priest nodded, then leaned back and shrugged. "More than that. Like I said, it's like the last five years were a sort of fugue. And that's much of my story. Mrs. Finch and her husband raised the child, good people that they are—or were, I should say. For they changed as the baby grew. At first Mrs. Finch would mutter and pray and talk about the child's ugliness and unnaturalness, but then, over time these complaints lessened, until they became endearments. And this puzzled me greatly, because I felt nothing from the child. As I told you, the blind can sometimes see with their other senses—but from this child I got nothing. No cold, or warmth, nothing at all. Like a blank slate. I ran my fingers lightly over her face once, when I thought she was asleep, and I had the oddest feeling that I was touching just that—a blank slate.

"They named her Anna, though I thought the name was not right. I could think of none that would be right. Does that make sense? And they kept her in the back bedroom and let her play—though I don't know if I would call it that—in the attic room and the hedged backyard. And no one outside of this little house ever knew she existed. Samhain was often about, though he never spoke to me again."

"Where is she now, Father?" Grant said quietly. The blood was pounding through his veins.

The priest looked distracted, then reached for his scotch. When he had finished with it he said, shaking his head, "This is all so strange. Like waking from a dream. All of it, from beginning to end, from the day that cold fellow arrived until now, this exact moment. As it was happening I knew it was unnatural, and perhaps even wrong, but I told myself that a vow was a vow. But of course it isn't, not if it's wrong. Even putting that television on before you came here was part of my dream, Detective. Do you understand?"

"I'm afraid I don't," Grant said. There was a slight edge in his voice, and he felt like reaching for his holstered .38, which, like his spare badge, he had not turned in to Captain Farrow.

"Where is the girl, Father?" he said, slowly getting up. He could feel the tension in the room, even though he knew it emanated from himself.

The priest looked up at him, and there was a tear tracking his cheek from his blind right eye. "What have I done, Detective? What great evil have I helped perpetuate? That cold creature was always about, and the police have already been here about the poor little girl Beatrice who was murdered, and the Lincoln is gone. I'm afraid the diocese will be very upset . . ."

"I don't know what you're talking about, Father."

"I'm afraid the police will be back." Coughlin put his head in his hands and began to weep.

Grant edged away from the chair, drawing his .38, looking out into the hallway.

"Anna should never have been here." The priest looked up, and his face was awash in tears. "I'm a priest! A man of God! And that thing was in my care for five years! Oh, I was asleep . . ."

Grant backed into the hallway and quickly mounted

the creaking stairs. There was a landing with two doors, and he opened one, a storage room, and then another, a girl's bedroom.

He went in. There was a bed, made up with white starched tucked sheets and a light pink summer blanket. A doll that looked untouched and new was propped against the foot of the bed. The walls were bare. There was an oval rag rug on the floor and nothing else. No toys, no keepsakes. The closet was open and empty.

Grant backed out of the room and slowly mounted the steps to the attic. He could hear the priest moaning and sobbing below. There was a stained wooden door with a glass ovoid handle. He turned it with his left hand, feeling the coolness of the glass, and pushed it open, aiming the .38 in his right hand into the room.

Two skylight windows sent sharp shafts of light that fell on the floor like painted distorted yellow rectangles. There were two bodies, half in the light and half in shadow. A man and a woman, older. Sensible shoes. There were no visible wounds, but they were cold as potato salad. There was a note under the woman's head.

Grant pulled on a pair of latex gloves from his pocket, just so that the local police wouldn't find his prints on anything later, and picked up the note, angling it into a shaft of overhead sunlight. He read it:

HOPE YOU ENJOYED THE PADRE. LONG TIME NO SEE. HAVE GONE HOME, DON'T FOLLOW. S.

Samhain.
Grant carefully folded the note and put it in his pocket.
Don't follow? the note warned.
"My ass," Grant said, out loud.

CHAPTER THIRTY

The car drove itself, which was good. There was precious little else she could do without Samhain around. Which annoyed her greatly, because she had thought her powers would be greater in this world. She had discovered, at the age of three, that she could kill—on a warm summer afternoon, as she sat in the shade of an elm tree in the tiny, secluded backyard of the rectory, a butterfly had alighted on her bare arm. She was still amazed by the flesh that enclosed her, baby pink and smooth and nearly flawless (there was a tiny mole in the curve of skin between her thumb and left forefinger, which she had not been able to wish away), and only her hair, which was unnaturally white blond, and which the fool humans who had taken care of her had cut in short bangs to minimize its effect, and the deep empty pools of her gray eyes, identified her as anything other than of the human race.

To the butterfly: she was sitting still as stone in a webbed folding chair, feeling the warmth and slight waft of breeze which brought flower and tree odors to her, when the insect, a beautiful monarch of bright orange and black, had settled on her motionless arm. She looked down at it. It moved its wings up, down, up, down as if completely oblivious of her presence. A cloud blotted the sun, and the neatly mowed square of backyard was plunged into sudden shadow. She looked up; through the sway of elm leaves she saw a single fat white cloud moving leisurely from west to east; already the bright fringes of the sun was showing at its trailing edges. The cloud looked vaguely like a rabbit, crouched and ready to eat.

She looked back down at her arm. The butterfly had ceased the beating of its wings and looked asleep. Could a butterfly be content? This one appeared so.

The sun burst out of its cloud cover and a shaft of light fell on the butterfly, making it radiant. As if startled from slumber it took flight, turning for a moment toward the girl, who stared at it while reaching out a tentative finger.

The butterfly brushed the finger with one wing, and fell to the ground motionless.

The girl looked at it for a moment and then closed her eyes and let the afternoon wash over her.

She met the other little girl quite by accident. Sometimes she got in the black Lincoln and rode, just to get out of the rectory and away from Mr. and Mrs. Finch, the minder humans, and sometimes just to vex Samhain. She liked to do that. Though lately he seemed more distant, less his old self, less prone to jest. Sometimes she wondered about that.

The car was spacious in the back, all windows clouded by tinted glass, and it went where she willed it to. She had taken jaunts into Boston, to see what a city was like up close; but it was noisy and crowded and filled with too much antlike activity and mindless motion. And, they had gotten lost in the maze of one-way streets, until

Anna had willed, *Just go home.* That had been close to exhausting, and she hadn't tried it again—though it did provoke an amusing tirade of invectives from Samhain, along the lines of "What if—"

"But it didn't happen, Samhain. We didn't get stranded, or run into a parked car, or stopped by a policeman, or set upon by hooligans."

"But what if—!" Samhain had persisted, and then Anna had laughed in his face and told him to stop.

Which made her almost sorry for him, because he had gone into one of his funks, then, all the spunk gone from him.

So the car trips had become more localized—to a shopping mall parking lot, to watch the humans frantically purchase; to the county jail, to watch the faces going in and coming out, and playing a guessing game of who was judge, who was lawyer, who was prisoner; to the park, to watch the humans at play.

Which was where, on a warm autumn day, she saw the other little girl.

The town park was a huge flat square plot of land, with a baseball diamond at one end, a soccer field at the other, basketball courts in the middle to one side, and the other left to no sport save leisure. This was the area closest to the parking lot. There were picnic benches, and metal barbecue grills permanently mounted next to them and an abundance of trees that reminded Anna of the rectory backyard. She was tempted to leave the Lincoln, but decided to heed Samhain's warnings about interacting with humans—until she saw something that almost startled her. A little girl, nearly her mirror image, was sitting under an oak tree alone, acting in the most curious way. She sat quietly for a few moments, then suddenly pushed herself off the ground and ran this way and that, then threw herself on the ground. Then she slowly rose and quietly returned to her original spot.

This was too much of a temptation, and Anna ordered the car, "Open the back door," and she got out.

She approached the other girl cautiously, and was also aware of everything else that went on around her. If the girl had a parent, it was nowhere near. There were no other children close by—the closest was a group playing basketball in the caged court forty yards away.

As Anna approached she saw that the girl wasn't as much like her as she had originally thought—she was taller, and probably older, and her hair was ash blond and not nearly white like Anna's. Still they were dressed similarly, in blue dresses and white blouses, though the other girl's blouse had a red bow tied neatly at her neck.

Anna stopped short of the tree—the girl had risen abruptly and was running to the far edge of the shaded area. She bent down, looking back and forth, and then dived onto the ground.

"What are you doing?" Anna asked.

Startled, the girl got up, dusted a knee with her left hand and said, "Oh!"

"What's the matter?" Anna asked dispassionately.

"I thought I was alone!" It didn't sound like a lie—the girl's face showed no fear or revulsion or any other emotion that would have sent Anna scurrying back to the Lincoln.

Silence stretched between them, and then the other girl held up her cupped right hand. She opened the palm to reveal what was hidden there.

"I'm playing acorn," she announced.

"What's that? Aren't acorns just seeds?"

The girl walked past Anna and sat down with her back against the bole of the oak tree. Now Anna saw that there was a pile of acorns next to her on the ground. She added the new one to the pile.

"Acorns is a game. You sit quietly, and concentrate very hard, and when you hear the tree drop an acorn you get up and run very fast and retrieve it."

"Why?"

"Because it's a *game!*" the other girl replied in explanation.

The other girl closed her eyes and waited—and then Anna suddenly heard a tiny *thump* off to the right. In an instant the girl was on her feet and running to the spot. She bent down and retrieved the acorn, and returned, adding it to the growing pile.

She looked at Anna. "It's you against the tree, you see," she said. "That's the game." The end of her sentence was punctuated by another faint *thump*, and again the girl ran to the spot and retrieved it.

While she was returning there was another *thump* very close by, and Anna looked down to see a fresh acorn, green and with a light brown crinkly cap, lying at her feet.

She bent quickly down and scooped it up, and looked up to see the other girl standing close by, with an excited look on her face.

"Now you're playing, too!"

Anna stared at the acorn in her hand, and then followed the other girl back to the bole of the tree.

"Make your own pile! I'll start you with half of mine!" She cut her acorn pile in half with her palm, and moved it off to one side. "That'll be yours! Whoever has the most at the end wins!"

Anna looked once more at the acorn in her hand, then dropped it onto the new pile.

There was a *thump!* followed by another *thump!* and

before she knew it Anna was running this way and that, and adding to her pile.

The afternoon grew late, and suddenly the other girl stood and said, "I have to go."

She began to walk away, and Anna said, looking at the two huge piles of acorns, "We haven't seen who won."

"Who cares! You can have them all—you won!" She laughed, and turned to keep walking. "My name's Beatrice, I'll be here tomorrow afternoon if you want to play again!"

And then she was gone, running, across the parking lot, out of the park and across the street into the human neighborhood beyond.

Anna stood for a long time, first looking in the direction Beatrice had gone, the maze of two-family houses almost on top of one another, of red and white with dark roofs, the jumble of telephone and electrical wires hither and yon making them look like they were caught in a web. The sun was dropping to the west, which meant it was at least five o'clock, probably later. Samhain would be beside himself.

Then Anna stared for a few long moments at the two piles of acorns. She noted that her own pile was wider and higher than Beatrice's.

With only a moment's hesitation she kicked the two piles, scattering the oak seeds, and walked to the black Lincoln.

She was back the next day, but Beatrice was nowhere to be found. She waited for an hour at the oak tree alone. An anger swelled in her, and she wanted to rip the oak tree from the ground by its roots and destroy it and its seeds. She waited another twenty minutes and then went home.

"What is it that makes these humans what they are?"

she asked Samhain that night. She was sitting in a comfortable chair in the blind priest's office—the most comfortable chair in the rectory.

"Why do you ask?" Samhain replied slowly; there was caution in his voice.

"Answer me, Samhain," she said, hating her little girl voice, even when she modulated it to its deepest. It was another of the prices she paid to be human in this world.

"I have been telling you for a long time that they are interesting creatures," Samhain began.

"They are creatures, first and foremost," Anna interrupted. "No better than any other life on this miserable planet. Beast, bug," she hesitated before adding, "butterfly."

"They are creatures, true," Samhain said. "But I've developed a certain interest in them, as you know. They show sparks of nobility, and selflessness, and kindness, that are totally alien to their base nature."

"I don't understand them," Anna said simply.

"Do you have to?"

"No."

Anna rose abruptly from the chair and marched to the hallway and up the stairs, saying nothing more. Samhain, floating like a black wraith, the bottom of his cape moving in the breezeless room, watched after, and heard the door slam to her room.

Beatrice was at the park two days later.

"Where were you?" Anna demanded.

Beatrice laughed; today she had on a green blouse, which nearly matched the color of an acorn. There were newly fallen acorns around the shaded perimeter of the tree.

"My mother kept me in—I was being punished." She laughed again.

"For what?"

"Are you always so serious? How old are you—three?"

"I'm five," Anna responded.

"Well I'm almost seven, and I don't like to do homework. Mrs. Greene sent home a note, and I was punished." She smiled. "But here I am!"

Beatrice noted the scattered acorns at the base of the tree. "We'll have to start with a new tree—if you want to play acorns again."

"I do."

Beatrice sighed. "Well I don't. It's too much work. Why don't we just sit and tell stories?"

Anna stood still, and watched as Beatrice sat herself down with her back against the tree, brushing acorns out of her way.

"Well?" she said, looking at Anna. "Has anyone ever told you you're funny looking?"

Beatrice laughed, and Anna walked purposefully to the tree and stood above her. She squatted on her haunches and touched the other girl.

Touch, look.

She stared into Beatrice's eyes, and Beatrice gave a little gasping sigh. Her head fell to one side and she sat motionless, staring into nothing.

Anna stared at her for a few moments, before straightening and walking to the black car.

"Take me home," she said.

Samhain was as close to livid as he ever became. "You must understand," he said, "how important it is for silence. The police were here, because of the car. Someone saw it leave the park. The priest did a good job of explanation, but this cannot happen again."

Anna said nothing.

"Do you understand?" Samhain almost screeched.

"Of course."

"The sixth Halloween is almost here. Detective Grant has found us, and we must leave. I have made arrangements. Mr. and Mrs. Finch—"

"I will attend to them."

Samhain grew calmer, but his voice was now filled with something like curiosity. "I must ask you: why, exactly, did you kill the little girl?"

But Anna was already on the stairs, and did not answer.

CHAPTER THIRTY-ONE

The biggest bender of his life.

Grant had no idea how long it had been, though by the length of his beard stubble and the chill now in the air outside the open window, he knew it must have been at least a week. Maybe more. It had started innocently enough, with him staring at the wall or at the piece of paper Samhain had left for him in Massachusetts. "Don't follow," It had said, but of course Grant had come back to Orangefield and tried to find Samhain in every corner of the town. He had waited for a rash of what the locals called Sam Sightings, when the Lord of Death was supposedly (and sometimes actually) sighted by locals, in the woods, by certain trees, sometimes in town itself. There had always been Sam Sightings this time of year, ever since Grant had come to Orangefield as a young cop a lifetime ago.

But this year there had been none.

Grant had spent whole afternoons sitting in the lawn chair at Riley Gates' farm, facing the fallow pumpkin ruts and waiting for Samhain to appear. The Lord of Death had done so before. But all he had gained was a stiff back, and all he had witnessed was, amid the bang and buzz and whir of machinery, and the distant shouts of workers, the near-completion of Halloweenland next door. The Ferris wheel was done; Grant had watched as they tested it, the giant metal orb turning at a stately pace. He saw the main tent through a yawning burned-out gap in Riley's house—it was a lurid shade of orange, with white piping.

One day before going back to the hotel he had driven to the front gate and stopped to see two more rides erected—a giant hollow can with straps on the inside to hold passengers in place while it spun and tilted, and a magnificent carousel, which must have been trucked in whole, and which now dominated the area just behind the ticket booth and just to the right of the nearly completed midway.

And there, one moist palm on the flank of a painted horse whose head was thrown back in a permanent open-mouthed scream, was Dickens, staring out at him calmly.

The flapper of a hand raised in mock salute as Grant gunned the engine and turned around, leaving dust in his wake.

And that day, the last before the bender began, was when?

Grant shook his head, and went to the room's sink and turned on the cold water. He lifted handfuls up, shocking his face until his eyes focused. He vigorously toweled himself dry and looked out the window. It was either dawn or dusk, the sky purpled.

He beheld the room, the perpetually-on computer screen glowing like a rectangular ghost, the litter of liquor bottles and beer cans and take-out food cartons and pizza boxes, a scatter of dropped clothing.

And nothing else.

No answers, not from the bottles, not from the cryptic note in his pocket, not in the streets or woods of Orange-field.

I've gone home.

Don't follow me.

"I did, and you aren't here. I know it. I know it in my gut."

Long time no see.

That was the puzzler: why would Samhain even bother to taunt him? He had the girl, had hidden her for five years. Why give Grant any hint at all of where he was?

One thing Grant had come to know after all these years was that there was always a reason for what Samhain did.

Grant looked around for a partially full scotch bottle, but there wasn't one. He went to the window and stared out at what he now realized was the rising sun in the east. So it was dawn.

Don't follow me.

I'm going home.

And, suddenly, Grant knew where Samhain was.

Home.

He searched in the wreckage of his hotel room for his cell phone, and dialed a number, and made an airline reservation.

PART THREE

IRELAND

CHAPTER THIRTY-TWO

It was raining in Dublin when Aer Lingus flight 332 landed. It was four-thirty in the morning, Irish time, and the rain streaked the window next to Grant's head. Everything looked surreal outside: rain, blue dark night going toward morning, the sharp pinpricks of airport lights. Grant could feel jet lag trying to grab him already—it was just around the time he would be going to sleep back in Orangefield. But, between driving and the overhead airline television sets glaring and just plain anticipation, and the fact that it wasn't time to sleep yet, he hadn't slept a wink.

Grant had been amazed: as soon as the Airbus 310 had hit the clouds over JFK Airport, the stewardesses and stewards had hit the aisles, selling merchandise. And they did a brisk business in the packed plane: cigarettes and booze at duty free prices, and there was even a catalog they distributed with all kinds of Gaelic goods for sale: crystal, woolen shawls, even a bodhran, a goatskin Irish drum. And then the televisions had flickered on overhead, showing American shows like the animated

The Simpsons, as well as some insipid laugh-tracked BBC programs, and Grant had known he was in for a long flight. No old John Wayne movies for him tonight. Already he wanted one of those cigarettes they were selling, but of course smoking on the plane was prohibited.

And here he was now, snaking his way through customs with his passport clutched in his hand, towing his wheeled luggage like every other visitor to the ancestral homeland, and already wondering if he had made a mistake.

No—in his gut he knew he had done the right thing.

He was sure of it.

For the first time in days, weeks, Grant allowed himself to feel something like hope.

This was what Samhain had meant by "home."

Samhain was in Ireland.

CHAPTER THIRTY-THREE

"Bill Grant, you old bastard!"

Weary as he was, Grant had to smile at the sight of Tom Malone's face. It had hardly changed in the ten years since Grant had last seen him, in this same airport but in a different world.

Malone took him by the shoulders and then gave him a bear hug. They stood in the nearly empty Dublin Airport terminal as the day began to break on the streets outside. Grant saw through the big glass doors that it was still raining.

Malone held him at arm's length, studying him closely. "My God, man, what's happened to you? You look a hundred years old."

"And you don't," Grant growled, trying to smile but failing.

"You'll tell me all about it, yes?"

Grant nodded. "I can't thank you enough for taking my call, and coming to get me, and everything else."

"Bah," Malone said, and Grant was amused by the faint brogue the former New York City cop had picked up in Ireland. "Anything for an old friend. But then again, you're still in the game, right?"

Grant shook his head. "Not anymore. Threw the badge on the desk a few weeks ago."

"That bastard Farrow. I should have strangled him when he was a rookie in Queens. I'm sorry I ever sent him upstate to bother you. I should have stopped after I sent Riley Gates to Orangefield."

Malone looked down at the Styrofoam cup in Grant's hand. "Where did you get that swill?"

Grant pointed to a coffee machine against the far wall. "Nothing open yet."

Malone pried the cup out of Grant's hand and threw it in a nearby waste bin. He took the handle of Grant's rolling suitcase away from him. "Follow me," he said, and Grant followed.

An hour later found them in the lobby of the Burlington Hotel. Grant was amazed at the amount of activity—everywhere he looked were young businessmen and woman holding breakfast meetings. Waiters bustled, and there was the constant clang of placed silverware. Grant pushed the plate of scones away from him, full and content, and drained his third cup of good coffee. Malone's fleshy, florid face regarded him closely.

"You really do look like shit," he said.

Grant made a face. "Been a rough few years, Tom."

Malone nodded. "I wanted to get back to the states when Rose died, but—"

"I told you not to come. I told everybody not to come. There was more going on than Rose dying."

Malone looked puzzled.

Grant decided to back off. He let his voice go soft. "She was bad for a long time, and then she got worse, ended up in Killborne mental hospital. That was the second time. She was just so . . . unhappy all the time."

Malone sat back in his chair and blew out a breath. "Nothing like that first time we all came over here, eh? You and Rose, me and Florence, and Riley and . . . what was her name?"

Grant smiled. "You knew about them breaking up before Riley died, yes?"

"Of course! He called her The Witch, for Pete's sake!"

Grant let himself remember for a moment.

"Riley was a great guy, and a damn good cop," Malone said. "Better than any of us."

Grant nodded. "Amen."

"God, we were all pretty young back then. Only you were even younger, you and Rose. The babies of the bunch. We had a good time that trip. Saw everything there was to see. Remember that bus tour? Only the six of us and those two couples from Michigan? We had the whole damn bus to ourselves! And that fellow, the bus driver, with his tour itinerary pointing out this and that with his microphone and driving that damn huge bus around curves the rest of us couldn't have negotiated with a motor bike! What did we see, then? Nearly the whole western part of the damn country! It was great, Bill. And when it was all over . . ."

"Riley and I went home, and you and Flo stayed here."

Malone nodded with satisfaction. "Yes! Hell, I just had my twenty years in by then anyway, and I knew love when I saw it. Would have been crazy to do anything else. And it was really great until Flo passed on, and now it's just merely wonderful."

Grant nodded, letting the moment pass.

"So . . ." Malone began, diplomatically.

Grant leveled his gaze at his old friend.

"What do you know about Samhain?" Grant asked.

Chapter Thirty-four

They set out the next morning, which dawned blue and bright. Grant didn't want to get out of bed, but forced himself to. He felt as if he'd been rolled over by a log. He knew it would take a couple of days to get the jet lag out of him, and that there was nothing to do but fight through it. The bottle of Paddy Irish whiskey they had shared the night before (Malone had scoffed when Grant requested scotch, and after the second drink Grant had to agree with his old friend that Irish whiskey was, indeed, smoother and easier on the belly than any scotch) had helped him sleep but also made him even more reluctant to rise.

But Malone was there in the doorway, hitting the back of a frying pan with a spoon and yelling, "Get up, you bastard! No laggards in my house!" and ten minutes later Grant was in the tiny toilet, shaving and making himself presentable in whatever way he could.

"I forgot they called you Captain Iron Ass," Grant growled.

"Trouble with you," Malone said over their breakfast of

coffee and scrambled eggs with salmon, "is you've had no one to kick your ass for a while. When you were little you had your momma, and then you had the Marine Corp for a bit, and then you had Rose for a good long bit. And now you have nobody but yourself, which is bad company." He gave Grant a mock hard look. "Well, now you've got me. As long as your in my care, little Bill, you'll snap to. You were talking a lot of nonsense last night, and not all of it out of the whiskey bottle, which I had to mull over, and I definitely don't like the shape you're in, so I've decided on a couple of rules. And if you don't like them or want to comply, then you can get your butt back to Dublin Airport. In short, it's my way or it's back to New York. Agreed?"

Grant made a sour look. "What kind of rules?"

Malone lifted a thick forefinger. "One. While you're in my care you'll be clean and sober, 'least till after dinner. Then we'll share a drink or two. We might have a pint along the way, at lunch and such, but no drinking alone. Yes?"

Grant nodded slowly. "I can live with that. Maybe."

"You'd better do more than that." He held out his beefy hand. "Give me your flask, then."

Grant started, then began to laugh. He reached into his jacket pocket and removed the flask of Dewar's he kept there. "Once a cop . . ." he mumbled, putting it in Malone's palm.

Malone raised a second finger. "Two. Knock the cigarettes down to a pack a day. You know you can't smoke in pubs here anyway, right?"

"Christ! When did that happen?"

"Couple years back. It was thought there'd be an uprising and general anarchy, but nothing happened except that there's no more smoke in the bars. You can't afford the good smokes here anyway."

"I should have bought them on the plane."

Malone nodded. "Yes, but you didn't. I'm not telling or asking you to stop, just cut it down. I don't like it in the house anyway."

Grant looked down at the lit cigarette resting on his plate and stubbed it out.

"Christ . . ." he muttered, "you sure you were a real cop?"

Malone grinned, and raised a third thick finger. "Three. Moderate the crazy talk. The way you were going on last night about this Lord of the Dead and The Little Girl Who Must be Stopped was worrying the bejesus out of me, and not for any boogeyman I might see. You were raving like a madman, Bill! You can't do that, especially in public. Act like a cop, not like a crazy American."

"Do *you* believe me?"

Malone lowered all three fingers. "I don't know. But that doesn't matter. You're a fellow police officer and Riley Gates, rest his soul, vouched for you, and that's good enough for me. I don't think you're a lunatic, at least not a whole one, and I do believe you've seen a lot of what you called 'weird shit.' Riley used to mention the strange goings-on in Orangefield from time to time. As for the rest, we'll see. The way I look at this is, this is police business, and we're looking for someone. What we find at the end, well, I'll keep an open mind." He jabbed all three fingers up again, into Grant's face. "Which isn't to say everyone in Ireland will. The Irish don't like meddlers, and they don't much suffer fools, especially if they're not homegrown. This may be the home of banshees, leprechauns, pookas and changelings, but that doesn't mean the average Irishman believes in them. Yes?"

"I get it."

Malone went back to his own breakfast plate. "How do you like the eggs, by the way?"

"Not as good as in the Burlington Hotel yesterday."

Malone made a face. "You're right. The trouble is the salmon. Everyone puts it in everything over here. After a while you get used to it, but that doesn't make it any better."

"It'll do."

"I would think so, compared to those Ranier Hotel accommodations you've been enjoying in Orangefield."

Grant shrugged and looked away.

"Well," Malone said, tactfully changing the subject, "I've got our itinerary all set for today. I made a few phone calls while you were sleeping half the morning away. We're going to see a man from Trinity College who knows a few things about Samhain. Soon as you make yourself presentable we can get to it."

"I already shaved," Grant said.

Malone laughed. "Ha! Not in my book, you haven't. Go back to the lav and look at yourself in the mirror. And do it right, this time. And comb your hair proper, and put on some aftershave. You look three days in the grave. That's going to quickly change, my friend."

"Christ! How did Flo put up with this?"

"She taught me every trick I know. The woman made me look mild and meek. I miss her greatly and I'm carrying on in her name."

"I don't remember any of this when we all came over here on that tour . . ."

Malone grinned. "We were on our best behavior then, for Rose and The Witch's sake. But it's a new day." He jerked his thumb in the direction of the bathroom. "Now."

Grant pushed his now-empty plate forward, and got up. "Christ!" he muttered.

Malone grinned with self-satisfaction, and held up four fingers. "And we'll have no more using the Savior's name in vain, either."

CHAPTER THIRTY-FIVE

Dr. Richard Farrely looked too young to know anything. He was short and very skinny, with sandy hair cut so that it almost looked like a mullet. He wore round horn-rim glasses and kept sniffing. Grant was reminded of a mouse.

They met in the middle of Dublin Park and sat on one of the benches near the gardens which, incongruously, were still in bloom in late October. Grant had forgotten about the strange flora of Ireland; on their stroll over, before passing over a bridge at the River Liffey, they had seen palm trees, one of the signs the isle's temperate climate. Before meeting Farrely, Malone had steered him around the park to stand before the mounted bust of James Joyce.

"Anything you'd like to say to the great man?" Malone asked.

"I couldn't get through *Ulysses*."

"Bah. Riley and I didn't even make you try to read *Ulysses*. It was *Dubliners* we pushed on you on that trip."

Grant stared at the blackened head of Joyce. "Good stuff, James," he said.

Malone laughed and took his arm. "Let's go see the Boy Wonder," he said.

"You have to realize, Detective Grant, that Samhain is not a person."

Farrely, unable to sit down, was pacing in front of the two cops, sniffing and moving his hands as if they were on fire. Grant was surprised at his accent: Midwestern American.

"Can you possibly stop shaking your hands, Doctor?" Grant asked.

"Hmm?" Farrely said, and Malone jabbed Grant in the ribs.

"You were saying, Doctor?" Malone said.

"Ummm . . ." Farrely looked at the ground, sniffed, put his hands into his pockets and took them out again. "I was saying that Samhain is not a person. Samhain is a festival, marking the beginning of winter and the completion of the harvest. In Irish it's pronounced 'Sah-ween.' The Druids were deathly afraid that once winter came it would never end, and that there would be no more crops to plant. Samhain was marked by the offering of harvest bounty—and sometimes human sacrifices—to the Lord of the Dead, in hopes that the next planting in Spring would be a good one. It wasn't much of a jolly celebration at all."

Farrelly paced, sniffed.

"But—" Grant began, but the teacher went on, not minding him.

"However . . . this harvest festival, eventually, became what is known as Halloween. You realize that Halloween isn't much celebrated here in Ireland. In America it's a different thing, of course, but the roots are in the festival of Samhain."

He suddenly stood stock-still and stared at the ground.

Grant tried again. "But you said there was a Lord of the Dead."

"Oh, yes! And, actually, there are a few texts where his name became merged with that of the festival. It was said that on one night of the year, on what became Halloween, that the Lord of the Dead had the power to let the spirits of the departed roam the earth."

Grant was about to speak when the teacher answered his question: "Therefore, yes, over time—centuries, long after the Druids were gone—the name Samhain has been blurred with that of the original festival."

"And is there really a Lord of the Dead?" Grant asked.

"Hmm?" The teacher looked up, startled. He thrust his hands in his pockets and rocked back on his heels. Suddenly he laughed, a dry blurting sound. "A Lord of the Dead? Of course not! Are there banshees? Leprechauns?" He stretched out the last word to a ridiculous length, making it sound silly. "Look, there are all kinds of manifestations of the Death Lord in nearly all cultures. The Archangel Gabriel was known as the Angel of Death. In Hindu mythology—"

"We're done here," Grant said, in disgust. He started to rise but Malone pushed him back onto the park bench.

"Doctor," Malone said politely, "aren't there folk who still believe in such things?"

The teacher barked another laugh. "Of course! I've been dealing with them my whole academic life!"

Grant wanted to ask him if that meant for the last twenty minutes.

Malone continued politely. "Have any of these folk been more . . . persuasive than others?"

"Yes! I've talked to people out by the Blasket Islands who swear they've seen witches and fairies! Once you get out of the cities nearly everyone still believes in changelings. Or at least many of the older folks do. I tried doing a treatise on leprechauns," again he pronounced it "leap-ree-cahns," "but I couldn't stop laughing enough to get more than a few pages into it. I have enough banshee stories to fill a book and a half! As a matter of fact I'm publishing a book on banshees next year, University of Michigan Press. The notes alone run forty pages. If it does well—"

"Doctor," Malone interrupted gently, "have you come across anyone who seems . . . familiar with the Lord of the Dead?"

"Yes! Megan Conner almost had me believing he was real. She knows where he used to reside, claims she knows all about him." He laughed. "In fact, she called me not two days ago, said she had just seen him! I tried to corroborate a few of her other claims, banshee sightings and such, and nothing came of it. She's quite unreliable, in my opinion."

"And where might we find Megan Conner?" Malone asked, pulling out his notebook at the same time as Grant.

"Hmmm?" Doctor Farrely stood up straight and said, "I can give you her address, if you like. She lives on the way to the Dingle Penninsula, in a beehive."

CHAPTER THIRTY-SIX

"Like I told you, boyo, it's my way or the highway. We're staying in Killarney tonight, and we'll talk to this Megan Conner tomorrow. I won't hear of anything else. Ten to one it'll be a dead end, anyway. You heard what the professor said about her."

Grant already didn't like the way Malone drove—but everyone in Ireland seemed to drive like a madman. Not as bad as Rome, but almost. Once they got out of Dublin the roads were way too narrow, and more than once Grant thought they would collide with a tour bus, all of which drove nearly as fast as the tiny cars on the winding roads. At least the roads were well paved.

Malone had taken on the annoying traits of a tour guide. They had already stopped at the Rock of Cashel, an outcrop of limestone with a tourist trap attached: a group of one-thousand-year-old church ruins that jutted like white stone fingers at the blustery sky. The tour buses, huge rectangular dinosaurs, were lined up in rows, and Grant could hear the clicking of cameras, like crickets. There was a wall around the ruins, which made them inaccessible, but at least there was a restroom near the parking lot.

Then back in Malone's cramped Toyota, and through the Ireland Grant remembered: the wide dairy farms consisting of impossibly green fields, a bright rich green like no other on earth, which ranged down into valleys and up mountainsides, some fields looking almost vertical, partitioned by low rock walls. And the flocks of sheep, marked with stripes—blue, red—for identification.

"The Galtee Mountains," Malone explained cryptically, identifying the gentle rise of the slopes around them. They weren't much, even compared to the Adirondacks where Grant lived, but the scenery in its own way was just as spectacular.

The road straightened and they came into a town that looked vaguely familiar to Grant. Malone turned to him with a mischievous grin.

"Remember this, Bill?" he said.

They parked, and stretched their legs and crossed the road—a dangerous task, since there was a blind hairpin turn to the right and the cars negotiating it didn't slow down.

It looked even more familiar: the walk across another parking lot with a small cluster of buildings on the right, one of which was marked with a TICKETS sign.

Grant peered ahead; as if on cue the sky had clouded and it began to trickle a misty rain.

"My God, not this!" he protested.

Malone laughed; the uppermost round curve of Blarney Castle met his eyes over the trees in the near distance.

"Time to kiss the Blarney stone again, boyo!" Malone roared. He was already disappearing into the ticket office and emerged a few minutes later with two entrance passes in his hand.

"It's the damned dumbest thing in Ireland!" Grant said, torn between laughter and anger. He wanted to get to Killarney, to the woman Megan Conner.

"That it is," Malone said, the smile on his face spread from ear to ear. "But here we are."

Grant blew out a long breath, resigned. "Then let's do it."

They walked the path to the castle, which grew as they approached. The rain intensified, a coating wet fog that exactly approximated the weather conditions of their first trip here.

"Do you remember what Eamon, our tour guide, said?" Grant asked.

"He said, 'Don't go up! You'll break yer head on th' wet steps! An' it 'taint worth it!'" Malone answered, affecting a heavy brogue.

The castle loomed—at the top was the ultimate Irish tourist trap, a line of pilgrims halfway up the rain-slick stone steps, and at the end, at the top, a slab of stone where the enraptured lay down, with the help of bored attendants, and were eased out over the edge of the parapets to kiss, upside down, the Blarney Stone.

At the bottom of the castle, at the entrance, Malone turned to Grant.

"Shall we do what we did the last time?" he asked.

Grant said yes, and the two of them marched forward and planted their lips on the castle wall itself.

"There!" Malone cried. "We've kissed the Blarney stone—only not the one at the top! Remember how Eamon thought that was the best thing he'd ever heard?" He laughed shortly and then became sober and looked at Grant. "I do miss the wives."

Grant nodded. "And I miss Riley."

"Me, too," Malone said. "Let's go get a pint somewhere, and miss him some more."

CHAPTER THIRTY-SEVEN

Killarney was as nice as Grant remembered. Of all the places they had visited on their tour, only Galway, a beautiful college town on the western shore, where the Atlantic Ocean gave it a climate just like Seattle in the States, with the spectacular Cliffs of Mohr, which resembled a staggered line of huge human profiles, including one known as "The Old Woman," nearby, had captured his heart more. Killarney was the perfect small city/large town—cosmopolitan and at the same time intimate. There were beautiful shops and even a mall, but even this had not taken away from its charm. Grant remembered a toy store run by a Czech immigrant, and Rose had bought a hat in a stuffy little establishment that had been the thing she most treasured from their trip.

Malone had booked them into the marvelous white old world–style hotel they had stayed in on their tour. It was, as the phrase goes, "centrally located," which in this case was an absolute fact. They could walk to anywhere they wanted to go.

They ate in the modern restaurant on the first floor of

the hotel, and Grant was pleased to see that mussels were still on the menu. He ordered and Malone shared, and over their Guinesses they planned the next day.

"I want you to look in the mirror later, boyo," Malone said.

"If you call me 'boyo' once more I'll kill you," Grant replied.

"Sorry," Malone said. "But you do look better already, you know. None of that boozing by yourself in your little room. You know, you've been as good for me as I have for you. I feel like I'm accomplishing something."

"When we talk to that woman tomorrow we will be," Grant said.

"We would have gotten nothing out of her today," Malone said. "The old Irish need to be finessed. If we'd barged in there at supper time she would have shut the door in our faces."

"I've got to trust you on this one. Back in the states—"

"Back in the states you would have drawn your police special and kicked down the door." He raised his glass. "And tonight, a little Irish music. There's a place a short walk down the street that pulls a good pint and puts on a good show. None of that phoney tourist cabaret crap. This is the real stuff."

Grant raised his own glass, but he was already thinking about tomorrow, and talking to the woman Megan Conner.

CHAPTER THIRTY-EIGHT

The Slieve Mish Mountains on the way to the Dingle peninsula were spectacular, covered from foot to tip with sheep pastures and stark white limestone rock outcroppings, with the Atlantic Ocean roaring below. The sky had cleared and again was that high, eye-hurting blue. They stopped in Dingle, a fishing town with a beautiful harbor dotted with red and green boats, and ate an early lunch of hamburgers, which seemed out of place. Across the street was a pub named Murphy's, with a brightly painted green fish-and-chip stand next to it, not yet opened.

"Does every town in Ireland have a Murphy's Pub in it?" Grant asked.

"Pretty much."

Malone threw down some euros and they left.

"Keep an eye out, Bill, it should be somewhere up here on the right."

More sheep on the left, down below the cliffs which led to the blue sea. Boats tore along the coastline. It was even brighter here, and the day had turned warm. Grant was in his shirtsleeves and peering to the right up the limestone jutted green grass.

"That's got to be it."

They had passed other beehive huts, which were originally built by monks centuries ago. They were stone structures, akin to American Indian teepees, and made to house a solitary worshiper.

But this one was different. There was a bus parked on the left of the road, and a swarm of tourists were snapping digital pictures without crossing. The beehive was beautifully constructed, and next to it was a farmhouse. In the doorway Grant caught a glimpse of an old woman with a cell phone in her hand.

Malone pulled up behind the bus and they waited.

In a few minutes the bus reloaded, and amidst words like, "Pay her to look at it up close—no way!" and with a chuff of diesel smoke the bus pulled out onto the narrow road and rolled away.

The doorway was empty now. Grant and Malone got out of the car and crossed the road. They climbed the gentle slope of the front yard and stood in front of the beehive structure. Grant peered in but it was empty save for a tip jar just inside the opening.

"Cheap bastards," someone muttered, and Grant straightened to see the old woman in the doorway of the farmhouse again, cell phone pressed to her ear. "Talk to you later, then," she said and folded the phone as she tottered down toward them, all smiles.

"Not you gents, o'course!" she said. "Meaning cheap and all. The bus people, I call 'em, and they hardly ever cross the road, so scared of parting with a euro they are."

She smiled as Malone opened his wallet and stooped to put a bill into the tip jar.

"Go in if ye like!" she said robustly. "Personal home of St. Thaddeus, in the fort' century, I have it on good autority."

"Are you Meg Conner?" Grant asked.

She put her hands on her hips. "In d' flesh. And who might you be?"

Malone said, "You know Doctor Farrely at Trinity College?"

"Sure I do."

"He sent us," Malone explained.

"A bit of a twerp, he is," Meg Conner answered, "but he has a good heart, I tink. His head's too much in the books, though, if you ask me."

Grant said, "He told us you knew something about Samhain—"

"God bless us!" Conner blurted, crossing herself. Her face became flushed, and she looked across the road as if expecting something to appear.

"Can we—" Grant began.

"Come in the house then, and I'll tell ye. This is no place to be telling stories, in the light of day. I'll make tea if ye like, but it'll cost ye a euro apiece."

"That'd be fine," Malone said, and they followed her to the door of the farmhouse and then inside. She closed and then bolted the door, and pulled down the shade on the single window facing the street.

"Sit down, then," she said. "I'll be gettin' yer tea." She nodded at the jar on the coffee table, which was stuffed with bills.

Grant added two more, and then sat down in two over-stuffed easy chairs, leaving the floral printed couch for Meg Conner. The room was small and stuffy, and a cuckoo clock ticked annoyingly on one wall next to a set of curio shelves holding tiny crystals birds.

In a few minutes they heard the whistle of the kettle, and then Meg Conner appeared with a tray with two steaming cups on it.

"None for me, not at this time of day," she announced, and put the tray down on the table and sat down with an "Oof!"

"So little Doctor Farrely sent you, did he? I'm sure he doesn't believe a tenth of what I tell him. But I've never lied a day in me life." She pointed to her eyes. "I seen changelings with these, I have, and once a banshee. Not something you'd like to see twice, I can tell you."

Grant sipped the tea, which was little more than hot water.

Meg Conner was staring at him, her hard little pinched face filled with sudden fury. "And I saw the Lord o' Death himself, I did, not two days ago."

"That's what Doctor Farrely told us," Malone said.

Meg was still staring at Grant, studying him, it seemed.

"And you've seen 'im too, you have. I can tell."

Grant nodded slowly.

"And he's done you a bad turn or two, I'd say."

"We've . . . had our run-ins."

She turned to Malone. "And you believe none of it, do you?"

"Actually, no . . ." Malone replied mildly.

"Well I would if I was you. Because you're going to see him soon, you are. I can read it in your face."

She turned back to Grant. "He's been gone from this place a long time, he has. And then he came back, for his own reasons, I'd say. Me grandmother used to tell us stories, only half of which I dared believe, and now I'm telling them to you. This used to be his place, and now he's come home. And I saw him as clearly as I see you."

"Where?"

"On the Burren."

Malone laughed. "The Burren? There's nothing on the Burren!" He looked at Grant. "It's an area of rounded limestone hills. There's so much limestone that it looks like the surface of the moon. Nothing there but rocks and a few wild flowers which grow in the crevices."

Meg said, ignoring him, "I was on my way with me son to visit me sister in Galway, and on the Burren at night I saw him."

"Did your son see anything?"

"Driving he was, and I didn't want to scare him half to death. But there outlined against the rising moon he was, big as death, a black cape and a pale white face. He turned to look at me but I closed my eyes I did, only I caught the faintest glimpse of his expression and it was the saddest thing I've ever seen."

"Sad?" Grant asked.

"That it was. Like the sadness of all the world on his shoulders. Then he turned away and stared out at the Burren, all alone. But that's not all I saw. I saw the Devil's own child the same day!"

Malone was ready to laugh again but Grant shot him a look that silenced him.

"What do you mean, 'the Devil's child'?"

"Would you like some more tea?" Meg asked. She nodded at the money jar.

Grant took two bills from his wallet and stuffed them into the jar. "You don't have to bother with the tea. Just tell me what you saw."

Meg settled herself on the couch. She stole a look at the cuckoo clock on the wall. "I'll be having to make this quick. There's another tour bus due in a bit, and I have to call me friend Eileen before that . . ."

"What did you see?" Grant persisted.

She folded her hands in her lap and looked hard at Grant. "Like I said, the Devil's own child. I was waiting for Curley, my youngest, to pick me up. He asked me to stand on the far side of the road, above the sheep pasture, so he doesn't have to put the car up the driveway. He's not so good a driver, and has trouble backing it up, he does. So I'm standing there, minding my own business, and I look down into Mr. Inagh's pasture and there's one of his sheep dead on the ground, and this girl standing over it."

"The girl killed the sheep?" Malone asked, incredulously.

"Oh yes, she did all right. Because I saw her do it again. All she did was look at it, and give it the lightest of taps, and down it went, dead as a fence post. And I was so afraid that she'd look up and see me that I ran across the road, and don't you know Curley nearly run me down. I got into that automobile faster than I've ever done anything in me life, you can be sure, and I'm almost eighty but a year. And then that very same night on the Burren I saw the Lord of Death himself."

She shut her mouth like a trap, and sat looking from one to the other of them. Finally Grant said, "Anything else, Meg?"

"Ain't that enough? The Devil's child and Death himself in one day!"

Grant peeled off a few more bills and jammed them into the jar as he rose. Malone was already out of his chair and heading for the door.

Suddenly Meg Conner scooted ahead of them, her cell phone already open.

"Eileen?" she said into the phone, as another tour bus pulled up in front of Malone's car and opened its door with a wheeze.

"Eileen, the three-thirty is here, it is! What's the bet, then?"

There was a mumble on the other end.

"Ha!" Meg chortled. "And take it I will! Stinkin' bus people! And I know that not one of the cheap bastards'll cross the street, just like the last one!"

She stood in the now open doorway staring at the bus as Malone and Grant walked down to the car.

As they got into the car Malone laughed sharply and said, "Did you believe a single word she said?"

Grant stared through the windshield.

"Every word of it," he said.

CHAPTER THIRTY-NINE

After an hour of argument, Malone agreed to take Grant to the Burren the next day. They ate dinner at the hotel in Killarney. Grant was already sick of the Irish custom of serving potatoes with every meal, sometimes in three different forms. The steak Grant had ordered (local Angus beef, which was excellent) came on a bed of mashed potatoes, with a bowl of boiled potatoes for the table. And every lunch and dinner he had had was also accompanied by family-style vegetables in the Irish flag colors: inevitably green beans, cauliflower and carrots, all steamed to tastelessness.

Malone speared a boiled potato and held it up. "Do you know where this comes from?" he asked.

Grant shook his head.

"Cyprus. They're imported, all of them. I have yet to eat a potato that was grown in Ireland."

Malone's face was more flushed than usual, and Grant asked, "Are you okay, Tom?"

"Just a little tired, is all. You've already given me more

activity than I've had in years. I must say I've enjoyed it, though."

Grant leaned across the table. "This stuff is real, you know."

Malone shrugged, put another potato on his dish and cut into it with his fork. "It's all the same to me, Bill. I don't mind telling you I don't believe a single bit of it. But you do, and it gets both of us out of the house. I forgot how much I missed real police work. I told you before, Riley Gates vouched for you and that's all I need. The rest is just recreation. Whether you find your boogeyman or not, the chase has been fun. And I want you to look in the mirror before you go to bed tonight. Two days off the hard booze and butts and you look like a different man. I'm proud of myself, I am."

Grant nodded. "I have you to thank."

"Yes, you do. It's been good for me to boss somebody around. Been a while." He pointed to Grant's plate with his fork. "Eat your potatoes, boyo. Good for you."

Grant groaned.

After dinner Grant was ready for bed but Malone dragged him to a singing pub in time to hear some traditional Irish music. It was crowded and noisy, but the music was good. The Guinness, though, only made him sleepier. He had actually nodded off at their tiny table when he was jostled awake by Malone's beefy hand.

"Time to go," the old cop said. "I'm tired myself and we have a bit of a drive tomorrow. We'll go on to Galway after the Burren, if you like. Cheaper than staying here another night. You'll like Galway, you will. Everybody does. We missed the Oyster Festival a couple weeks back but there's plenty else to see. And it's a college town, so maybe we'll see some pretty girls."

Malone smiled at him. "So what'll it be? On to Galway after tramping around the Burren looking at nothing?"

"Galway sounds fine."

"Good then."

Grant didn't tell him that he had no idea if they would ever leave the Burren alive.

CHAPTER FORTY

"They brought Neil Armstrong, the Apollo astronaut, here, and he said it was the only place on Earth that looked like the surface of the moon."

Malone stood with his hands on his hips, surveying the rocky landscape while Grant searched the four horizons. It was a raw, blustery day, clouds and blue sky occasionally trading places, and there had been a sprinkle of rain on the ride up. They had checked out of their hotel in Killarney, their bags thrown in the back of the Toyota.

Below and to their right lay a verdant green valley, as out of place in this alien landscape as a golf course on the planet Mars. All else was limestone, the rocks so densely packed together they looked in places like the bottom of a quarry. And yet tiny wild flowers, yellow and purple, had found purchase here and there in cracks, in the narrow spaces between rocks.

Grant made a slow surveying circle, and Malone laughed, then coughed.

"No sign of your boogeyman, Bill?" he asked, laughing

again. "We've been here a bloody hour and the rocks haven't changed, far as I can tell."

He coughed again. "I've got to sit down, boyo."

He ambled off to the car, and Grant looked after him with concern. Malone looked no better today than he had the night before—his ruddy complexion had washed to paleness, and twice they had to pull over for him to catch his breath. He claimed it was nothing, that he was "just tired and old," but Grant wasn't so sure.

"Maybe we should head out to Galway soon," he said, reluctantly, and Malone gave a wave as he climbed into the car and sat down, putting his head back on the rest and closing his eyes.

"Anytime, boyo," Malone said.

Grant shaded his eyes against the sudden appearance of the sun, and looked to the north, the west—

There was a figure to the west, darkly outlined against the gray-white rocks. A black cape, swirling independent of the breeze.

"Tom," Grant said, but the figure in the car looked asleep.

Grant began to climb over rocks toward the distant specter, who was unmoving, staring out across the Burren, seemingly unheedful of Grant.

The day darkened, gray clouds rising from the west behind Samhain and climbing the sky. The sun retreated and then was gone, and a chill rain began to fall.

"Samhain," Grant called, as he got nearer, but the figure refused to acknowledge him.

Grant drew close, and now Samhain turned slowly to face him.

"We meet again," he said, the slash of mouth forming something like a smile. But the hollow eyes were empty, and there was, as Meg Conner had said, a great aura of melancholy about him.

"Where is she?" Grant said.

Slowly, the specter shrugged. "Not here. Not anymore. She went on without me."

"Why?"

Samhain paused, then looked to the west once more. "Because I failed her. Because I won't help her."

There was a long pause. "Because, Detective, I discovered that there is another hand in all this."

Again he looked to the west.

"She has to be stopped, Samhain," Grant said.

"I agree. There are . . . things already in the works."

"What things?"

"The future," Samhain said, again turning his blank oval face to Grant, "remains to be seen." Without pause he said, "For millennia, I thought the Dark One was my master. I always knew who the Dark One was. But I never knew who *I* was.

"Do you know, this is where I started on this planet. It was a long time again. It was barren then and it's still barren. I used to treasure the barrenness. But now I don't. Something has happened to me and I don't know what. There were other places, before this planet, and I don't have a clear memory of them. Only hints that have come back to me. Don't you find that sad, Detective? I have no memory of my own . . . beginnings.

"In a way I thought myself a god—but what am I god of? Death? It happens every day, every hour, every second. It's happening as we speak, all around us. I could raise one of these sterile-looking stones and we would find some vile insect eating some other vile insect. Within twenty miles of where we stand, someone is dying.

"I thought I hated life, Detective, but I don't. This is the odd and dangerous truth, and something I never fully realized.

"And I served a false god, it seems."

"If we don't stop her, she'll destroy everything."

Samhain sighed. "Oh, yes, she certainly will. It's what the Dark One has always longed for—the absolute negation of life. And, if there is no more life, there will be no more death. I knew that, of course, but I'm afraid the finality of it escaped me."

Samhain turned slowly to face Grant. "There are a few things I want to get . . . straight, Detective." He smiled grimly. "Off my chest, if I possessed one. You see, I've never actually . . . killed anyone. I'm powerless to do so. You must believe me. It's one of my tricks. I can cloud a man's mind into thinking or doing something, but only if he is susceptible, and only if he is willing. Bud Ganley, for instance. He unhooked the chain holding that car engine himself. All I did was . . . suggest."

"What about Marianne Carlin?" Grant snapped.

Samhain's stone face regarded him silently for a moment.

"It was the Dark One who caused her death. Though I do now regret it. I suppose you might call me an . . . accessory, if you like. A tool. I've never been able to influence you. And I must tell you that I've grown quite fond of you over the years. I have come to regard many of you as interesting creatures, deserving, even, of an amount of respect. All the bugaboos I've tossed at you were in your own mind. I have no power over anything. I didn't kill your wife, you know—I only let you believe I did. She was not a bad woman, but she was tired of life. I merely . . . abetted her, if you will. And sometimes I was a conduit for the Dark One himself—which was, I suppose, my greatest crime."

"You'll help me, then."

It began to rain harder, a mist rising over the rocks which had turned chalky white with the wetness. Samhain turned away. "You? You can do little, Detective. And I don't know if I can even help myself."

"Where did she go?"

"To Orangefield. To Halloween. Where else? Though neither of us will find her until she wants to be seen. Midnight on Halloween, four days from now." He sighed again, a sound beyond sadness. "Your friend, the other policeman, please believe that it was not me. It was merely his time."

"What do you mean?" Grant said in alarm.

Samhain began to slowly drift away over the rocks, his black cape swirling as he receded. "You must talk to Reggie Bright, Detective. She is our only hope in this matter. And you must hope that I am truly strong this Halloween."

And then the wraith was gone, melting into the rain and mist, and Grant was running back to the car.

PART FOUR

ORANGEFIELD

CHAPTER FORTY-ONE

It took almost two days to arrange things for Malone's burial and the disposition of his possessions. The police in Galway, and then in Killarney, had been helpful and even respectful, but they made it clear that Grant wasn't to leave the country until the coroner was finished with his report. Malone had a brother in Milwaukee, who flew over, and finally Grant was able to hand him the car and house keys and head for Dublin airport.

It was raining, had been since the funeral, and Grant was relieved when the Aer Lingus Airbus climbed above the clouds and the sun emerged, glaring coldly off the tops of the clouds below. Soon the sun set and the stars shone even more coldly. And then Grant sank into blessed sleep.

New York looked strange after the wet bright green of Ireland, but by the time he drove onto the Northway into the Adirondacks he began to feel at home. The trees had dropped many of their leaves, but there was still a riot of colors from the elms and oaks nestled in with the upstate pines. The radio said it was thirty-eight degrees, and

Grant thought of the light overcoat packed in his luggage in the trunk and turned the heat on in the car.

Orangefield was bedecked for Halloween, pumpkins everywhere. An orange stripe had been painted down the center of Main Street, and Grant was relieved to see that the Pumpkin Days Festival was over and that the tents had been taken down in Ranier Park. The MAYOR GERGEN WELCOMES YOU TO ORANGEFIELD, THE PUMPKIN CAPITAL OF THE WORLD banner was still up on City Hall, though, Grant noted wryly.

Out of habit, Grant slowed down as he passed the police station, but then he drove on, turning ten minutes later onto Sagett River Road.

The Bright house had a real estate sign on the front lawn that looked like it had been there for quite some time. Grant noted the phone number and punched it into his cell phone.

"Boskone Realty," a hopeful chirpy female voice answered.

"I'm looking for the Bright family. One of your signs is on the front lawn."

"You interested? Haven't been able to move that property in almost two years. Now it's the market but it should have sold in a minute twenty-four months ago. Beautiful place, a little high end for the area but that's a plus. The newest asking price is"—Grant heard shuffling papers—"three twenty. I'm sure I can get them down near three at this point."

"I'd like to get in touch with the Brights."

A short laugh. "So would I! They owe me a fee or two."

Grant asked if there was a forwarding address.

"Only thing I have is her sister, who's handling the

house sale. They split up a while ago. I think he's dead but I'm not sure."

Grant told her he was a police officer and obtained the sister's phone number.

"If you decide you like the place lemme know—I bet I could get her down to two ninety at this point."

Janice Hoffer, the sister, lived in Albany and wouldn't talk on the phone. An hour and a half later Grant was at the door to her condo a short way from the Albany University campus.

"Sorry to make you drive all this way but I don't like talking about my sister on the phone. It's the husband."

"The real estate agent thought he was dead."

Janice Hoffer humphed. "If only. He's the problem. If you ask me, Marcia should have dumped him sooner. Turning that kid of theirs into a circus freak, for heaven's sake, and just to make a buck."

"Reggie?"

"We called her Gina. She was fine until all that weird stuff happened when she was five."

"I was with her when she . . ."

"Came back from the dead?" Janice Hoffer humphed again. "Give me a break. Anyway, as you know, something weird-ass happened to her, and she was never the same."

"I checked in on her a few months later and she was fine."

"Define 'fine'—she was already acting screwy by then, believe me."

"That's not what her mother told me."

"Marcia bullshitted you! Ted had her on one of those late night shows almost right away, claiming she'd seen

161

the other side. Gina told a pretty good story, too, and convincing. Ted tried to get a book deal, but that never went anywhere because the kid didn't have any real proof. Only stories about weird shapes, and Mr. Death himself, all kinds of nonsense. That's when the trouble started, people coming to the house asking for an audience with 'the dead kid.' Things like that. They moved a couple months later, to the midwest, and then the real trouble started. Reggie started talking to 'her friends' again, supposedly dead folks, and Marcia freaked out. Gina stopped eating and went into catatonic episodes. They put her in an institution for a while, but then even the nuthouse wouldn't keep her. Too weird. Then Ted tried to turn her into an attraction again, local talk shows, radio, TV, newspapers, and finally Marcia kicked him out and divorced him. She got custody, but Ted took off with the kid and that was that."

"What do you mean?"

"We don't know what happened to her. And now she'd be, what, thirteen years old?"

"Twelve, actually," Grant corrected.

"Whatever. The point is, Marcia didn't try too hard to find her. I think she was burned out, and didn't know what to do with Gina anyway. I mean, when the nuthouse kicks you out . . ."

Janice Hoffer seemed to have run down, like a windup toy, and had nothing else to say.

"Is there anyplace I can start?" Grant asked.

Hoffer shrugged. "Try Cattersville, Ohio. That's the last any of us heard of Ted and Gina."

CHAPTER FORTY-TWO

It was amazingly easy to find Ted Bright. Grant immediately thought of what Janice Hoffer had said—apparently Marcia Bright had just decided not to deal with it anymore. Ted Bright was listed in the Cattersville phone book, and Grant found his number with a simple online white pages search. The man answered the phone on the first ring.

"Baker?" a hopeful voice said.

Grant identified himself, and the voice became instantly wary.

"Is this about Marcia?"

"No, it's about your daughter."

"Oh. Are you working for some collection clown?"

Grant found that he was losing his temper. "I need to know where your daughter is, Mr. Bright."

"Like I've told every collection clown and shithead lawyer I've dealt with for the past three years, I have no idea where Gina is."

"She's been gone for that long?" Grant asked incredulously.

"You said you were a cop, right?" Bright asked, the wariness in his voice deepening.

"That's right," Grant lied.

"I remember you now. From Orangefield, right?"

"I was there the night your daughter . . . returned."

There was a moment of silence, and then Bright's voice came back, altered to friendliness.

"Bill Grant! Hey, how are you! Shit, I should have gotten in touch with you long ago!"

"Why is that?"

"Sure! We could have made a lot of money, you and I. Wow! Why didn't I think of it before? I should have talked to you seven years ago, when this all began. Hell, I could have gotten you on Leno! The guy who was with Gina when she came back! You looking for a manager, by any chance? Why didn't you get in touch? We were on a couple of daytime talkers, too! Though none of it ever made the local paper, that bastard Mayor Gergen afraid of bad publicity. Maybe that's why you never called . . ."

Through his sudden rage Grant managed to get out: "The only thing I'm looking for is your daughter."

"Oh." The voice deflated. "Like I said, she's been with Carperon, Inc. for the past three years. I can't tell that to the collection clowns or they'd put a lien on the money I get from them twice a year. And they pay in cash."

"What is Carperon, Inc.?"

"Stands for Carnival Per Onus. They book acts all over the country. Believe me, I've been through this with everyone, and there was nothing illegal about it. They treat her just fine. Hell, once they kicked her out of the nuthouse there was nothing the social services idiots could do about it. They feed and clothe her and they're certified. Though the last year the payments have dropped. I've been getting the guaranteed, and not a penny more. Maybe people aren't interested in freak shows anymore—"

Grant had had enough. "I could be in Ohio in ten hours if I drove, and I would very much like to beat the piss out of you."

A pause and then Bright laughed. "And I'd have the local police on you in five minutes!"

"Do you realize what you've done to her?"

"I haven't done a damn thing to her!" Bright shouted. "Do you know what *I've* been through since she turned into what she is? I used to have a regular job, a regular home life, a regular wife. We went out for ice cream every Sunday, for shit's sake! I put clothes on their backs, food on the table, gave them a nice house on Sagett River Road and presents under the Christmas tree!" He was nearly hysterical now. "And then my kid goes . . . *somewhere else*, somewhere where no one has been before, the effing afterlife, if you believe it—*and she comes back!* And overnight my life turns to shit! My wife is hysterical, my kid is catatonic, my boss tells me he can't afford the publicity and fires my ass! And where am I then? WHERE AM I, DETECTIVE GRANT? I'm nowhere, that's where I am. I have nothing I ever wanted, after I had everything. So what do I do? What would you do? What would anyone do? I take care of business! That's what I was trained to do, the only thing I was trained to do. The only thing I'm effing good for! My old man always said, 'Take care of business, son.' That's the only damn thing he ever said to me! Never, 'Nice catch, son!' or 'That's okay, son, you'll get it right the next time' or 'I'm glad you're my son!' Only 'Take care of business!' WHAT WAS I SUPPOSED TO DO?" Bright was weeping now, and Grant heard a pounding noise, as if the man were hitting something with his fist—a wall, a desk, himself.

"Mr. Bright—" Grant tried, lowering the anger in his own voice like he had been trained to do in a high-tension situation.

"I TOOK CARE OF BUSINESS, DAMMIT!" Bright shouted, sobbing, and then the phone went dead.

Grant stared at his cell phone for a moment and then turned it off.

CHAPTER FORTY-THREE

Carperon, Inc. was not listed on the New York Stock Exchange. Not that Grant thought that it would be, but it was a place to start. The single overhead bulb in his hotel room had burned out, but he didn't even notice. The glow of his computer screen illuminated the room.

The room was cold, and he got up to slam the window shut. Outside, the sky had taken on a tepid late October glow from the setting sun in the west. There was a brighter glow that was not part of twilight, and he heard the faintest tinkle of what sounded like calliope music.

He reopened the window all the way. He shivered and noted that the heat had been on all the time, offset by the chill coming through the window.

The tinkle became a low and steady susurrus of music, the chiming of bells and the occasional sharp snick of a cymbal.

And now he saw it, over the trees, over the low buildings and houses of Orangefield: the very top portion of the Halloweenland Ferris wheel, turning slowly and majestically, outlined in lights: red, green, yellow, blue.

He listened for another moment, and thought he could hear the far-off murmur of crowd noises, and a barker's sharp tongue.

Another shiver went through him, and he slammed the window shut.

He wanted a cigarette or a drink, but pushed those thoughts out of his mind.

When he Googled Carperon, Inc. nothing came up. The same with Carperon. Which left him with a long and tedious search through carnival management and then just plain carnival, which naturally brought him a string of Carnival Cruise Lines hits.

He leaned back in his chair—now it was too hot in the room. He rose and reopened the window a crack. The ancient radiator was hissing.

An unopened bottle of Dewar's sat next to the television on the floor where he had placed it as a reminder. His body and head ached to open it, but he walked back to the computer and sat down.

He typed into the search engine "CARNIVAL FREAKS."

For the next hour he waded through nonsense, sites for Tod Browning's 1932 film *Freaks* and a gaggle of less interesting junk. He kept looking at the Dewar's bottle, which he had set there as a test.

Then he went back to the search engine line and added "BRIGHT" after the word "FREAKS."

More nonsense, even worse: "BRIGHT TEETH! DON'T BE A FREAK!" Two sites for a band called "Brighty Mites."

He got up again, opened the window a little more, didn't look at the scotch.

He marched back to the desk and typed in "CARNIVAL FREAKS GINA."

Nothing.

Then: "CARNIVAL FREAKS REGGIE."

Bingo.

There were three entries, one of which was a bogus come-on for pornography. Of the other two one was a newspaper article and the other some sort of list.

He went for the list first.

It proved to be a list of notes for a graduate school paper on freak shows. Grant had no idea why it had been posted to the Web. There was a "Gina the Otherwordly Little Lady" listed as a footnote reference note for page 76 but no other information. No matter what Grant did he couldn't access the paper itself; he kept getting a nonaccess page for Columbia University. The name of the thesis, "The Treatment of the Disabled and Noncomformist in America, a Legal History" was listed at the beginning of the notes section but there was no author listed.

The other Web page was for the Mobile, Alabama *Register*, which, apparently, was no longer in business because the page came up as expired.

He searched for the newspaper and discovered that it had gone belly-up two years ago. It was also listed under "Alternative Newspapers." That listing had a phone number but it proved to have been reassigned to a family named Porter.

So . . .

He spent the next hours trying every variation of "freak' and "Gina" and "Regina" and "Bright" and anything else he could think of. It got cold in the room again, and he shut the window.

His back ached; he rolled the computer mouse away in disgust and sat staring at the unyielding screen.

He looked at his phone, which was sitting flipped open on the desk.

He snatched it up, punched in a New York City number. "Murray?"

A groggy voice said, "This is Murray Chase. This is an unlisted number—"

"This is Bill Grant."

"Grant . . ." Silence for a moment. "Sure, Bill Grant! How are ya?"

"Not too bad. I need a favor."

"That depends, Bill . . ."

"Let's just say it's for Riley Gates and Tom Malone."

A moment's hesitation. "I heard about Riley. Damn shame. If it wasn't for him I never would have made detective, never mind lieutenant. And I just heard about Malone today through the grapevine. Damn shame. Another good one."

"That's what I'm counting on. Do you know anybody at Columbia University?"

"Give me a sec. You do realize it's two in the morning, Bill."

Grant looked at the lower right-hand corner of his screen: the time icon confirmed what Chase had said.

"Shit, I'm sorry."

"You don't sound loaded, so it must be interesting." Chase laughed. "Yes, I know somebody at Columbia University who can get into the records. That's what you need, yes?"

"Yes."

"Call me at this number tomorrow morning and I'll see what I can do."

"Thanks."

"And call at a reasonable time—say ten a.m."

"You got it."

The call ended in Chase's laugh and then yawn.

CHAPTER FOURTY-FOUR

The next morning, after a fitful night alternating between bouts of sleep during which he dreamed of alcohol, and insomniac stretches during which he sat in bed and thought about alcohol, he arose soaked in sweat and realized it was Halloween. An electronic bell the mayor had installed in the garret of City Hall proclaimed the day precisely at eight, with eight funereal *bongs*. At twelve noon the farce would be repeated. The *Orangefield Herald* had tried to mount a mild campaign against what they had called "ghoulish tendencies," but it had come to nothing, since the mayor's brother owned the paper. Ted Bright had gotten that part right. The people and especially the businesses of Orangefield loved it because it was good for business—and whatever was good for the almighty buck in Orangefield never failed to fly.

Sure enough the date icon on Grant's computer screen seconded the motion: it was the thirty-first of October.

"Shit," Grant said.

He automatically reached for a cigarette, found the

pack in his shirt pocket (deliberately) empty, and cursed again, balling the fragrant pack into a ball and throwing it at the wall.

He called Murray Chase, risking the cop's ire.

"Hey, Bill, for Pete's sake, it's—"

"It's important, Murray."

"Gimme what you want."

Grant told him.

"You gotta realize this guy might be teaching an early class. I'll call you when I know something."

"Thanks."

Ten minutes later the phone rang, and Grant pushed the talk button, holding his breath.

"I got him, but it may take him a bit to get what you want. I gave him your number so he can call you himself. His name's Professor Jeff Harmon."

"Thanks again."

But Chase had already hung up.

Grant dressed, put the fully charged phone in his pocket and drove to a diner to fill himself with bacon and eggs. He didn't look at the Dewar's bottle on the way out. He drank three cups of coffee, and it tasted like turpentine in his mouth. All he wanted was a drink.

He willed the phone to ring but nothing happened.

Near the diner was a newsstand, and he stopped there and bought a package of cigarettes. There were carved pumpkins lining the counter of the stand. As the attendant handed him the cigarettes, Grant nearly tore the cellophane off and had a butt lit as soon as it was in his mouth.

"One out of two ain't bad, Malone," he mumbled.

Still he willed the phone to ring, but it was silent.

He knew what would happen if he waited around doing

nothing. He would smoke most of the cigarettes, then he would march into the nearest bar as soon as the phony clock tower in City Hall struck twelve gloomy bell peels.

Then he would proceed to get very drunk.

"This one's for you, Malone."

He threw the half-finished cigarette down and climbed into his car, turning it toward the highway.

He barely glanced to either side as he drove out of town. He already knew what he would see: a barrage of orange fruit, face after face carved into grotesque grins. Every shop in town put their pumpkins out first thing in the morning, and tonight as darkness fell the air would be filled with the spice of thousands of burning pumpkin guts. Every house had not one but two or three or twenty pumpkins. Each street was a riot of Halloween decorations: house-long webs with spiders that jangled down as the unwary walked through what looked to be the one open spot; Frankensteins sewn together with mechanical and electronic parts, which growled GRRRRRRRR! and reached out to grab you as you passed; bats on wires that danced around one another; the howl of wolves instead of door chimes when you pushed a front door button. Blocks had contests for best decorations and best lights (orange and white that flashed "Happy Halloween" in letters two feet high; lights strung in trees to look like rain and lightning; light shows strung over three houses running, coordinated by computer). Every year it got worse, became bigger. Everyone loved it.

And the trick-or-treaters—they started earlier every year, the kindergartners out way before dark, and no curfew until midnight. They wore costumes now that looked like designer clothing: rapper outfits complete with bling, little girls as runway models, space creatures designed by special effects experts (complete with more electronics and lights).

Grant looked at none of it and didn't take his eyes off the road until he was on the Northway.

He took the north ramp, thinking to drive until he was tired of it. The trees of the Adirondacks were in last full glory: a riot of bright orange and red leaves that outshone even the pumpkin-suffused town of Orangefield. There were some stretches where the foliage would be spectacular.

The phone in his pocket suddenly rang, a harsh chirping sound.

Grant simultaneously slowed from 65 miles per hour while fishing the phone from his pocket. He flipped it open as he came to a stop on the shoulder of the road.

"Yes?" he said, pushing the talk button.

In his haste he had jabbed the end button instead.

"Shit!"

The phone rang again a moment later, and Grant carefully pressed the talk button.

"Is this Detective Grant?" a thin, reedy voice said.

"Yes, it is. Professor Harmon?"

"Yes. But I'm a little confused. I had a talk with a New York City policeman this morning—"

"Yes, he said you'd call me directly."

"The information you're asking for, I can't release. There's student confidentiality involved—"

"Didn't Lieutenant Chase tell you it was important?"

"That's really beside the point. We have university procedures that prohibit us from releasing any student information to anyone but the student. Even their own parents can't access their own sons' or daughters' information."

"That's insane! You have to tell me—"

"It's all tied up with federal law, Detective. We could actually lose funding if we broke procedure on something like this. Even Columbia Law School is bound by it." He gave a short laugh.

"Professor Harmon, I can't tell you how important—"

Grant noted the rising hysteria in his own voice.

"I'm very sorry, Detective. There's nothing I can do."

"You said Columbia Law School, right?" he nearly shouted.

The phone went dead.

Grant sat looking at the phone, a useless object in his hand, and then he jammed it onto the seat beside him.

He viciously turned the engine on, gunned it as he threw it into drive, and pulled out onto the Northway, cutting off a tractor trailer. The truck threw its brakes into a scream as Grant slammed ahead, pulling into the left lane and looking for a turnaround.

He found one, and as he completed the U-turn and pushed the pedal to the floor he flipped open his glove compartment, took out what was in there, and put it in his shoulder holster.

CHAPTER FORTY-FIVE

He entered the Columbia campus after leaving the car in what must have been the last parking spot in New York City, on 116th Street. There were some students in costume, a party going on in the grassy area in front of the domed Low Memorial Library. He asked a girl dressed like a vampire where the Law School was located. She asked a companion dressed like a flying monkey from *The Wizard of Oz*, who hitched his thumb to the right.

"Walk between Philosophy and Kent and across the sculpture area. It's on the east campus, over Amsterdam Avenue. Jerome Greene Hall. You can't miss it. It looks like a friggin' toaster."

Grant did as he was told, passing some incredibly ugly sculptures. He entered the building. An atrium cut through the building from top to bottom, letting in a lot of light. He asked a few passing students where he might find Harmon, with no success, walked down to the second floor, which looked like an airport lounge with a café, quickly dismounted the ceremonial staircase to the first floor, consulted a roster behind glass on the wall and found Harmon's office number. He got lost in a maze of classrooms and lecture halls but finally found it, tucked away next to a stairwell.

The door was ajar and he pushed it open.

"Are you Professor Harmon?"

A lanky man with a mop of reddish hair swiveled his chair away from the computer screen he had been hunched over and said with a quizzical, almost bored look, "Yes?"

Grant removed his .38 from its holster, toed the door shut behind him and stepped forward, putting the gun to Harmon's neck.

"Hey, is this one of Dan's jokes—?"

"No joke. My name is Grant. I spoke to you on the phone four hours ago. You know what I want."

Harmon began to open his mouth to protest, but when Grant pressed the muzzle of the .38 harder into his neck he kept his mouth shut and lost most of his color.

"I don't want to hear any bullshit about confidentiality," Grant said. "And don't faint. Let's go."

Harmon turned back to the computer, pulled up a new screen that said "Student Records," and punched in a code. Another screen came up telling him that he had been granted access.

"What was the name of that paper again?" Harmon said. He began to wheeze and complained, "I'm not going to faint but I do have asthma."

"Then take care of it," Grant ordered.

Harmon pulled out an inhaler from his pocket and shoved it into his mouth, taking a deep breath. He put it away and Grant told him the name of the thesis.

"I don't give a shit who wrote it, I don't give a shit about anything but this reference on this page." Grant shoved the piece of paper he had written the information on.

Harmon ran his fingers over the keyboard, squinted at the screen, tapped more keys.

The screen went dark, then the name of the thesis came up, with a few lines of information under it.

"It's not online," Harmon reported. "The author, Anne Simmons, never turned in the final version. And she didn't complete her course work."

Grant pushed the muzzle harder into Harmon's neck. "What does that mean?"

"It means the thesis hasn't been published, so we can't look at it here."

Harmon slowly looked up at Grant. "Why are you doing this?"

Grant lowered the gun. "It's very important."

Harmon studied him for a moment. He had regained his color, and wore a pensive expression. "I've watched a lot of cop shows, Detective, and either you're nuts, or what you say is true. If you promise not to point that gun at me again I'll help you. For a price."

Grant opened his mouth but Harmon was already out of his chair, putting on his jacket. "There will be a copy in her advisor's office. Either on computer or in manuscript. You're lucky—he's a good friend of mine."

Grant holstered his gun and followed Harmon out the door and down the corridor.

Harmon stopped in front of an adjacent office and rattled the doorknob.

"Dan?" He banged on the door. "Dan, open up!"

A slouching young man who was passing by said, "Law and Civilization, lecture hall one-twelve. I just cut it."

He continued his slouching shuffle down the hall.

Grant followed Harmon in a run to the stairs.

CHAPTER FORTY-SIX

Grant was reminded of the lecture hall in *The Paper Chase*. It was half-full with half-asleep-looking students, but even the most bored of them had an open notebook and was holding a pen in his or her hand.

Harmon marched to the lectern and said something to the short, rotund teacher, who stopped in midsentence and followed Harmon out of the hall. At the doorway the teacher turned and said to the class, "We'll pick it up next time."

The teacher, who was introduced as Dan Stein, looked Grant up and down and said, "You're really a cop?"

Grant opened his jacket and showed him his gun.

"Hey!" Stein said. "We can put this in the teleplay!"

"Dan and I are writing a teleplay for *Law and Order*," Harmon explained as they went back to Stein's office. He looked suddenly sheepish. "It's not sold, yet, just on spec. I'm sorry, but that's all I could think about while you held your police special to my neck."

Stein's eyes went wide. "He held it to your neck?"

Harmon waved a hand in dismissal. "We'll use it in the teleplay, Dan. Open the door."

Stein fumbled his keys out and opened the door. They entered a cluttered office with papers and books stacked everywhere.

"We need Anne Simmons' thesis."

"Who?" Stein said. He frowned.

"Two semesters ago. She didn't complete."

"Wow, two semesters. I can't remember them a week after they're gone. We'll check the machine."

They followed him around a wall of law books topped with stacks of spiral notebooks at a precarious angle. Behind the wall was a desk covered in junk—pens and pencils, more notebooks, stacks of loose papers, more law books, thriller novels—and in the midst of it all the largest computer screen Grant had ever seen.

"Great for DVDs, when I can't stand grading anymore," Stein commented, as he pushed a button hidden behind a pile of books. There was an uneventful moment and then the screen filled with what looked like a homemade movie, a handheld camera recording a flight down a concrete set of steps in what looked like Central Park.

Stein uncovered his keyboard and tapped some keys. "We filmed part of the teleplay, borrowed some film students," he said.

The screen went blank, then bright blue, hurting Grant's eyes. Then a white screen came up with a cursor in the upper left corner.

"What was the name again?" Stein asked.

Harmon told him.

Stein typed it in.

A name came up, followed by rows of information.

"Hey," Stein said, suddenly wary, partly covering the

screen with his hands, "does Mr. Detective here know about the confidentiality laws?"

Harmon said, sighing, "It's all right, Dan."

Stein shrugged and pushed his face close to the screen. "Oh," he said.

"What?" Harmon replied.

"It says it's here. She never finished it, right?"

"Correct," Harmon said.

"Then all we have to do is find it," Stein said, sweeping his hands around the room, the endless stacks.

CHAPTER FORTY-SEVEN

"Jeez, Dan, haven't you ever heard of organization?" Harmon said, after a half hour of plowing through one stack of old papers. They had each taken a quadrant, leaving the least likely corner of the room (*"Really* old stuff," Stein had explained) for last.

Stein laughed. "I took a course in Labor Organization once," he said. "They gave me the choice of dropping out or flunking."

Grant threw aside a bound thesis titled "Labor Union Strife of the 1960s and Its Long-Term Effect on the American Economy" and picked up another called "The Rembrandt Effect: Labor Law in Seventeenth Century Holland."

"Don't you remember anything about Anne Simmons?" Harmon asked Stein.

There was silence, then Stein said, "No. Oh, wait, yes. She was either tall and thin with blond hair, or short and heavy with blond hair."

"You're sure she was a blonde?" Harmon said.

"No."

Grant looked at his watch. "Would you two screenwriters please get back to work?"

"You will promise to let us use you as a consultant, right?" Stein asked.

"If you find what I want, you can pick my brains clean."

"Cool."

There was the sound of papers shuffled, riffled, the thump of theses tossed aside.

After another half hour the three of them stood in the midst of a sea of discarded paper staring at the remaining corner of the room.

"How old?" Harmon asked.

"Well, there's always the chance it was misfiled."

Grant stepped forward and grabbed the top of the nearest pile, and his two companions dug in beside him.

Twenty minutes later Stein announced, "I've got it."

The two others stopped immediately and looked over the short man's shoulders. He held in his hand a maroon-colored binder with a typed sticker on the cover which read: "The Treatment of the Disabled and Nonconformist in America, a Legal History" and under that "by Anne Simmons."

"This is important?" Stein laughed, and Grant tore the thesis out of his hand and pulled it open. He quickly thumbed to page seventy-six and moved his index finger down to the footnote number, which was at the end of a long sentence. His heart pounding, he tore his finger back to the beginning: ". . . and Gina, the Otherworldly Little Lady, who, her father claimed, had visited a land beyond the grave and then returned to the land of the living. Managed by her father, she appeared on talk shows before abruptly disappearing into the strange world of the carnival freak. Whether she is catatonic or delusional, her rights were obviously abused, and as of this writing she is a member of a team of carnival attractions owned by Carperon, Inc., a midwest purveyor of traveling shows, the most recent of which, Halloweenland, owned and operated by a so-called Mr. Dickens, whose real name . . ."

Grant read the name, dropped the thesis and turned toward the door.

"Hey, Detective, you okay?" Stein asked.

Harmon voiced concern and curiosity. "Detective Grant? What does it mean?"

"It means I go back to where I started."

Behind him, as he ran for the stairs and his car, he heard Stein utter, "Wow! We can use that line in the teleplay!"

PART FIVE

HALLOWEENLAND

CHAPTER FORTY-EIGHT

For a lingering last moment, Grant stood by the door of his car in the Halloweenland parking lot and smoked a cigarette. There was a Halloween moon up, a thick lopsided smile hovering overhead, and it looked like part of the show. Orange and white Christmas lights were strung in sagging arcs between tall poles around the wide perimeter of the park, swaying slightly in the chill October breeze. More lights, orange only, outlined the ticket booth leading into the attractions. The huge lot was almost full, and families, some with license plates from as far away as Ohio, were pouring out of SUVs and vans. There was a line of charter buses at the far end of the lot, two abreast and ten long. Halloweenland was doing a brisk business.

Grant's heart was still beating fast, but his cop's mind was working. He watched the Ferris wheel, which had just started up with a new set of passengers, after coming to a jerking halt every thirty seconds to unload and reload. It was even taller than it had looked from his apartment, and its carnival lights were blinking tonight in

187

patterns. Its movement was as smooth and silent as a jeweled watch.

There was plenty of other noise, though: the calliope tinkled at full throttle, and Grant realized that the sound was piped into speakers mounted on the same poles that supported the lights. The Tilt-A-Whirl was in full canted flight, its passengers, just glimpsed at the height of the ride's turn, doing the wave and screaming happily as gravity made the bottoms drop out of their stomachs.

Grant dropped and crushed the cigarette, and lit a new one. "Like I said, Malone, one out of two ain't bad." Grant patted the reassuring curve of the flask filled with scotch, as yet untouched, in his jacket pocket. "But the night is young."

He walked to the ticket booth and bought an entry ticket. The ticket seller was pale and moonfaced, and gave him a slow, eerie smile as he slid Grant's ticket across to him with long, thin, long-nailed fingers.

"Have a good time, sir," the ticket taker said in a stentorian voice.

Grant felt the man's eyes follow him in, and the hair on the nape of his neck prickled.

"Shit," he muttered. "Here we go, the biggest, weirdest shit of all."

He walked toward the events tent, passing the expanded kiddie-ride section on the way. Besides the Cups and Saucers, which were in full spin, there was now a Caterpillar, a kind of small, bumped roller on wheels—the attraction was that as the cars went round in round in their small circle, a canvas covering painted to look like a caterpillar moved over the entire length of the contraption, leaving the squealing children in momentary darkness, until the cover retreated again. There was also something Grant hadn't seen since his own childhood: a small, steam-powered railroad, with real passenger cars open at the top and only wide enough to fit a few children inside. An engineer sat cramped in the open tender car behind the engine. It moved silently as Grant passed by, which meant that it wasn't steam after all, but probably filled with electronics and an electric motor.

"It actually runs on magnets—like the new high-speed trains in Europe," a voice next to Grant said, as a moist hand fell on his and squeezed lightly. "Of course we keep this train at four miles per hour, for the kiddies. Don't want to scare Mom and Dad, do we?"

Grant turned and looked into the slightly grinning face of Mr. Dickens. But the eyes were anything but merry.

"When I first met you, you never smiled," Grant said.

"Ah, so you're still a good detective. Excellent. Walk with me."

Dickens took Grant's arm and steered him away from the direction of the attractions tent.

"I want to see Reggie Bright," Grant said.

"Of course. But first we'll walk, and I'll show off my diversion."

"Is that what Halloweenland is?"

The grin was gone from Dickens' face, but the grim, hooded eyes remained dark and unreadable.

"Please, Detective, walk with me."

And then, as he had so many years ago, Thomas Reynolds, Jr. gave a little bow, which looked much more fitting now than it had when Reynolds had been a boy of thirteen, dressed in stiff clothes and with the mannerisms of a mannequin.

"What happened to your mother?" Grant asked, and Reynolds was silent for a long moment. Then he said, "She ended up in an insane asylum in Michigan. And then the authorities discovered that she was an illegal alien. In these times, there is not so much tolerance for foreigners, and she was a burden to the state besides, so she was deported back to Romania."

"I thought she was Russian."

Reynolds shook his head. "She never spoke of it to anyone, and only answered direct questions. My family has a long history in this . . . business, on both sides. The strange was never alien to either my father or my mother. But my mother, in the end, could not abide it, and so gave up. I have not heard from her since. And being involved in what I have been, I have not been able to visit her."

"I'm sorry to hear that."

Reynold's looked up at him, and his eyes were small and hard. "So am I, Detective."

They had come to the waist-high chain fence surrounding the carousel. Reynolds stopped and rested both hands lightly on the chain. A ride was just ending, and the merry-go-round seemed to stop for their pleasure. Grant noticed that there were many carved animals besides horses: a dragon, dark green scaled, with folded wings and carved fire issuing from its fearsome mouth; a gryphon, mythical creature, painted in gray and gold; a pair of stately white unicorns standing abreast a benched seat in deep red. A new herd of children mounted the platform and swarmed to their chosen places, and soon the ride slowly came up to speed. Now Grant saw, in a blur, a few other animals: Cerberus, the three-headed dog who guarded hell; a winged angel, looking fearsome and resolute, though white; and something that looked a lot like Samhain—a deep black cape topped with a barely glimpsed ashen face and flared open at the bottom to reveal a black-seated bench beneath, which was empty.

"A few of the pieces I had specially made in Germany,"

Reynolds explained. His voice dropped in timber. "Even when I was in Europe there was no time to visit my mother." His voice became suffused with bitterness. "Even though, once I came within a few miles of the institution where she is kept. There was always the work."

They left the carrousel, and Reynolds drew them slowly toward the midway. "Perhaps I should explain a bit, Detective," he said. "When we first met, I offered to let you see the second volume of my father's *Occult Practices in Orangefield and Chicawa County, New York*, which covered the period from 1940 until 2000 or so. Do you remember?"

"Yes. As you suggested, I started to read the first volume, which I borrowed from the library. That was when I had my first visit from Samhain."

Reynolds' eyes brightened. "Really? Did he destroy the volume?"

"As a matter of fact he did."

"Curious, since he must have known there were other copies. I'm sure he was just trying to impress you."

"He impressed me."

Reynolds smiled briefly. "If you also remember, during our first conversation I told you that Samhain, for all his fearsomeness and power and supposed dominion over the dead, is merely a servant."

"Yes, I remember that, too. Samhain calls him the Dark One."

Reynolds nodded. They were on the midway, now, which was illuminated with more orange bulbs that outlined each canvas booth: shooting galleries with rows of ducks and red and white targets; guess-the-number wheels which clicked as they were spun; softball tosses into angled bushel baskets. There were milling crowds and noise and the yell of barkers urging customers to try their luck, and the tart buttery smell of popcorn in the air.

Reynolds said, "We of course have known him as Satan, or the Devil, or the Evil One, or Uncreator, or one of countless other names. He is basically a destroyer, who wants to negate all life and unmake everything that has been made.

"We know that on the rare occasion throughout history, forces have aligned giving the Dark One the opportunity to enter our world. If he is able to do so, he then will have the ability to destroy all creation. The Earth, the moon, the stars, all life, everything.

"Reggie Bright was involved in such an attempt, of course." Reynolds paused and gave a slight smile. "You yourself played a part in it, though I doubt you understood the full import of what was happening. This is covered in the third volume of my father's work, which I have continued. *Occult Practices in Orangefield and Chicawa County, New York, 2000-Present.* Yes, Detective, I once told you I would write that book, when I was a very formal and very scared thirteen-year-old. Now I'm not quite as formal but still very much scared.

"Which brings us to the future."

They had exited the back end of the midway and passed through the back of a lot where unused equipment lay under almost total darkness. Only the sideways moon smiling down upon them.

They stopped before the rear entrance to the main event tent. Reynolds held out his fishy, moist hand and laid it gently on Grant's forearm. Grant saw now that it was deformed, had been burned or mangled, and was grown over with calluses and what looked to be new grafted skin.

"What happened to you, Thomas? You don't look like a twenty-year-old. You look a hundred years old."

Reynolds smiled, but his eyes were filled with anything

but merriment. "Older than you, yes, Detective? We have both been through a lot in the last seven years."

"But what—"

"A tale for another time. I've been many places, let's say, and seen many things. Not all of them were pleasant. All of my travels, and all of my ... actions, were in preparation for this day. Or night, rather." His smile deepened momentarily. "Soon we shall see. Remember, I once asked you to call me Thomas, Junior? That's how formal I was."

Grant nodded.

"And now," Reynolds said sweeping a flap open in the tent wall which Grant had not even seen, exposing the gray darkness within, "shall we begin?"

CHAPTER FORTY-NINE

As the flap fell closed behind them, Grant saw that the light in the tent was not so much gray as a kind of sickly pale green. They were in a walled-off section of boxes and more unused equipment. Reynolds led the way through a maze of paraphernalia, cautioning Grant to stay near.

"I thought it best we enter from the back," he explained. "She is stationed toward the far end."

They came to a wall made of tent canvas, which stretched clear across the width of the main tent. From behind it came muffled sounds. Without hesitation Reynolds found and pulled aside another flap. Grant was immediately blinded with a richer light, a deep suffused gold that would seem mysterious if one were to enter from the business end of the tent.

There was another midway, this one stretching into the near distance and roped off in the center to force entering patrons to view one side and then make a U-turn past where Grant and Reynolds stood, before viewing the other side, then exiting where they had come in. A few customers passed Reynolds, wide-eyed, and he smiled and made a slight bow.

"Enjoying yourselves, I trust, folks?"

The oldest of the bunch, a man of grandfatherly age, goggled and said, "Where in heck did you get all this?"

The impresario shrugged nonchalantly. "Here and there."

The man shook his head and hobbled on to catch up with the rest of his family, who were already making noises of amazement at what they were seeing next.

Reynolds consulted a huge white-faced pocket watch. "Would you like to see some of my amazements, Detective? We have a little time."

"Whatever you say."

As they made their way against the crowd down the left side, Reynolds regained some of his swagger. About halfway down he stopped and drew Grant through the filing customers until the two of them stood directly in front of a cage about four feet tall and three wide. Inside was what looked to be a man, less than half-normal height, with the sleek red and white head of a fox. As the crowd lingered Reynolds pointed to the sign above the cage which read MARLO, THE FOX MAN OF KASHMIR and said, "Indeed, ladies and gentlemen, I found him in the Kashmir region, which, as you know, has been a disputed land between India and Pakistan for generations. I lost two men in his capture, and another who, we might say, died of curiosity on the ship which brought him back. Notice!"

Reynolds stepped away from the cage and uttered a few words which were nothing but gibberish to Grant: "Peshti, Mahtu, Ree!"

The tiny animal-man immediately sprang forth, gripping the cage bars with his tiny hands and feet, and opened his mouth in a mournful screech like a wolf baying at the moon. His teeth were impossibly long, as were, Grant now noticed, his delicate fingers and toes, which ended in curling sharp pointed claws.

The crowed stepped back, gasping, and then Reynolds said, "Enough! Mahtu, Ree, Fashta!"

The fox-man immediately let go of the bars and shut his mouth, falling to all fours before curling into a ball and closing his eyes.

"You are lucky, ladies and gentlemen. He will sleep for hours now, poor fellow. I just reminded him of his lost homeland. We can only hope that he will dream of it."

"Is that true?" Grant asked, as they moved on to the next attraction, leaving the crowd behind them still bunched around the cage.

Reynolds shook his head. "No. His reality is much more terrible. I saved him from something much too horrible to think about." He moved his arm in a sweeping, inclusive gesture. "Everyone in this tent—every *thing*—is beholden to me. All would have been destroyed—or much worse—by the Dark One, if I hadn't intervened.

"And believe me, Detective," he added ominously, "they are all beholden to me."

They now stopped before an ornately carved huntsman's table protected by a plate of Plexiglas to keep the curious at bay. The carvings were tiny openmouthed heads. They looked to be screaming. On the table, Grant observed as he and Reynolds stepped behind the Plexiglas, were a row of jars, each larger than the next, the largest some two feet tall. They were made of dark-colored glass, blue, red, brown, green. Above them was mounted a sign which read THE HEADS OF HOOLOO.

Reynolds ignored the crowd this time and spoke only to Grant. "An area in western China, which is still untouched by Communism. We had a devil"—he grinned in the gold-dark at his own pun—"of a time getting these out." He peered up at Grant. "All in Volume Three, of course."

Without a beat passing, Reynolds tapped on the blue jar.

Instantly the color melted away, leaving an empty crystal clear space with a head suspended in it. It was the color of dark tanned leather. It floated, insensate, for a moment, and then seemed to awaken suddenly.

Then it opened its eyes—ice blue and piercing—and opened a mouth filled with two rows of perfect white teeth and began to yell, a sound that echoed from the jar as a hissing screech.

In quick succession Reynolds tapped the other jars—one, two, three—and they in turn produced screaming heads, each larger than the one before. The bottle green jar yielded a head nearly half again as large as Grant's own. Between the four of them they filled the area with a bone-rattling moan, like an organ's deep chord of regret and horror.

Grant turned to peer through the Plexiglas—the crowd had once again stepped back, their eyes wide with wonder and fright.

Again in quick succession, Reynolds tapped each jar—one, two, three, four—and they instantly went dark and silent.

As they moved on Reynolds said, "It is good for them to remember, but only for a few moments. Otherwise they would die of fright. And before you ask," he added, turning to Grant, "yes, they did have corporeal bodies at one time."

"Is that what they are crying for—the loss of their bodies?"

Reynolds turned away and said, simply, "No."

They had almost reached the entrance to the tent. Reynolds consulted his bulbous watch and quickened his pace. They passed two attractions, The Man from Siam, consisting of a full human skeleton walled off in a brightly lit room with a glass front; the skeleton was posed sitting in a simple chair, apparently asleep, its head dropping upon its ribbed breast, with a small table by its side upon which lay an open book.

As Grant passed by, the skeleton suddenly roused and stretched, then took the book in its bony-fingered hands and began to read: "Break, break, break . . ."

Beside that was a similar space, this one square and again brightly lit from the inside, which was empty. Reynolds hurried on but Grant stopped as the space abruptly filled with colored blank masks trailing multicolored streamers. There must have been thirty of them. Not one interfered with another, and yet they flew at a faster and faster pace, seeming to fill the entire space with a blur of multicolored motion.

And then as suddenly as they had appeared they were gone, as if a flame had been snuffed.

"Please, we must hurry along," Reynolds said, returning to retrieve Grant. He stopped for a moment to stare into the lit box which was now again empty.

"Emma," his whispered, his face filled with loss and sadness.

"Who—"

"Another time," Reynolds said, shaking himself from his reverie.

They strode past the attractions near the entrance, fish tanks that gave off a faint formaldehyde odor, filled with two-headed calf fetuses and three-tailed kittens. There were shelves arranged with huge dinosaur bones and tiny skeletal things that appeared half fish, half animal. Patrons were two deep, ogling in wonder.

Reynolds waved a hand in dismissal. "Mostly fakes. They expect it, so I provide it." He added as an afterthought, "Their gullibility makes me ill."

They stopped at the very first attraction, what Grant assumed to be a moldy-looking re-creation of a long-dead pharaoh's burial chamber. There was broken pottery and a few trinkets and, in the center of the chamber, up on a shelf, what looked to be a mummy. It was in a decrepit state, brown bandages falling from the half-rotting corpse, hands clasped across the body, eyes staring heavenward in a frozen rictus of pain.

"Fake?" Grant asked, as Reynolds lingered momentarily.

"Oh, no," Reynolds answered. "And he was not dead when we found him."

Reynolds gave a short bow to the corpse, and then drew Grant away and to the opening to the attraction tent. He looked again at his watch and briefly consulted the attendant there, who nodded and whispered into Reynolds' ear.

Reynolds hurried back to Grant. "We haven't much time," he said. "She's arrived, just now. Her black Lincoln has just entered the gate and parked."

Grant stiffened, and reflexively reached for his .38.

Reynolds' hand stayed him; he shook his head and said, "Come."

They walked to the other side of the tent, and stopped before what was actually the last attraction. It was a furnished room, a larger box than the others and without glass to protect it. The lighting was mellower here. The room itself was furnished like a real sitting room, in the style of the Victorian period, with billowy curtains framing a faux window against the back wall. The window was backlit with a soft glow to look as though the sun was either rising or setting. To one side of the window was a bookcase filled with leather volumes; to the other side was an ancient Victrola, its curved black horn pointed into the center of the room. A tune played something soft and barely distinguishable as "Goodnight, Irene."

There was a Sheridan couch (Grant hated Sheridan couches)—which, Grant realized with a start, was the same one that had been in Thomas Reynolds, Jr.'s house when Grant had visited him there. It was upholstered in a very dark fabric, black or the deepest navy blue. The ebony coffee table from the house was there also, stationed in front of the couch. And one of the two red damask chairs that Grant remembered, in the center of the room, in which sat a woman dressed in a long Victorian dress, with buttoned black shoes.

"Regina Bright," Reynolds announced firmly.

Her hair was as white as flour, pulled back in a severe bun. She looked thirty years older than her age, not a teen but a middle-aged woman, her face lined with the beginnings of old age. Her skin was nearly as pale as her hair.

Grant would have thought her an albino except for the eyes, which were open and piercing. But they did not seem to register the world around her. Though they stared unblinking, Grant had the feeling that they were completely turned inward.

Reynolds said to the gathered crowd behind them, "Sorry, ladies and gentlemen, but this attraction is closed."

There were groans, but he ignored them.

He pulled at ropes to either side of the boxy room, and a canvas flap fell down over the front of the room, hiding it.

Reynolds motioned for Grant to follow him, and they went to the left side of the room where there was a door. Reynolds produced a key from his pocket and opened it. They entered.

"Gina, I've brought an old friend," Reynolds said softly.

Regina Bright made no movement; it was as if she were a statue.

"It's Detective Grant, who helped you once before. Do you remember?"

Still no sign of life; her hands rested in her lap, her eyes stared straight ahead.

"Gina—"

"The Dark One is close by," Regina's mouth said. Grant swore the lips hadn't moved, and the voice was unearthly, faraway, little louder than a powdery whisper.

"Yes," Reynolds said. "It's true."

"And it is Halloween and nearing midnight."

"Yes," Reynolds repeated.

There was silence in the room, and Grant became very uneasy. The very atmosphere was strange, as if all of the oxygen had been sucked out. He was finding it hard to concentrate, or breathe.

"What's going on?" he asked Reynolds.

"I don't know." The impresario had sat down on the Sheridan sofa, and looked pale and ill. He was blinking his eyes furiously.

"Gina, what's going on?" he gasped. "Where's Samhain?"

She said nothing, only stared.

Grant drew out his .38 and turned toward the door. "I'll take care of this. I'll go out and find the girl and end it."

"*No.*"

Regina Bright's voice was loud in the room, a booming

command, and Grant stopped in his tracks and looked back at her. He could not move.

"Let me go!" he shouted.

"It will not work." There was silence and then she said, "Nothing we can do by ourselves will work."

"What!" Reynolds said. "Gina! All these years, all this time! You can't tell me—"

"We have failed." The whisper-voice was resigned, and suffused with what sounded like fear. "There is nothing we can do to stop her . . ."

"I won't accept that!" Reynolds shouted.

"Come with me . . ."

The room clouded, was filled with a gray mist that boiled all at once from the floor, the walls, the ceiling. Grant felt himself being pulled toward Regina Bright. Her eyes widened, became huge, kept growing until they were the only thing in the room. And then there was one eye only, gigantic, and Grant and Reynolds were drawn into it. Grant burst through her cornea, which shattered like glass, and was pulled into a blue darkness filled with what looked like approaching stars.

And then he cried out and saw no more.

CHAPTER FIFTY

The child that was the Dark One moved with a reptilian grace unknown to any other five-year-old girl. She was dressed in pink, had picked the outfit out herself that morning in the house filled with the bodies of the family she had murdered with her touch just outside Montreal, close to the New York border. A touch, a look; she had rung the doorbell, the black Lincoln at the curb, and when the woman had answered she had merely held her hands up and smiled. When the woman had laughed and picked her up she had merely looked into the human eyes, touched her lightly with her little finger and the woman was dead.

And then the rest, the dog, the cat, the man in his study and the children, including the five-year-old girl in the pink dress.

"Do you like it?" she said sweetly, on the ticket boothline, to the teenaged boy in front of her with the mullet haircut and leather jacket.

He turned and looked down on her with a sneer on his acned face. "Get lost."

She looked up at him with her gray eyes and touched his ripped jeans.

He gave a short cry and fell dead to the ground.

"*You* get lost," she said, the voice no longer phoney-sweet, but hard and raw and deep as a cold well.

She touched and looked, touched and looked, and the line melted in front of her.

The ticket booth was empty now, and she walked unimpeded into Halloweenland.

She looked up at the moon overhead, and smiled. "Last night for you, too," she said.

By now there was a commotion by the ticket booth, shouts of alarm, so she quickened her steps and went to the Ferris wheel. She stood looking up at it curiously, as she had so many things on this strange Earth. It was round and perfect and she hated it. In a little while it would no longer exist.

"Are you lost, little girl?" a man said to her. He was holding the hand of a boy of about her age. "Where are your parents?"

Touch and look, touch and look.

She was alone again with two crumpled bodies at her feet.

She stared a the Ferris wheel for another moment, then wandered on, studying the carousel. Some of the carved horses looked to be in pain, and she liked that, but there was too much happiness, and the calliope annoyed her. *Touch and look, touch and look.* Now the humans were taking note of her. The carousel came to a gradual stop and the humans were screaming, making way.

One stood in her way, a fat man in bib overalls with a long iron bar in his hand; he had been running the merry-go-round and now stepped out of the center, where the mechanisms were, and stood before her.

"Is this some kind of Halloween trick?" he asked, his pig eyes narrowed. "If it is—"

Touch and look, and he was gone from her sight, on the floor of the platform, his head coming to rest next to the hoof of a froth-mouthed blue-and-white steed.

There was shouting behind her, and she slowly turned, looking at the crowd that had formed and was staring at her in horror.

"*Boo!*" she said, and laughed, not hiding her true voice, the deepest, richest, most frightening one, and held her hands up. "*Attention! You'll all be dust in an hour! Poof! Gone! Dead! Go home and say good-bye to EVERYTHING!*"

From somewhere to her right there was a whizzing sound, and she turned in time to see a stone making its way toward her.

Look, and it blew to pieces, the pieces to dust, and settled to the ground.

Another stone, and another, and she did the same.

Some of the crowd began to peel off, move away, run.

She laughed again and screamed, "*There's nowhere to go! After tonight there will be nothing! Not even death will help you!*"

The crack of a rifle shot from the left.

Look, and the sound was swallowed by the night.

She jumped down from the carousel, a five-year-old little girl with eyes as old as time, and after the bravest of them came at her in a rush, *look, touch, look, touch, look, touch*, soon she was all alone.

The lights of Halloweenland blinked, went out, came back on and went out again. The moon was lowering toward the west, its smile now a sickly frown. The night air was colder, and the breeze had built to a whistling wind, which whipped the strings of lights and made wires bang against their poles. The calliope music was gone; the roar of the last of the cars and buses screeching away died to silence, leaving only the tapping of empty soda cups across the empty parking lot. Signs on their hinges at the entrance to stopped rides creaked.

A little girl whistled.

"Where are you? Where are you?" she called in her little girl voice. This was the night she had waited for forever. This was the evening—the last evening—when all the thousands of years of creation, the millions of years of life, were snuffed into nothingness. This was the night—*finally!*—when it all went away.

She whistled and lingered for a moment on the midway at a game where ping pong balls were tossed into little goldfish bowls. She amused herself by putting her finger in each bowl, watching each tiny reddish fish— *touch, look, touch, look*—stiffen and die.

Tent flaps flapped around her, and the night grew even colder.

"Where *are* you?" she called sweetly, walking on, toward the big tent.

She wished this night, this moment, could last forever.

"Ready or not, here I come!" she shouted, walking through the abandoned opening.

The canvas walls rattled around her, and the huge tent poles down the center aisle swayed and creaked, strained by the building cold outside wind.

She walked slowly, dispassionately taking in the attractions: the mummy; the glass vases with their screaming heads (*look, touch*, four times, bringing silence); the curious fox-headed thing; and then, after making the turn at the far end, walking past the rest—the Wide Woman (*look, touch*), the Amazing Mice (*look, touch*), the flaming hand (a fake, fed by a propane tank hidden behind)—she stood at last in front of GINA THE OTHERWORLDLY LITTLE LADY: ASK HER ANYTHING ABOUT DEATH AND SHE WILL ANSWER.

She stared for a moment at the dropped flap hiding the contents from her eyes.

Then she walked slowly to the door on the left, and opened it with her five-year-old fingers.

The room inside was dark.

Empty.

CHAPTER FIFTY-ONE

"We cannot stay here long," Gina said.

"Where are we?" Grant replied. He and Reynolds and the girl were on an obsidian plane that stretched to the four horizons. The sky was blue-black and untouched by clouds. There was a faint hiss in the air, like air escaping from a tire.

Grant bent down and touched the floor. It felt like glass, cold and smooth. He could almost see his reflection.

Gina said, "This is an in-between place. Not living and not death. It used to be called limbo."

Reyonlds said, "I take it we're safe from the Dark One here?"

"For a time," Gina said. She still spoke without moving her lips. "She will find us, eventually. And, like I said, we cannot beat her."

She sat on the ground cross-legged, and Grant noted how worn and tired she looked.

"At midnight," she said, "it will all be over."

"For a time," she continued, "I thought she could be overcome. Ever since I returned to Earth from the Land of the Dead I knew this day would come, and have prepared for it. But she is too strong."

Grant noticed a change in the west, a dark outline that drew nearer.

"Is that her?" Grant said, and Gina and Reynolds turned to look.

"No," Gina said, and now Grant discerned the figure of Samhain making his way toward them.

He drew up close and hovered in place, his cape swirling, his bone white face impassive.

"Are you hiding too?" Grant asked.

Samhain turned his face slowly toward the detective. His empty black eyes were unreadable, his red slash of a mouth silent. He looked at all three in turn, and then turned his attention to Gina.

"I'm here to help you," he said. His voice was filled with sorrow. "There is only one way to stop her, and you must do exactly as I say."

CHAPTER FIFTY-TWO

Three minutes.

Anna was amusing herself with the sky. There were big holes ripped in it, showing dead nothingness beyond. She had cut the moon into quarters, and moved it to the western horizon, where the four pieces twirled like tops.

Somewhere in the distance a siren was wailing, and she thought she heard screams and moans. Around her the wind had picked up even more, nearly to gale force, and it was much colder. Already she had destroyed much of Halloweenland—rides overturned, the light poles yanked from the ground and tossed aside like matchsticks, the big tent punched in and collapsed on itself like a deflated balloon.

She stared at the Ferris wheel now. It began to turn, slowly at first and then faster and faster. She blinked the lights on, and they made the Ferris a circle of blurred lights.

Then she raised a finger, and with a grinding snap the wheel flew from its hub into the sky, still whirling madly, up and up, half as high as the scudding clouds—until it stopped suddenly, and came flying back down to Earth, crashing in a nearby field. The ground shook, and there was a mighty grating of metal against metal.

And then: only the wail of the October wind, and far-off cries.

Two minutes.

Like a conductor Anna moved her hands, her head, and things flew apart and into the air and crashed against other things. The ticket booth blew to pieces as if a bomb had gone off. Great rents appeared in the parking lot.

In her head, the time ticked down toward midnight. And every moment she grew stronger. More sirens wailed, distantly. Steam rose from the cracks in the parking lot and, with a wave of her hand, Anna turned the entire area molten and then into a lake of fire.

Overhead, the stars began to disappear.

One minute!

"Hello," a voice said behind her.

She turned like a snake snapping its head around, and then she smiled.

"You!"

"Yes," Gina said, and now when she spoke her lips moved.

"I looked for you in your little side show," Anna said, and laughed. "I imagine you went to your little hideaway. Limbo. I would have come to get you soon, after I was through here."

Gina stood motionless.

"Where are the other two? The policeman and the impresario of all this?" She waved her hands, indicating the remains of the amusement park around her.

"They're safe."

Anna laughed, a booming sound. "*Safe?* No one is safe!

Nothing is safe! When I'm finished there won't be anything anymore!"

She took three quick strides and stood before Gina. "Don't you understand?" she screamed. Her white face was livid with triumph. "In a few seconds none of this will exist anymore! ALL OF IT WILL BE GONE!"

Gina said nothing.

Anna grabbed the other girl with both hands and stared into her calm eyes.

Midnight, the twelfth stroke.

"TOUCH! LOOK!" she roared.

Gina fell dead.

And the world went away from Anna, who screamed once as she was yanked from the Earth.

CHAPTER FIFTY-THREE

"SAMHAIN!" The voice, filled with a bottomless fierce rage, tore through the Land of the Dead. In the tall tower of the jagged stone structure he called home, the Lord of the Dead faced his two guests, who stared out across the ledge that bordered one side of the tower at a blasted alien desert landscape pocked with pale canyons and stone walls. The sky was the color of mustard, flecked with wan gray clouds. It was hard to breathe in the thin, hot air.

"Then Reggie is dead," Reynolds moaned. There was pain in his voice, and he put his head in his hands. "She didn't tell me that was the price."

"Yes," Samhain replied. "She knew it was the only way."

"And it's not over," Grant added.

"No," Samhain answered. He seemed oddly distant, preoccupied. He turned toward Reynolds, and Grant was startled to see him reach out a long slender white finger and touch the impresario lightly on the shoulder.

"There is no need to mourn," he said, in a voice that was almost gentle. "You will see her again."

Reynolds raised his tear-streaked face. "I loved her."

"Yes. And as for your father—"

"I know. It was the Dark One. Not you."

Samhain stared out over the spotted plain which surrounded the tower, out past the miles of arid emptiness, toward a distant range of low mountains that resembled blunt pointed teeth.

Grant had noticed a series of movements in the near distance, strange shapes barely visible—geometric squares and rectangles, balloon shapes, stringy things and things that looked like crawling insects. They were all headed vaguely in the same direction.

Samhain explained, "Those are the dead. They come here for a time, and then they leave. This is only a way station, you know."

"Where do they go?"

"That is the great question, isn't it?" Samhain answered cryptically.

The boom of the Dark One's voice, imbued with savage rage, came again:

"SAMHAIN!"

Samhain pointed to the distant mountains. "That is where I must meet him," he said. For a moment his voice regained its old witty edge. "For better or worse."

Grant put his hand on his .38 and drew it out. "I'll go with you."

Now Samhain laughed. "That won't do you any good here, Detective!" As Grant's look turned sour he gestured with his hand. "Please! Fire it at will! At me, at the sky, anywhere you like!" Again he laughed.

Grant shrugged and aimed the police special at the Lord of the Dead. "Something I've always wanted to do," he said, and pulled the trigger.

The gun discharged, but it was as if the bullet didn't

exist, or was absorbed by the very air around it. There was a bullet, but it had vanished.

Samhain roared with laughter. "You humans continue to amuse me to the last! Surely I will miss you, Detective Grant."

"What's going to happen to you?" Grant asked.

"Oh, we shall see," Samhain replied, still cryptic.

"Can the Dark One still get back to Earth?"

"Oh, yes. If I fail, I'm afraid everything will be destroyed, after all. This world, your own, everything."

The booming cry of rage sounded again in the distance.

Samhain said, "I'm afraid I must leave soon."

"Please let me go with you."

Samhain shook his head. "I must do this alone."

Samhain stared down at the dry plain below them and said, "Ah! Mr. Reynolds, I believe your prayers are answered."

A shape—a wisp of smoke in the shape of a ring—had detached itself from the line of pilgrims on the plain below and was making its way to the base of the tower. It passed out of their sight and Grant imagined it floating across the wide entryway and up the huge set of stairs—one flight, two, a third, and then, finally wending its way up a spiral staircase.

The three of them watched as the wisp of smoke, the lightest blue in color, made its way onto the platform and stopped before them.

"Gina?" Reynolds said hopefully.

A voice came, a faraway whisper, tentative. "I . . . knew that name."

"Do you remember anything about Earth?" Reynolds asked.

"Very little. I know I was in another place. And now I am here."

The roar of the Dark One's voice rattled the stone around them: "*SAMHAIN!*"

"That voice I know," the ring of smoke said, with a trace of fear.

"Don't worry, Gina. Samhain told us that you must stay here with us."

Reynolds stepped forward and attempted to touch the smoke ring, but it backed slowly away from his touch.

"Yes. I will stay here."

The ring seemed to solidify a little and settled gently to the floor of the platform.

Grant turned to address Samhain.

"Now what—?"

But Samhain was gone.

CHAPTER FIFTY-FOUR

A stranger in my own land.

These words went through Samhain's mind as he made his way away from his stone palace into the wilderness. There were parts of his own world that he hadn't been to in ages, and this was one of them. He remembered the mountains as being low and ugly, nothing like the magnificent peaks he had seen on Earth, but he remembered little else about them.

He missed Earth already and was surprised at the fact. He missed Ireland, and he missed Orangefield, the Adirondack mountains which ringed it like a halo of lush green. Though he had not been blessed with the sense of smell, he could almost feel the moist fecundity of those evergreens, those thick forested areas and even the wet furrows of the pumpkin patches after a rain. The air had shimmered then, and the soil was so rich and dark, it was a living thing itself.

Living things.

And he, the Lord of the Dead.

Perhaps that was it: after all these centuries, all this vast

217

expanse of time since the beginning of life on Earth, when he had suddenly found himself there and knew he had a job to do—after all these countless days and years of ushering the dead from Earth through his own kingdom—he suddenly realized that he didn't hate life at all. That had been the Dark One's biggest trick—to make him feel that he despised life as much as the Dark One did—and to believe that, as the Dark One did, that he wanted to erase every speck of life from the Earth wherever it was found.

But he didn't want this at all.

After all this time, life was as mysterious to him as ever—a mystery he could not understand and which, he now knew, fascinated him.

Though he was Lord of the Dead, he loved life itself.

The braying cry of his name rose over the distant mountains and flowed over the dry plains and washed over him.

"SAMHAIN!"

"Coming, master," he said, to himself, and allowed himself a thin red smile.

He passed through the line of pilgrims and, as if they knew, they parted for him. And still they continued their trek to the east, where their ultimate destination lay. He only knew that they went and then were gone. When he had tried to investigate this phenomenon he had found himself stopped by a gentle wall. The pilgrims passed beyond, and he was not allowed. It was the only place in his whole domain from which he was barred.

The pilgrims closed their line again after he had passed through, as if he had not been there. A few turned to regard him—a thing shaped like a triangle with three eyes; an impossibly slender thing which slithered along the ground, pushed by four sets of tiny legs; a box with eyes on all sides—but quickly lost interest and resumed their separate journey.

Once, long ago, he had sought to map the four corners of his world and discovered that it was not round, as he had supposed. When he had reached a certain point in his landscape he merely found himself back where he had started.

He remembered that the mountains were at the edge of the world. As they grew closer he began to study his surroundings more closely. The pale patches of brown and tan which dotted the land were more numerous here. There were less of the dry-rooted plants which sprung up here and there near the tower, and almost no boulders or other markings. Soon the plants had disappeared altogether, leaving him with a flat, dry, blotchy vista.

His name, louder now, blared out at him from the rising hills.

He noted that there was a darkening patch in the sky above the central mountain, taller and sharper-toothed than the rest. So, she was trapped, but fighting. Samhain remembered how the Dark One had, the other time she had attempted destruction, eaten away part of the sky of the Land of the Dead, and how long it had taken to heal.

As he watched, and as his name was roared out once more, the patch darkened to a ragged angry cut.

Samhain quickened his pace, floating like a black-caped wraith toward whatever came.

Hours later, as he reached the base of the mountain, the sky had darkened overhead, making it look like night. Samhain looked back the way he had come: in the far distance lay his tower, sitting serenely in the pale light of its own sky.

Another roar, another gouge in the sky overhead.

"Where are you?" Samhain called, and in answer was the girl's voice deepened to despair and rage.

"Inside! Come to me now!"

Samhain passed along the base of the mountain and began to climb. He looked up, the naked peak devoid of foliage or snow, like a single snaggle tooth high above.

"Where?" he called.

When his name was called again, in a fitful scream, he saw, a third of the way up, a cut in the side of the peak.

He made his way up to it; it was a tall and narrow opening to a shadowed cave.

He went in.

Immediately, the cut closed behind him, with a rending bellow of rock and stone.

Samhain passed deeper into the cave, following the cry of the Dark One's voice.

And there, in a cavern within the belly of the mountain, chained to the smooth floor of a cavern lit by the surrounding walls which glowed a sickly green, was the girl.

There was no longer a pretense that she was a young girl. Though her body was still small, her face was ravaged with the deep lines and creases of an aging beast. Her eyes were hooded black pits, her lips cracked.

"Let me go, Samhain," she spat.

Samhain shook his head. "It took much to get you here, and this is where you will remain."

"I COMMAND YOU!"

Samhain hovered over the writhing thing. "No. And you never did."

Calculation and desperation crossed the thing on the floor's face. She became calm, and she showed something that was supposed to be a smile.

"I will share *everything* with you."

"Everything of nothing?"

"Why not? There will be a kingdom of nothingness, and you and I will rule. No life, no humans, nothing to stand up to our domination."

Samhain slowly shook his head. "More lies, Dark One? You would destroy this place, and me, if I release you."

"RELEASE ME AT ONCE!" she screeched hoarsely. "RELEASE ME OR I WILL TEAR THE SMILE FROM YOUR FACE AND TURN YOU TO DUST!"

"We both know that you cannot do that, either. Not as long as you are here."

The voice became calm. "Let me go back to my own place, then."

"Yes," Samhain said, and lowered himself over the chained figure. "You may return to your realm, but you will offend this one no more."

Anna smiled.

"Do it, then, Samhain."

Samhain lowered himself even farther, and, sighing, kissed her.

She grabbed his cape in her clawlike hands and howled, "*Die, Samhain!*"

"Yes . . ."

The cape dissolved, the white face turned to dust, and there was nothing.

Anna, screaming triumph and vindication, vanished from that place.

CHAPTER FIFTY-FIVE

Grant and Reynolds, and the thing that had been Regina Bright, heard the echoing scream from the far mountains.

"It is over," Gina said, a whisper.

And now, as the other two watched, her smoky form began to lengthen and fill out. The smoke vanished, and, slowly, in its place appeared something that looked very much like Samhain. The face was less rigid, the eyes less hard, the long-fingered hands softer-looking.

Before Reynolds could speak, Gina said, "Yes. I will be the new Lord of the Dead. It is fitting, don't you think?"

She turned to Grant, and her thin red lips smiled. "Things may be a bit different from now on, Detective. I don't know if Orangefield will be seeing quite as much of me."

"Samhain?" Grant asked.

"He is provided for." She looked out at the line of pilgrims making their way across the barren landscape. "Those are my charges. Perhaps I can make their time here more pleasant than it has been."

She regarded Grant again. "And you, Detective, must

return to Orangefield. It is not your time." She smiled again. "Yet. And if you forego the cigarettes and alcohol, I may not see you again any time soon."

"What about you?" Grant said to Reynolds.

The impresario smiled. "I'll be staying here, of course. I could never leave Gina again. And what better place to write the third volume of my history than the very place that inspired it!"

Reggie nodded.

"We will miss you, Detective," she said. "I can tell you that your friend Tom Malone is in peace. In fact, he is about to leave us. You have learned a very great secret, one that no man who returns to Earth should know. I will take the knowledge from you, but not the certainty. That will be my gift. Good-bye."

She leaned over, and kissed him.

And then Grant was suddenly gone.

CHAPTER FIFTY-SIX

Another Halloween gone.

Grant found himself in Riley Gates' old folding chair, facing Riley Gates' empty pumpkin patch, with a cigarette in one hand and a half flask of Dewar's in the other. Overhead, the moon was in its accustomed position and shape. Off in the distance he heard a police siren, which abruptly stopped.

There was silence in the new November night.

To his right, about a hundred yards away, lay the twisted remains of what had been the Halloweenland Ferris wheel. Grant stared at it hard, having no memory of how it got there.

Where have I been? he thought. *What did I miss?*

Vaguely, he knew that momentous things had happened. But he had no memory of them.

He closed the flask and tossed it away, suddenly not thirsty, and flicked the cigarette into the cold, still night.

He reached for another cigarette, then shoved the pack back into his pocket. The thought of nicotine made him ill.

He pushed himself up out of the chair, hearing his own bones creak.

At the edge of his memory something flared, and for a moment he was sure that he had seen wondrous things.

But then the half memory, a place with thin air and a yellow sky and a parched landscape, dissipated like cigarette smoke.

Just a dream.

No: something more.

He knew that if he walked over to Halloweenland that there would be little left to see, that the impresario Reynolds was gone, and Reggie Bright, too.

Reggie . . .

Again a memory flared, then faded.

There was a girl named . . . Anna, but she was gone now, he was sure.

It had been important to find her, but it was no longer important. He was sure of that, too.

He stretched, feeling his bones settle into place, shivered, and turned to leave.

The moon, which was just the moon, made him feel suddenly secure, for some reason.

And Orangefield was still Orangefield.

And there was always next Halloween . . .

EPILOGUE

For the first time in eons, Samhain felt at peace.

There was no job to be done, no impetus driving him on—no false prophet to follow.

He looked down at his body and laughed: a child's balloon shape, with two rubbery arms, and two rubbery spindle legs which wobbled when he walked. He laughed again and the cardboard cutout next to him turned its three eyes on him and scolded, "Is it funny, pilgrim?"

"To me it is, yes," Samhain answered.

The line stretched for miles behind him. In front was the wall that had been impenetrable to him. But when he came to it he passed through with ease, feeling a pleasant tingle over his shape.

And now the yellow sky he had beheld for so long changed into a deeper color, almost blue. In front of him a whirlpool had formed, and, in its center, a fiery hole.

He felt light as air, felt his body melting away as he moved into the whirlpool, which became a tunnel of light. He was drawn forward, forward, and watched the cardboard cutout that had been with him sucked into the light and away, dissolving with a sigh.

And then he was through, and someone was there in this new place, this glorious landscape, to welcome him.

He felt his body again, his true body, and now his memory returned to him in a flash, and he knew who he was, and was filled with a stunning instant realization of fulfillment and happiness.

He felt his wings, strong and rigid on his back.

"Welcome home, Gabriel," someone said.

A SHORT, CURIOUS
HISTORY OF "THE BABY"

Where do stories come from?

They come from all kinds of places.

"The Baby," the novella you're about to read, came from a rather curious place—and taught me a rather valuable lesson about the differences between long short stories and novels.

Here's what happened: a couple/three years ago, a dynamic young writer and editor named Kealan Patrick Burke got in touch with me and asked if I'd contribute to a book of novellas he was editing. An Orangefield tale seemed just the thing, and before long I had dived into it head first.

Immediately, I realized that it had the makings of a novel, and tucked that fact in my back pocket. I already knew where it would go, and what it had to do to be a novel.

The present problem was to make it into a fully rounded novella.

That turned out to be fairly easy. As I approached the end (a little over 16,000 words) I knew how it would wrap up—and in suitably lurid fashion.

I also already realized that the same material used in

the novel, which turned out to be *Halloweenland*, would set out into uncharted waters, and that the ending of Part One, which would incorporate much of "The Baby," would be nothing like the novella version.

To make a short story shorter: I finished the novella for Kealan—and then his project, through no fault of his own, rolled over and died.

So now I had this beautifully rounded novella, with a horrific ending that would be nothing like the novel version, and it was an orphan.

Cue: Richard Chizmar to the rescue.

It turned out Rich had just started a series of beautifully illustrated, oddly shaped-lengthwise books called The Signature Series—and it turned out that the novella "The Baby" fit it like a glove.

"The Baby" was finally published, and sold out in a matter of months.

In the meantime, I began *Halloween*, which melded "The Baby" into the first part of the book, the way I had always planned.

I had, in the end, two versions of the same basic story with utterly different conclusions. The novella had to end with a bang, and the novel version had to open a portal to further adventures.

A valuable lesson, indeed, for any writer to learn—and, I think, a vivid illustration about the elasticity of language and, especially, of story.

Following, for your enjoyment, is the original version of "The Baby," lurid ending and all.

I hope you enjoy it in a whole different way—and learn something, as I did, about the difference between long short stories and novels.

—*Al Sarrantonio*

ONE

"I'm asleep, Jack."

Annoyed: his cold hands on her at one in the morning, she could see the illuminated clock face now that her eyes were open, hear his breathing, the catch in it that would make him snore later. Even facing away from him, she could smell the beer on his breath.

"I promised—"

"I don't give a *shit* at this point," she snapped, still curled up in a fetal position, legs pulled up, defensive, half-asleep. "You were supposed to come home five hours ago. We were going to try tonight. But instead you went out beering with your moron friends. Don't deny it, Jack—"

She gasped, not letting him hear it as he slid into the bed behind her, naked she could tell, his hands ice cold but soft as they had always been when he had first caught her eye, this boy of a man with the lock of hair in front that wouldn't stay put, and the violet eyes and the crooked smile. Her heart had melted the first time he looked at her. Melted like the saints and the nuns could not articulate, melted like time stood still and the moon froze solid in the sky and she knew her life was changed forever. His mouth on her later that first time and a kiss unlike any she had dreamed about, two mouths becoming one and then, much later, after fumbling and some laughing, two bodies becoming one. This was nothing like the fairy tales, or the dirty books, or the cable channels only for women where everything was clean and bland with guitar or piano music and then the commercials. This was magic that no one could write or sing or tell you about in the bleachers behind the soccer field when you shared a cigarette with your friends and felt the first chill of autumn blowing up under your Catholic skirt like Marilyn Monroe's in that movie with the sidewalk grating. What the hell were the nuns thinking? Plaid skirts that looked like nothing but delayed sin, in navy knee socks and those black shoes shined to mirrors that made boys look up at your panties—

"Jack, at least let me turn around!" she gasped, surprised at his ardor which was never lacking.

And then turning in the dark to meet his lips and hands and her nightgown pulled up over her head and the panting and the arched back and then three wonderful bit-lip screams while he tasted her nipples and nipped her neck once and then again as he always did, little bites that left pale red marks and she had to wear a turtleneck for two days.

The nuns couldn't change you but they could make you blush at your own body still—

And then it was over. He ran his hand through her short hair and whispered, "I promised," and then added, which made her heart flutter, "a baby," and she murmured, sleepy, and then rolled over away from him again, naked, too tired to pull on the flannel, and returned to sleep.

TWO

Then:

Six hours later in the police station in shock, with her sister Janet with the pinched look and Baby Charlie asleep in the stroller behind her.

Detective Grant: he looked old, tobacco stains on his teeth and the index and middle fingers of his right hand. A sot's nose, webwork of tiny broken veins. But the eyes: they were hooded in the shadow of their sockets but wary as a hawk's. He was definitely paying attention.

He had a notebook out and a pencil, and kept looking from the pad to her and back again.

"Mrs. Carlin, let me make sure I have this right." He flipped back a couple of pages and read to himself, lips moving silently. Then the eyes were on her. "You say your husband came home at one o'clock this morning?"

She nodded, and Janet, beside her, shifted in her chair, plastic seated, uncomfortable. "Only tell him what you want to, Marianne."

Detective Grant ignored Janet. Those eyes of his, still waiting . . .

"Yes," Marianne said. "He . . . woke me up when he came in. I was asleep facing the clock. I'm sure it was one."

"And he was gone when the phone woke you up an hour later, at two o'clock?"

"That's right."

Cold. She felt so cold and numb and dead.

The eyes looked down at the notebook, then back at her. "You're *sure* of this?"

She hesitated, looked at the floor. Embarrassed. "We . . . made love when he came home. Then I went back to sleep."

The eyes. But she said: "I'm *sure* it was one o'clock when he came home!"

"Don't say another damn thing, Marianne," Janet snapped. Baby Charlie snuffled in the stroller behind her, then settled back into sleep. "We'll get a lawyer. I'll call Chuck now. He'll know what to do."

She made to get up, huffing her pregnant belly out of the chair, but now Grant turned to her. "Mrs. Larson, I'm just asking your sister some questions. This isn't an interrogation and I'm certainly not charging her with anything. I'm just getting the time line straight in my mind."

Janet glared down at him across the desk. "Then why are we in an interrogation room? I know that's what this is. I watch TV."

Grant leaned back in his chair. "As I told you, I thought it would be more comfortable, especially since they're painting the area where my desk is today. I didn't want you to have to inhale those fumes . . ."

"So you said," Janet said. She was studying the far wall, a mirror, and walked toward it. "There anybody behind there? Like I said, I watch TV—"

"No, there isn't," Grant said, trying to hide his impatience. "Though you're right, it is a two-way mirror."

Before Janet could say it, Grant heaved himself out of his chair. "Let me show you." He walked briskly past Janet to a door beside the mirror and held it open for her. "Have a look."

Janet peered in, noting the short, empty hallway, the view into the room through the visible part of the two-way mirror. "Just like television," she said.

Grant waited for her to have her look, then waited for her to return to her seat before reclaiming his own. As Janet sat down with an "Ooof," she commented: "If this was a real interrogation, you'd offer us a Coke or coffee."

Grant looked up from his notebook. "Would you like something?" he asked.

Janet shook her head. "That's all right. We won't be much longer, will we?"

"We're almost done." The detective studied his notebook and then leaned across the desk to face Marianne again. "You're absolutely positive about the time?"

Marianne nodded. She barely heard him, Jack on the table, under the sheet, the cold room, colder than his hands had been, he was so white, albino white except for the bruises. The side of his chest that looked like it had been crushed, purple, broken, worse than the veins on Detective Grant's nose, almost black. They wouldn't show her anything lower, his legs cocked at an odd angle under the sheet.

Baby Charlie awoke with a squeak, as if thrown out of a dream, and abruptly began to cry. Janet instantly heaved herself back out of the chair and fumbled with a blue bag that hung from the back of the stroller. She produced a half-filled bottle which she thrust at the child without looking at him.

The room was quiet again.

"The reason I ask . . ." Grant began, and then added to the silence in the room.

"You've asked her twelve times," Janet said bluntly.

Grant looked at his notebook and then flipped it closed. "I talked to the driver who hit Mr. Carlin myself. We gave him a Breathalyzer test, which he failed at three o'clock this morning, and a blood test, which he also failed. He's in custody now. He drove home after his car struck your husband, Mrs. Carlin, and he went to bed. We picked him up at his house. He was so drunk he didn't remember the accident. There were two eyewitnesses who saw the accident, both of them friends of your husband, and one of them, Petee Wilkins, gave us a partial license plate number. A couple of pedestrians also saw it from farther away . . ."

Marianne didn't want to hear, she was so tired, so frozen in time, this wasn't happening. His body so white, the black-and-blue on his side and they wouldn't let her see the rest, "I promised," he'd said, "a baby . . ."

". . . everyone we talked to," Detective Grant was saying, "was sure your husband was killed last night in front of Loughran's Bar at just before one o'clock in the morning . . ."

THREE

How many days?

She had no idea. Whatever they had given her worked too well. The wake, the funeral, the burial, all of it had been surrounded in fuzzy light. She felt as if she was packed in cotton candy. Janet, thank God, had acted like a commander in chief, leading her like a zombie, telling her when to sit, to stand, everyone else in the church on their feet and she was immobile, sitting down, staring at anything but the coffin. And then a soft tug, the hissed, "Get up, Marianne, for heaven's sake," and then a push here, a pull there, and then, finally, the empty house and even Janet gone.

Only the pills left.

How many days?

It was sunny out, Indian summer. It had been raining the day of the funeral. At least one day, then. Had the burial been on a Monday or Tuesday? She didn't remember.

She sat up in bed, already claiming the middle, and groaned. She was staring at the red numbers of the alarm clock, staring at them, the bottle of pills next to the numbers—

With a howl of pain she lashed out with her left hand, knocked the pills and the clock to the floor.

"Dammit!"

She sobbed, and kept crying, hands balled into fists against her eyes, rolling over onto her side of the bed and curling up against herself as she had that night.

"Jack, Jack . . ."

She opened her eyes and saw the blank face of the broken clock radio staring at her, the red numerals extinguished.

"Oh God, oh God . . ."

After another half hour she crawled like a zombie out of the bed onto the floor. She felt around until her hand closed on the bottle of pills, which had rolled under the bed.

Something gently brushed over the top of her hand, like the tips of trailing fingers, and tried to take the bottle from her.

"No!" she said, out of it, holding the bottle tight. "I want to!"

She ripped the top of the bottle off and quickly shook a mountain of pills into her palm, then into her mouth.

She crawled back into bed and slept again, still clutching the bottle like a precious keepsake.

Four

"That's it. Enough is enough," Janet announced.

Marianne forgot that she had given her sister a key to the house. Through a very thick fog, she heard Janet storming around downstairs, then clumping up the stairs.

She tried to feign sleep.

"Get the hell out of bed," her sister ordered.

Marianne felt something in her hand, opened her eyes and stared at the empty pill bottle. Her sister was there, yanking the bottle from her and holding it up for examination.

"How many of these damned things did you take?"

"Lot . . ."

"Goddamned idiot . . ."

Janet threw the bottle down. Marianne heard her sister on the phone, the tap of three buttons before sleep came again . . .

FIVE

A brighter yellow light, sharp edged like the world.

She opened her eyes and smelled starch. The sheets were still white in hospitals. There was a cool autumn breeze smelling faintly of pumpkins and leaves, an open window to her right. To her left was a white panel screen in sections that covered the length of her bed as well as the foot. The sound of a television behind it. A game show, *The Price is Right*. Audience laughter.

She took a deep breath.

As if on cue, the panel at the foot of the bed was folded abruptly aside and her sister was there, glowering.

"About time," Janet said. There was a chair behind her, Baby Charlie asleep in his stroller next to it. Two vases of unattractive flowers were set on a dresser behind the stroller. She could see the edge of the television now, mounted on the wall and swiveled toward her sister's chair.

"Catatonic in the other bed," Janet explained, reading her mind. "So I bogarted the TV. Feel like watching?"

"No."

"You're not going to keep up this gloomy shit, are you? It's getting tiring, and Baby Charlie's been missing his play group."

"How long . . . ?"

"You've been in this rat hole for three days. The candy machines don't even work. But they take Jack's insurance, thank God, and no one's asked me to sign anything." Her eyes dilated for a moment. "Except for Detective Grant."

Memory failed Marianne, then kicked in. "Grant . . . ?"

"The cop. They wanted to swab your business end, so I said go ahead."

She was more awake now, and frowned. "Why?"

"Apparently Detective Grant didn't like what Jack's buddies had to say when he talked to them. Especially that moron Bud Ganley. And since you were so insistent about . . ." She waved her hand, suddenly embarrassed. "You know."

Threads were slowly weaving together, her mind unfogging, a clear picture . . .

"He thinks I was *raped?*"

"Something like that. The detective thinks you may have been mixed up about the time, that ol' Bud paid you a visit after he brought Jack to the hospital. You know Bud, always on the make. And since you and Bud had a history . . ."

She was speechless, and Janet went on.

"He's a weird one, that Detective Grant. Looks haunted, to me. And a lush, too. Remember Chip Prohman? In my class at Orangefield High? He's a desk sergeant, now. I talked to him yesterday. He told me Grant's wife is dead, and he's been involved in some *real* weird stuff the last few years. You remember those Sam Sightings everyone talked about a few years ago? Folks tramping through the woods, looking for Samhain, the Celtic Lord of the Dead? The rumor was Grant was somehow mixed up in that. And all those rumors when the house at Gates' farm burned to the ground—he was in the middle of that, too, according to Chip. But Chip always was an asshole, so who knows . . ."

Janet's voice trailed off. Her unease hadn't left her. She glanced briefly at Baby Charlie for help, but he was snoozing contentedly, head tilted slightly to one side, a river of clear snot flowing from one nostril.

"Look," Janet said, "I didn't think it was a big deal. You were out like a light, and Grant was persuasive. He said they'd be lucky to get a sample after that much time, but apparently they did. A female nurse did it. I was right here, outside the curtain, the whole time. Took two minutes."

"You always hated Bud Ganley."

Janet's unease evaporated. "You bet I've always hated him. What's not to hate? And I wouldn't put it past the prick . . ."

"To come to my house and rape me after my husband had been hit by a car and killed?"

Janet looked at the floor for a moment, then shrugged. "When you put it that way, it sounds pretty damn stupid."

"What did Petee say?"

"You know Petee Wilkins. He'll nod his head at anything Bud says. He swears Bud was with him the whole time. That they put Jack in Bud's car and drove right to the hospital. Then after they called you they went back to the bar." She snorted. "That part sounds right."

"Bud told me on the phone from the hospital that they couldn't handle what happened, that they had to have a drink. He was almost crying."

"So he and ol' Petee get drunk and leave you alone to handle it. Like I said, that sounds about right. Well, Detective Grant doesn't believe either of them. He thinks Bud paid you a visit after they left the hospital."

"It was *Jack* who was with me!"

Janet just looked at her.

Baby Charlie came awake with a sudden intake of breath. Before he could start wailing, Janet expertly slid his bottle from its bag and plugged it into his mouth.

"Like I said, Marianne, I'm not going to be able to keep doing this."

"You've already done too much."

"Tell me about it." She locked eyes with Marianne, and her expression grew serious. "You still look a little out of it. You gonna try to kill yourself again? Can I stop worrying about that, at least?"

"Yes. It was stupid. And the weirdest thing is, I think someone was in the room with me."

"Come again?" Janet asked.

"A . . . spirit, trying to keep me from taking those pills. There was a hand . . ."

Janet stared at her as if she had just landed from Pluto. "You think *that* was Jack, too?"

Marianne looked away. "I don't know . . ."

There was a sudden chill in the room—as if clouds had pushed the sun away, and autumn had flipped over into winter. The pumpkin and fallen leaf odor had disappeared, leaving a chill. Marianne shivered, and looked at the window, which darkened for a brief moment, ushering in silence and cold, before snapping back to normal.

Her arms, she saw, were covered with goose bumps.

Her sister was speaking, fussing with Baby Charlie, making sure the straps on his stroller were secure.

"I've gotta go," Janet announced. "Now that you're awake, they'll probably want your bed and release you. I'll talk to the nurse and come back later to bring you home.

Your house is clean, most of Jack's things are packed up and in the garage. You can decide what you want to do with them later. You're having dinner at my house tomorrow night. No argument. And you're going to call me before you go to bed tonight, and again when you get up tomorrow morning. And if I hear anything I don't like in your voice, a slur from pills or alcohol, or even cough syrup, I'm going to come over to your house and strangle you. Got it?"

Janet turned away from Baby Charlie to her sister, who was staring out the window blankly. "Earth to Marianne!"

Marianne turned and gave her a weak smile. "I've got it, Janet. Again, thanks for everything."

"You bet." She turned back to Baby Charlie and made a sudden sour face as an odor wafted upward from him. "Whew, little man, we need to make a stop at the changing station on the way out."

SIX

She felt like a visitor in her own house.

She remembered a similar feeling when she came home to her parents' house from college the first time. Janet was already married by then, right out of high school the year before, and the bedroom they had shared, which was still essentially unchanged, looked almost strange, as if someone else lived there. Everything was where it had always been—her bed piled high with stuffed animals, the shelf over the headboard lined with books, the rolltop desk open, a row of knickknacks, figures from the *Wizard of Oz* across the top, the bed tables with the funny-shaded lamps, little gold pom-poms hanging from the shade rims, two of them missing on her lamp, victims of their cat Marvel's hunting ardor. She knew every inch of this space, the messy closet, the red-and-white curtains, the floral wallpaper. She had lived in this room since she was a little girl—and yet, today, it all looked new to her, as if she was visiting herself.

That was how Marianne felt in her house today.

But there was a difference, because she was not coming home to the same house.

Jack's half was . . . gone.

It hit her immediately, when she looked at the hat rack in the front hallway and saw his baseball caps gone. There was only her own gardening cap, on its single peg. Normally it would have been hidden behind one of Jack's hats, which had always annoyed her. There were certain places—the living room closet, stuffed with his golf clubs, baseball glove, bowling ball—where he tended to crowd her out. The garage had been his, the basement his, even though he had been promising her for years to set up her sewing machine down there.

All of *him* was gone, now. The living room closet was nearly empty, three of her coats hanging forlornly. His side of the bedroom closet was bare. Even his muddy shoes and ratty sneakers had disappeared.

Marianne sat on the made bed, folded her hands in her lap, and stared at the open closet door.

Gone.

A movement caught her eye in the corner of the room to her left. The room was dark, the window open a crack, October twilight descending outside. Light washed in from the hallway closet.

"Jack?" she said, tentatively.

The shadow thickened, seemed to take shape, then drew into itself and was gone.

"Jack! Are you there?" She rose, walked to the corner of the room and put her hand out.

Something trailed along the top of her hand like a bare caress, and melted away.

"*Marianne* . . ." the faintest of faraway voices called.

She stood staring at her hand, at the blank corner of the room, listening to the wash of distant traffic outside.

SEVEN

"He was there."

Janet was getting tired of rolling her eyes. Chuck Larson had been truly interested in the beginning, but now that the dessert and coffee was gone he just wanted to escape to his TV room and a baseball playoff game.

"Honey—" he began, trying to rise.

"Shut up and sit down, Chuck. Unless you want to put Baby Charlie to bed."

Chuck sighed, settled back into his dining room chair.

Marianne looked from her sister to her brother-in-law. "I'm sorry, I shouldn't be going on like this."

"What we've got here," Janet said, "is you still trying to deal with your husband's death. My own feeling is that it's time to kick your own ass and move on. But you were never me, Marianne. So in the short run I'd say go with it. If it doesn't stop, we'll get you a shrink."

"I think it was really him."

Chuck, trapped in the sisters' conversation, tried to revive his own interest. "But all you saw was a shadow, and felt something on your hand, and heard someone whisper your name?"

"It sounded like Jack."

"Sounded like? Or was? Is there any of it that could have been something else? The shadow maybe from a passing car in the street? The touch on your hand a breeze from the open window?"

Marianne said, "And the voice?"

Chuck hesitated, shrugged. "In your head? A noise in the house, misinterpreted?"

"It was the same kind of touch as when I took the pills, when the bottle rolled under the bed and I reached for it."

Janet snorted. "That was a dust bunny, kiddo. I cleared them out myself. By the way, don't you ever clean that place of yours?"

Chuck smiled, hoping the evening was over. His grin didn't carry the room, however.

"Honey—" he began again.

"Yes! Please! Leave!" Janet said, exasperated. "Watch your damn game!"

Relieved, her husband raised his bulk out of his chair and headed for the door.

"But put the baby to bed first!" Janet commanded after him.

He physically flinched, but kept walking.

Janet turned back to her sister. "How did you sleep last night?"

"Fine."

"Marianne, what the hell is it you aren't telling me?"

"What do you mean?"

Janet gave a grim smile. "You've never been able to hide anything from me. You know that. And you're trying now."

Marianne tried a blank look, then gave up. "I'm glad you let Chuck go. I didn't want to talk with him around."

"So he's not around. Talk."

Marianne took a deep breath. "I think . . . I'm pregnant."

"*What!*"

"I started throwing up this morning, and, well . . . I just know."

Her sister's face grew florid. "I'll kill Bud Ganley. So help me God, I'll kill him with my bare hands."

Janet suddenly pushed herself away from the table and got up. Somewhere in the depths of the house, Baby Charlie was crying, Chuck's voice trying to soothe him.

"I'm calling Detective Grant right now," Janet said. "He may be weird, but he'll take care of Bud Ganley." She stomped off toward the kitchen, and the wall phone.

"Janet, don't!"

Janet stopped and turned around. Her face was flushed with anger. "Why the hell not! You were raped, and now you're pregnant! And I want to watch that son of a bitch Ganley swing by his balls in jail!"

251

EIGHT

Bud Ganley stretched out and crossed his long legs and wanted more than anything to put his boots up on the desk. But he instinctively knew that wouldn't be a good idea. He had the feeling Grant would kick them off, and there were a half dozen other cops of various ranks in the room who would like to take a poke at him. He'd already gotten rid of his tobacco chaw at Grant's insistence, and knew from the murderous look on the detective's face that if he gave the old man reason enough to pound him, Grant just might do it. And every other cop in the place would surely look the other way.

"Smells like paint in here," Ganley said, stretching his arms over his head and yawning.

"You know something?" Grant asked, tapping his pencil on the desk and staring at Ganley.

"No," Ganley said, looking at the ceiling.

"Well, I'll tell you anyway. The older I get, the more tired I get of guys like you. I've known you since you were, what, seventeen? And you're still the same punk at thirty-four."

Ganley smiled, showing white teeth through his thick handlebar moustache. "Thirty-five next week, Detective. You gonna throw me a party?"

Ganley looked down from the ceiling. For a moment their eyes locked, and Ganley's smile went away.

Man, this guy has weird eyes, Ganley thought. *The rest of him is a complete wreck, but those eyes have seen way too much.*

For a brief moment, a pang of something almost like pity went through the young man. Then that, too, went away.

Ganley grinned. "Can we get to it, please? I've gotta be back at work."

"As long as it takes, Bud," Grant said, lost in his notebook now.

Suddenly Ganley sat up straight and put his hands on the desk. "Look," he said, trying to make his voice sound reasonable, "you know I didn't lay a hand on Marianne—"

"I'm not sure of that, Bud."

The way Grant's voice sounded sent a chill through Ganley. "You're not gonna try to tell me that DNA test—"

Grant was regarding him with a level stare now, then gave a nearly imperceptible nod.

"That's *impossible*! I didn't do anything to her! I swear I didn't! Petee swore up and down I was with him the whole time! The nurses at the hospital—"

"You had time after you left the hospital," Grant said evenly. "And you certainly had motive."

Ganley exploded, standing up. His face grew red. "That was fifteen years ago! And those charges were dropped!"

Grant tapped his pencil against his head. "Not in here they weren't. You tried to rape Marianne when she was in high school."

"I was in love with her! And I got drunk and a little bit out of hand!" Ganley abruptly sat down and put his head in his hands. "Oh, man . . ."

Grant waited patiently. Ganley looked at the floor for a few breaths, then looked up at the detective. "Look," he said earnestly, "straight talk, okay?"

"Fine with me."

"What I did back then . . ." He took a deep breath. "What I did back then was way wrong. I even knew it at the time. I guess they call it date rape now. Or at least attempted date rape. But I was nuts about her, absolutely out of my head. And I knew we were going to break up, and my head was just full of snakes and I was drunk—"

"No excuse. Not now, not back then."

Ganley took another deep breath. "Okay, you're right. And thank God I didn't really do it."

"But you would have, if Jack Carlin hadn't knocked you on your ass."

Ganley nodded. "Yeah."

"I always found it puzzling how you and Jack became such good friends, especially after he and Marianne hooked up after that night."

"It just happened, man! Jack's a great guy—*was* a great guy . . ." He put his head in his hands again and looked at the floor.

"You can leave, Bud," Grant said.

Ganley looked up, puzzled. "But you said about the DNA—"

"I didn't say anything. And like they say in the movies: don't leave town."

Ganley bounced out of his chair, suddenly grinning, his trademark bopping gait evident as he wove his way through the maze of desks in the bull pen. At the front desk he stopped and smiled at the sergeant. "Chip! How's it hangin'!"

Chip Prohman tried to put a dispassionate look on his fat face. "Hope you didn't get yourself in big trouble this time, Bud."

"Nev-ah, my man! Nev-ah!"

He was out the door, all eyes on him, except for Grant's, which were set like lasers on his notebook, while he frowned.

NINE

Something in the corner again.

Marianne came awake at a sound like two pieces of soft fabric being drawn one over the other. Reflexively, she looked over at the bedside table, but the clock, set back in place, was blank, broken. It was deep night, the window open a crack, cold breath of breeze barely bothering the curtains, no hint of moonlight in the darkness behind the curtains.

The sound came again, from the corner.

Marianne pulled herself up in the bed and stared into the gloom.

"Jack . . . ?"

The sound increased in volume. Now she heard a louder, more distinct sound, like a cape flapping. The shadow in the corner grew deeper in the soft darkness surrounding it, and a hint of blank white, like an oval, peeked out at her and then was gone.

"Jack, is that you?"

"*No.*"

The sound of the voice, suddenly loud and deep and

distinct, sent a bolt of ice through her. She clutched the sheets to her like a life jacket.

"Who—" she began, her voice trembling.

"Someone . . ." the voice said, and now the form took on more edges, moved out of the corner toward her. The pale oval appeared and disappeared again, cut with a slash of red at the bottom: a mouth.

The figure stopped at the foot of the bed. Now the face became wholly visible: a pale oval the color of dead fish, two empty eyes like cutouts of darkness, that bright red slash of mouth like a wound. He was enfolded in a black cape that swirled and snapped as if it were in a stiff breeze.

The temperature in the room dropped; dropped again. Marianne shivered.

"Where's . . . Jack?" she managed to whisper hoarsely.

The figure tilted its head slightly to one side, but said nothing. Marianne noticed now that there were arms of a sort, also dead fish colored, and hands with unnaturally long fingers, enfolded in the cape.

"I wanted to see you," the thing said. It's voice was deeply neutral, without inflection.

Marianne shivered, hid her eyes as the thing drew up over the bed toward her.

"No!" she gasped.

She clutched the sheet and blanket to her face, felt a wash of cold unlike anything she had ever felt before. It was like being dropped into a vat of ice water. No, it was worse than that—like being instantly locked in a block of ice.

There was a wash of breath over her, colder still—

She opened her eyes, gasped to see that face inches from her own, the empty black cutout eyes regarding her, unblinking.

The mouth opened, showing more blackness still—

"No!"

She covered her face again, and, instantly, she knew the figure was gone.

She lowered the blanket and sheet.

The room was as it had been, the corner a stand of gloom, empty, the cold gone.

A breeze from the open window rustled the curtains, and she drew in her breath.

Something beyond them, in the night, moved past the window, a flat retreating shadow.

TEN

Bill Grant hated his empty house.

It was full of memories, all of them bad the past few years. Even when his wife Rose had been alive the house had not been a happy place, her depression regulating their lives like a broken wristwatch. When they had bought the place on his lousy beat cop's salary twenty years before it had been filled with nothing but good memories. But when the dark moods began to overtake her, the parties stopped, and then the socializing altogether, and eventually even the amenities with family.

And then, abruptly, she was gone, leaving Grant with only his job, and all that other business—what Grant liked to call *weird shit*—that seemed to happen in Orangefield every Halloween.

And *weird shit* left nothing but more bad memories, which made his empty house feel even emptier.

So he did what he often did now, especially as Halloween approached, which was to sit in his chair in his finished basement with an open bottle of Dewar's scotch, get drunk, watch old movies, and hope to God that *weird shit* wouldn't happen.

Grant poured two fresh fingers of scotch into his favorite glass—what had once been a jelly jar from the sixties encircled with pictures of the cartoon character Yogi Bear (outlined in yellow), his friend Boo Boo (outlined in blue) and Jellystone Park (drawn, originally in a garish green). Over the years and thousands of dish washings, all but the faintest outline of Yogi's fat head was still visible, none of Boo Boo but one of his feet, and some bizarre section of Jellystone Park that may or may not have been a picnic table, Grant no longer remembered.

Grant used the jelly jar because it reminded him of himself: slowly fading away with each new washing of *weird shit* . . .

He downed the two fingers in two neat swallows, and refilled the glass with two more fingers of scotch.

He hit the remote change button hard, angry that AMC had started to show commercials with their movies—he liked his westerns as neat and unblemished as his whiskey.

But Turner Classic Movies was showing a period piece, something along the lines of a 1930s version of *Dangerous Liaisons* without sex, so, grumbling, Grant hit the button hard again and put up with the few commercials breaking up the old John Wayne western *Stagecoach* on AMC.

"That's more like it!" Grant toasted the TV as the movie came back on. What a great John Ford flick. The only one he liked better was *The Searchers*. He'd have to buy it on tape someday to avoid all the breaks.

He was refilling his glass yet again when a tap came on the casement window to his left.

He nearly spit his whiskey back into the glass, remembering the last time that had happened (*weird shit*), but then he went smoothly into cop mode, rose, and drew his 9mm out of the drawer in the side table next to his lounge chair.

The tap came again as he reached the window. Reaching up, he pushed the dirty white curtain abruptly aside.

There was a face there. A young girl . . .

She made a motion, and he recognized her. He nodded and pointed up.

The face retreated and Grant dropped the curtain back into place.

He grabbed the scotch and his glass on the way, thought better of it and put it back.

Leaving the TV on, he went upstairs, hearing his own heavy tread on the creaking stairs.

She was not at the back door, which was closest to the basement window, so Grant went to the front door and snapped on the porch light as he opened it.

"Come in, Marianne," he said, holding the screen door open for her.

"I'm s-s-so sorry—" she began, but he cut her off.

"Nonsense. Come in and sit down. Can I make you some tea or coffee?"

She looked like a scared rabbit. "C-c-coffee would be great."

"Are you all right?"

She nodded, but was shivering like a leaf.

Grant moved past her into the kitchen, and she followed, sitting at the kitchen chair he pulled out for her. He fiddled with the coffeemaker, which had already been preprogrammed for tomorrow morning. After a few minutes of trying to fool the computer chip in it, he was able to get it to work. In a few seconds the comforting *blurp* and *drip* sounds commenced.

Grant sat down at the table across from the young woman. She was looking at her hands, locked in a prayerful grip on the top of the table, as if she had never seen them before.

"I haven't seen you in . . . what, two weeks?" Grant said, mustering his soothing cop voice. He knew he was pretty drunk, but was able to overcome it. He tried to lighten his tone and gave a small smile. "What's bothering you? Besides everything, that is?"

The girl continued to stare at her hands on the table. It was obvious she was trying to bring herself to say something, so Grant continued his monologue.

"I know what you're going through, Marianne. I lost my wife a few years ago. That hole still hasn't filled up completely. But it does get better, I can tell you from experience."

She was still fighting with herself.

"I . . . heard about your pregnancy, of course," Grant went on. "As you probably know, the DNA results on Bud Ganley were negative."

This was the spot where, like it or not, he would have to harden his voice a little. "You obviously did have relations with someone that night, Marianne. What I have to ask you is a hard question: who was it?"

Her eyes darted up from her hands, and Grant saw that they were filled with terror. For a moment, darker thoughts than Marianne Carlin's private life assaulted him.

"Detective—"

Her hands were trembling, now, and when he reached over to steady them they were cold as winter.

"Don't say anything yet."

He abruptly got up and went to the coffee machine.

The cycle wasn't finished yet but he yanked the carafe out and poured a cup for her anyway. He pushed the carafe back into its place and noted the spilled coffee hissing on the hot plate beneath it.

He wanted very much to go back to the basement and get his bottle of scotch. But after putting the steaming mug down in front of Marianne and taking a step toward the cellar door, he abruptly turned back and poured himself a cup of coffee.

"Milk or sugar?" he asked the young woman.

Her teeth chattering, she answered, "Milk, p-p-please."

He yanked open the refrigerator door, pulled out a quart of 2 percent milk, let the door close.

He sat down in front of his own black coffee, pushing the milk carton over to Marianne. When she made no move to open it, he did so himself, pouring it into her mug.

"Say when."

She focused on him, not on the coffee.

"Someone in a black cape with a white face was in my bedroom tonight," she said in a rushed, terrorized voice.

It might as well have been shouted through a loudspeaker. Grant dropped the milk carton, which hit the table and began to spill. He stared at it for a moment and then reached out and righted it.

Oh, God. Weird shit.

Marianne's eyes had never left his face.

To take his mind off of what she had said, he grabbed a dish towel from its rack behind him and sopped up the spillage with it. His mind was tightening and loosening like a fist.

Samhain.

When he was finished he tossed the wet towel into the sink and sat back down. She was staring at him with a pleading look in her eyes.

"Just tell me what happened," Grant said.

She did, every detail, and Grant's faint hope that she might have been delusional, or worse, faded.

"Detective Grant, what's happening to me?"

He opened his mouth to speak, thinking of a hundred ways to answer her question, but then said nothing. Mustering all of his cop's resources, he forced his lips into the same small smile he had showed her at the beginning of the interview.

"Drink some of your coffee. Believe me, there's nothing to worry about."

Like hell there isn't.

For a brief moment, her face showed relief. "You know what I saw? I'm not crazy?"

With all of his effort, he made his smile widen. "The last thing you are is crazy. I've seen this kind of thing before in Orangefield. For now, I just want you to forget about it."

"Really?" Her voice was filled with something like hope. "I called my sister, and she said it sounded like a Sam Sighting. She was laughing when she said it. But I heard—Janet heard—that you've been involved with this kind of thing before. The trouble at the Gates farm—"

It took all of his effort not to scream. "Leave it to me, Marianne. I'll look into it for you. If it makes you feel any better, other people in Orangefield have reported the same kind of thing you have."

And almost all of them ended up dead.

Her hands had stopped trembling, and were cradling her coffee cup.

His forced smile widened even more. "You'll do what I say?"

She suddenly nodded. "All right. But what was that thing I saw?"

His smile was locked into place, and he let his tired eyes crinkle in what may have looked like merriment. "It may be something, or nothing at all. Let's call it a 'Sam Sighting' for now, if you want."

In all innocence, she said, "What if I keep seeing it?"

"Just . . . don't worry. It won't hurt you."

A lie. You don't know that.

"Do you feel better now?" he asked.

She looked down at her coffee cup, nearly empty, and nodded, then smiled. "Better than I have in . . . a while. Thank you, Detective Grant. I . . . usually end up talking to my sister, and she's . . . well, a bit overbearing."

Grant forced himself to laugh in concurrence.

"Are you seeing a doctor?" he asked.

"Doctor Williams."

Grant nodded. "I know him. That's good, Marianne."

Without realizing it, he had risen and was ushering her out of the house. At the front door he stopped her and gently took her arm.

"If you need me, anytime, night or day, call me." He fished one of his ever-present business cards out of his wallet and gave it to her. "All the numbers are on there, at the station, home and cell. Don't hesitate. I'll . . . protect you, Marianne."

"Protect me?"

He forced a smile back onto his face. "Don't worry. I'll call you to make sure you're all right."

She took the card and suddenly raised herself on her toes and pecked him lightly on the cheek.

"Thank you, Detective."

"I need to ask you one more time, Marianne. Are you absolutely sure it was your husband with you that night?"

Her eyes were unblinking. "Yes."

"All right."

She was out the door and gone into the night.

He closed the door, locked it.

Samhain.

Ignoring the dirty cups in the kitchen, the coffee still warming which would taste bitter in the morning, he stumbled to the basement stairs and forced his feet to descend them. He sat in his lounge chair and, after looking at the curtained casement window, stared at the television. *Stagecoach* on AMC had been replaced by another, inferior western, riddled with commercials he didn't even register.

Weird shit.

Slowly, methodically, he emptied the Dewar's bottle, hammering himself down into sleep, and false peace.

ELEVEN

"Bud?"

The voice was deep, not at all friendly, and Bud Ganley didn't even bother to stick a hand out from underneath the truck and give the finger. After all, he was earning a buck now, and didn't owe anyone anything. This clown could wait. If it was a cop, screw 'im, if it was a customer, screw 'im, too. Whoever it was, he could talk to the boss, Jim Ready. Bud was just the hired help.

"Bud Ganley?"

"Eff off," Bud said from beneath the truck, continuing to work on mounting the rebuilt engine. He'd been sloppy with the chains and the block and tackle, he knew, but if he got it in place soon everything would be fine. If he didn't have this truck finished and ready to go today, Ready would really fire him for sure.

"I'd like to talk to you, Bud."

"I said—" Ganley began to snarl, but suddenly it became very dark around him and he was no longer beneath the truck in Ready's Garage.

"What the—"

"I was polite, and that didn't work. So, now I'm not polite."

It was so dark he thought he was in the middle of the woods somewhere. But it had been broad daylight, eleven-thirty in the morning, almost lunchtime, so this couldn't be . . .

He tentatively reached up and felt the engine block, swinging slightly on its chain cradle, above him.

"Jesus, I'm blind!"

"And dumb, and deaf as well, Bud. I've watched you for a long time, but never been much interested in you until now."

"I can't see!"

"You'll see again. Don't worry about that."

Now there was something in front of him in the darkness, where the engine block should be—a swirling black thing that came closer and then hovered above his face. He saw something rise out of the folds of black—a pasty face with no eyes and a smiling red mouth.

"Let's talk, Bud."

"Who the hell—"

"I'm someone who wants to talk."

"What do you *want?*" Ganley said in a panic.

"I want to know if you planned on seeing Marianne Carlin again." The thin red mouth added with emphasis, "And I want you to tell me the truth."

"Yeah, sure, why not? I mean, her old man's gone now, right? Why shouldn't I see her? Who knows, she may fall for me yet, right?"

"Didn't you try to . . . hurt her once?"

"What are you, some sort of cop trick machine? Is Grant in there behind the costume?"

The thing looked for a moment as if it were going to laugh, then the red lips became straight and grim.

"How would you feel about leaving Orangefield, Bud?"

"What! Eff you! I've lived here all my life! No way!"

"What if I asked you to leave, and never come back, and never think about Marianne Carlin again?"

"Christ! Now I *know* Grant's in that costume! Eff you, Detective! You can't tell me what to do and I don't listen to anybody but me!"

"That's what I thought. You've always been that way, and I'm sure you always will be. Thank you for talking, Bud, and thank you for your honesty."

"Eff you!"

The black thing with the white face was gone. Now the blackness dissolved around Ganley, as if someone pulled a blindfold away. He saw the engine above him at the exact moment it slipped its chains and fell toward him.

He got out one puppylike squeal before it hit.

TWELVE

"Thanks for seeing me, Doc."

Williams smiled his crusty old doctor's smile. "Country doctors always like seeing their old patients, Bill. I miss Rose a lot. I remember all those bridge games years ago—"

Grant cut the doctor off before he could go into one of his ten-minute reminiscence sessions.

"Doc, I'm here to talk about Marianne Carlin."

Williams' long, hound dog face formed a frown. He rubbed his chin. "Well, gee, Bill, we might be getting into doctor-patient confidentiality areas there—"

"I already know she's pregnant," Grant said. He wanted to reach for a cigarette but thought better of it here in Williams' office. Out in the hallway a nurse stopped at a doorway directly opposite and slid a form into a plastic holder mounted on the wall. A moment later she ushered a woman and a young, sniffling child into the room and closed the door after them. She gave a quick glance into the office and nodded at Williams.

"I'll be there in a minute, Martha."

The nurse nodded again and walked briskly away.

Williams leaned back in his desk chair and put his hands behind his head. "If you know she's pregnant, then why are we having this conversation?"

Grant said, "I need to know if she's *really* pregnant."

Williams frowned again, then nodded. "You mean an hysterical pregnancy, something like that?"

"Right."

The doctor scratched his cheek, rubbed his chin, looked at the ceiling. "Well, then, once more we enter that gray area, Bill . . ."

"It's important. I think she may have been raped the night her husband was killed. I thought it was Bud Ganley, but a DNA test cleared him."

"Bud Ganley." Williams frowned. "I just got off the phone with the coroner not twenty minutes ago about Bud Ganley."

"What about him?" Grant asked. The hair on the back of his neck began to prickle.

"He's dead, Bill. Surprised you haven't heard about it yet. Truck engine slipped its block and tackle chains while he was mounting it from below, crushed his head like, well, you provide the image. Grape, tomato, whatever. I was on duty at Orangefield General earlier today when they brought him in." He made a sour face. "If it had been yesterday, would have been my friend Gus Bellow instead of me looking at him. Wish it had been."

"Is his body still at Orangefield General?"

"Probably transferred it to the funeral home by now. He'll be in the ground in a few days. Won't be much of a wake, I imagine. I never did like that kid much. He was the kind that would take two lollipops from the jar."

Grant said nothing, which caught the doctor's attention. "You okay, Bill?"

"Just thinking . . ."

The nurse appeared again in the doorway and made a scolding motion at Williams.

"All right, all right," the doctor said, nodding. He pointed to the watch on his wrist. "One more minute, Martha. I promise."

As the nurse retreated Williams turned back to Grant. "They're stacking up out there like planes over an airport. Gotta go."

"Is she really pregnant?"

"Now, Bill—"

"I told you, it's important. She seems to think she is."

Williams asked, "When was the last time you saw her?"

"A week and a half ago. She came to my house. I've talked to her on the phone a few times since then, but haven't seen her."

Williams rose and came around his desk as Grant got out of his chair. The doctor put his arm around the detective's middle, brought it up to his shoulder and squeezed. "You know, if I was your doctor, and I am, I would tell you to cut down on the cigarettes, which I can smell on your breath, and your drinking, since I felt what is probably a pint bottle in your raincoat pocket as I reached around you just now to bring my hand up to your shoulder. You see, I have to be a detective in my work, too." He sighed. "I remember ten years ago, when your Rose and my Gladys, God rest both of them, dragged us to all kinds of things, it seemed every Saturday afternoon . . ."

His extended reminiscence was cut off by Grant's stone face and the reappearance of Martha in the doorway. The doctor nodded to her and then leaned over to whisper into Grant's ear.

"Point is, you're a lousy detective, Bill. She's got a belly on her you can see a mile away."

"Wha—"

Williams whispered, "She's five months pregnant, Bill."

THIRTEEN

"Think of it as a favor, Mort. A big one."

"You got that right. You think I've got nothing else to do than run lab tests on closed cases? That kid Ganley's dead, right?"

Grant spoke evenly into the receiver. "Right."

"And he was your number one, right?"

"Correct."

"And he came up neg, right?"

"Correct again."

"And now you want me to run not the other idiot, what's his name, Petee Wilkins, but—"

"Yes, Mort. That's what I want you to do."

A long-pause on the other end, then a snort. "You got it, hojo. Though God knows why I'm doing this."

"Tomorrow, Mort?"

"A.M."

There was a click in Grant's ear.

FOURTEEN

Marianne Carlin didn't answer her phone, so Grant drove to her house. It was chilly and getting chillier, October marching steadfastly away from Indian summer and toward winter. The sky was a stark, cold, deep blue, a shade particular to this season. The elms and oaks were in full riot, bursting with red and yellow, already starting to shed. The road was littered with a beautiful blanket that had not yet become a nuisance and danger, waves and dunes of leaves that filled gutters, washed over curbs and clogged storm drains.

Already, a few pumpkins were out on stoops, uncarved but waiting for nearing Halloween.

Grant avoided the center of Orangefield, where the leftover bunting would still be strung for the Pumpkin Days Festival, which thankfully had ended. A week of drunken teens, greedy locals and a bloat of tourists in the Pumpkin Capital of the World living by the twin unwritten Orangefield codes of "Have A Good Time" and "Make A Buck." Ranier Park had been turned once again into a mecca for commerce, with two huge circus tents erected—one filled with aisles of Halloween wares, the other a haven for lovers of bad live music, with seven days of varied fare: country, rock and roll, jazz and, heaven forbid, rap music. For the first time in ten years Grant had avoided Pumpkin Days duty, taking part of the week off and burying himself in administrative work the rest. It had been a kind of blessing.

Marianne Carlin's house, a tidy ranch, was on a tidy street. The lawn was dotted with leaves not yet in need of raking. There was no pumpkin on the stoop, but a clutch of Indian corn hung from the front door, which was painted red.

As Grant parked his Taurus, Marianne emerged from the side of the house, wearing gardening gloves. Sure enough, now that he looked, she showed a belly, even beneath her painter's overalls.

Grant caught up with her as she entered the yawning opening of the garage next to the house. He found her fumbling around in a wheelbarrow, which was filled with gardening tools.

He cleared his voice and she turned around, startled.

"Oh! Detective Grant!"

Grant smiled. "Sorry."

She smiled, too, and regained her composure, handing Grant the trowel she had plucked from the wheelbarrow. "Would you carry this for me?"

She walked past him, and led him back to the side of the house, where a tangle of dead weeds and still-blooming annuals clogged a small plot.

"It's a mess," she explained, taking the trowel from him. "I pretty much ignored it this year. But I thought going at it might be good for me. For the plants, too."

"Marianne, why didn't you tell me you were five months pregnant?"

She had knelt down to plow at the black loamy soil, and looked up at him. "Because I didn't know. I didn't know until the day after Jack died. I started to feel sick, and then I started to show. And every day I seem to show more."

Grant heard a car door slam. He turned to see Marianne's sister Janet trudging toward them over the lawn. In the backseat of her Buick, Baby Charlie waved his arms from his car seat. His face was red and he looked to be wailing, but the closed car and the distance prevented him from being heard.

Janet stopped and put her hands on her hips, regarding Grant. "You again! Just the man I want to see!" She reached out and grabbed Grant by the elbow, tugging him away. As Marianne began to rise Janet pointed at her. "You stay there. I'll be back in a few minutes and take you to lunch."

Marianne obeyed, and Grant was hauled over the front lawn toward his car, parked in front of Janet's. She had a grip like a bench vise.

She let go of Grant's arm and faced him.

"Actually," Grant said, "you're the one I want to see. Did you know your sister was five months pregnant?"

"Five months my ass." She pointed to her own belly. "*I'm* seven months pregnant, and I've been puking since day one." She jerked a thumb at the Buick. "Same thing happened with Baby Charlie. Puking and feeling like puking for nine months straight, and showing after two. Big as a house. It runs in our family. *Nobody* escapes it. And I'm telling you, Marianne wasn't pregnant five months ago. I would have known. I've got radar. I can sense it. When she started to feel sick after Jack died, *then* I knew she was pregnant. But she wasn't till then. She *couldn't* have been."

"Why?"

"Jack had a vasectomy when they got married. In fact, he had it reversed the day he died. He and Marianne had decided to have a kid. Marianne told me he'd promised to come home early that night, so that they could start trying to get her preggers. But instead he went out celebrating with those two asshole friends of his. Macho manhood and all that crap. Did I mention I'm glad Bud Ganley is dead? One less loser in the world."

"Is there any chance Marianne was having an affair, and got pregnant five months ago?"

"*Ha!* My sister? She was wild crazy in love with Jack Carlin, and he was the same with her. No way in hell."

She put her hands on her hips again. "My turn. You're the guy who knows all about the weird stuff in this town, right?"

"Well—"

Janet didn't let him continue. "Marianne's been acting just plain strange. And getting stranger. She tell you about the guy with the cape?"

"She came to see me right after it happened. I've been calling her on the phone every few days since then to make sure she's all right. Every time I phone her, she says she's fine."

"Oh, you need to catch up, Detective. This cape character's been back just about every night. Now she says he's her friend, and that she's not afraid of him anymore. She even calls him Samhain. I stayed with her one night in her bedroom, but didn't see a damned thing but that dog shit ugly wallpaper of hers. The next night she claimed he was back. Either she's nuts, or there's still something mighty screwy going on."

Grant said nothing.

"It's like she's in a fog. A couple weeks ago, she was just

beginning to show. Now she's almost as big as me." Janet took a deep breath. "The thing I want to know is: if she's pregnant, five months or otherwise, how the hell did it happen?"

"I don't know."

"Well, I've said my piece," Janet continued, shaking her head, "and now you know everything I do. I gave you that stuff of Jack's you asked for when I was cleaning out the house, and I'll help any other way I can. I think my sister would have been just fine by now, after Jack's death, if all this other monkey business hadn't started. I'm worried about her, but I don't know what to do. Maybe you can worry about her, too. Between the two of us we can do a lot of worrying."

She turned and shouted to Marianne, "Come on! Let's go eat! I'm starving!"

Marianne threw down her tools and stood up. She looked even more pregnant than she had when Grant arrived.

Janet was shaking his hand. "Thanks for listening, Detective."

She dropped Grant's hand, and trundled over to help her sister into the front of the Buick.

Grant couldn't help but be struck by how much bigger than her sister Marianne looked.

FIFTEEN

"You're sure, Mort?"

"Ninety-nine point nine percent. I'm positive if we did the full test every marker would match. This is the guy, all right."

Grant was silent.

"Just to make sure," Mort said, "I took samples from both the hairbrush and the toothbrush. Same result."

Grant made a sound that was something like, "Thanks."

"And you said this guy was her husband? If he was dead how could he —"

Grant said, "Exactly," and hung up the phone.

Sixteen

It always seemed to rain at burials. There was a blue tarp over Bud Ganley's casket, which Grant had no doubt was a cheap one. There were only a handful of mourners: Ganley's mother, his employer, Jim Ready, a couple of like-aged slouchers who looked like pool room buddies, and Petee Wilkins, who stood off by himself. Grant had made his way into the back end of the cemetery, through a small stretch of woods, and stood at the top of a moderate rise looking down at the proceedings below. His raincoat collar was up against the chill, and his cigarette was used up.

He lit a new one and watched as the reverend finished his ministrations and the two slouchers, who turned out to be the grave diggers, began to lower the casket into the ground. They pulled the blue tarp off it then, and Ganley's mother threw a clod of dirt on it and turned away, not looking at Petee Wilkins. The way she walked told Grant that this was the last in a long line of disappointments.

Petee stood watching as the two grave diggers began to shovel the mound of waiting dirt into the hole. Grant ambled down the hill and approached him. Too late to flee, Petee noticed him and stood rooted to the spot, looking at the ground. Grant was struck by how much Wilkins looked like a skinny rat, down to the twitching nose and sniffles. He had always been a follower. Grant had first met him when Wilkins was twelve, and got caught trashing a house on Sagett River Road. The punk he was with got away, but Petee got caught. He was the kind who would always get caught.

"'Lo, Detective," Petee said, running the back of his hand across his continually running nose. He wouldn't look up.

"I just have one question to ask you, Petee," Grant said.

"Sure. Whatever."

"I want you to tell me the dead-ass truth, and if you do I won't bother you again. That's a promise."

Petee's nose twitched, and his shoulders spasmed up and down with what might have been a form of assent.

"Okay?" Grant asked.

"Sure."

"Just answer me this. Did you and Bud Ganley take Jack Carlin home before you took him to the hospital?"

Petee drew the back of his hand quickly across his running nose. His nose twitched twice. "No, Detective Grant."

"Are you sure? Look at me, Petee."

Wilkins glanced up briefly. Even his dark brown eyes were small and ratlike. "He wanted us to, but we didn't!"

"He was alive after that car hit him?"

Petee was staring at the ground again. Behind them, the two grave diggers went about their work, which lent a susurrus of shoveled dirt to the conversation. "Yeah, but just for a couple of minutes. At first he begged us to take him home. Then he got all glassy eyed and kept calling for Marianne, saying he had to go to her. That he had promised. He started yelling a bunch of stuff." He glanced up at Grant briefly again. "Then he was gone. He died right there in the street before we put him in Bud's car and took him to the hospital."

"Why didn't you tell the police that he was alive after the car hit him?"

Sniffle, wipe. "Bud was afraid we'd get in trouble. And I was afraid."

"Afraid of what?"

Twitch, shrug. "Afraid . . ."

"Tell me, Petee, or we end up down at the station with you in a holding cell."

"Oh, shit." He shuffled his feet, looked back at the grave diggers, who were wiping their hands, stared at the ground again. Grant noticed that his knuckles were white, his hands trembling. "Afraid . . ."

"Petee—"

"I was afraid of what he said, and what happened! I believed Jack, is all! Bud ran to get his car, and Jack was all busted up and dying, and he stared right through me and was yelling, 'I promised you a baby! I promised!' And then . . ."

"And then what?"

"And then he died, and . . ."

Grant was about to prod him again when Petee blurted, with a groan, "And something flew out of his body and away, Detective! Smoke, or fog, or . . . something that looked just like Jack!"

"Petee—" Grant began.

"Aw, shit, Detective," Wilkins said, wiping his nose and then his eyes. He was crying now. "Can't you leave me alone? Can't you just leave me the hell alone? All my friends are dead now, and my life is shit. Can't you just lay off me?"

Grant took a long breath, and said, "Sure, Petee. Like I promised."

Wilkins turned abruptly, almost stumbling into one of the grave diggers, who was loading his shovel into a wheelbarrow, and walked off, hitching sobs and wiping at his face with his hands.

Grant stared after him for a moment, then turned and made his way up the slope, lighting a cigarette. The rain had turned to a chill mist, coating fallen leaves and making their brilliant colors slick. The trees were almost denuded now.

It was two days till Halloween.

SEVENTEEN

Grant had never heard Doc Williams sound flustered, let alone frightened. But frightened was what he sounded on the phone.

"You'll come to see me right now, Bill?"

"Of course. But why don't you just tell me—"

"Not on the phone. And for God's sake not in the office. I'll be in the coffee shop in the strip mall across the street."

"I'm on my way."

Williams was not there when Grant walked into the coffee shop, but he walked out of the men's room a moment later. He was pale as a sheet, and looked unwell.

He motioned Grant to the booth farthest from the counter, in an empty corner of the shop. Grant sat down and the laconic waitress, chewing gum, ambled over and asked him if he wanted anything. "Doc here already ordered coffee for ya, new pot's brewin', be a few. Any pie? Cake? Pumpkin pie's good t'day."

285

She stared over his head, and Grant told her that just coffee was fine.

"Be back when it's ready."

She turned and shuffled back to the counter, where an open newspaper awaited her.

Grant turned his attention to Williams. "Let me guess before you tell me. Marianne Carlin is more than five months pregnant."

To his surprise, Williams nodded and waved that off. "Yes. Actually, she's almost reached term. I'm not even going to try to explain it." Williams stared straight into Grant's eyes. "I was threatened, Bill."

"By whom?"

"He was . . . very insistent. Told me that if I went near Marianne again he would kill my family, and me. And . . . he told me not to go to the police for help."

Williams glanced nervously past Grant to the front window. At that moment the waitress was shuffling toward them with two mugs of steaming coffee, which she set down ungracefully, managing to spill onto the table.

"Sure you don't want to try the pumpkin?" she asked, not quite stifling a yawn.

Doc said quickly, "Thanks, May. We're fine."

She turned and shrugged, shuffling back to the counter. "It's real good pie . . ."

"Why did you call me, Doc?"

"Because he said I could tell you, and only you. He said to tell you his name was Sam."

Samhain.

Doc Williams was still talking, and Grant had missed some of it.

". . . on the telephone. I thought it was a prank at first. I was sitting in my office, and picked up the receiver, and my hand up to my elbow went cold, as if it had been plunged into ice water. I thought for a second I was having a stroke. The voice told me what I just told you, and then said to tell you that Marianne Carlin was to be left alone until Halloween was over. He said you would understand. And that was it. When I put down the phone receiver my arm was back to normal, not ice cold anymore."

Williams looked at Grant with a special pleading. "In the afternoon, when I was leaving for my rounds at the hospital, something was waiting for me next to my car in the parking lot behind my office. It was this 'Sam' creature, all black swirling shadows and a white face like a horrid Halloween mask. He repeated what he'd said and told me to call you. He came up close to me and his breath smelled like . . . *nothing*. Like empty space. I thought he was going to kill me on the spot. What the hell is going on, Bill? Would this thing really hurt my family?"

"Yes," Grant said. "I think he would. Do what you were told. Let me worry about Marianne Carlin."

Williams stared at his untouched coffee. "I've never seen anything like this, ever, Bill! I'm a *doctor*! Who the hell is this 'Sam'?"

"He's the thing you fight every day, Doc."

EIGHTEEN

Grant's finger was getting numb from pressing the doorbell at Janet Larson's house. He'd peered through the front windows—everything looked normal, a scatter of toys on the rug, a half-empty bottle on the coffee table in the living room, a changing bag nearby. There was a Buick in the driveway, the same one Grant had seen at Marianne's house. The doors, front and back, were locked. An uncarved pumpkin sat on the porch next to the door, the outline of a to-be-cut face fashioned in magic marker.

"Y' won't find 'em there, mister!" a voice called, and Grant turned to see an old woman staring at him from the property next door. She had stopped precisely at the border between the houses, next to her driveway. She had a face like a lemon, and Grant noticed that there was no pumpkin on her stoop.

"Do you know where Mrs. Larson is?" Grant asked, stepping down from the porch to better talk to her.

"Left early this mornin', the whole bunch of 'em! Piled

into the SUV like Satan was chasin' 'em. Kid squawking like always."

"Do you have any idea where they went?"

The old woman made her face look even more sour, turned around, waved her hand in dismissal. "No idea, 'cept they had a couple bags with 'em. Usually means they're off to New Hampshire, to his brother's in Derby. Only place they ever go." She stopped and turned around, making a sudden fist and shaking it at the house. Her face became very red. "Used t' take in their paper when they went away, but they're ingrates! Not even a thank-you! Young and selfish."

Her face lost its color, and she turned and walked slowly back to her house. "Well, they'll get what they deserve when they don't dish out any candy to the little monsters tomorrow and the house gets egged."

There were three Larsons in Derby, New Hampshire, and the second was the right one. After some negotiation with Chuck, Janet's wife, Janet finally got on the phone.

"Make it quick, Detective. Baby Charlie needs a change."

"Why did you leave so quickly?"

There was a long silence on the other end of the phone. "Let's just say I was asked to."

"By whom?"

"He said he knows you. He also said he'd kill Chuck and Baby Charlie if we didn't go."

"Did you—"

"I don't have time for this, Detective. I'm too busy being scared to death. As you've seen, I put on a good bluff, but underneath I'm just a grade-A chickenshit like most people. I believed what I was told."

"When—"

"I stayed at my sister's house again last night, Detective. Most of the night there was nothing to look at in the corner of her bedroom but that ugly wallpaper. And then there was something else. And, well, here I am."

"What if your sister needs you?"

"She's on her own, now. All she did was coo and sing, anyway, when this thing appeared. He seemed pretty fond of her, too. Me, I don't like ghost stories, much less the real thing."

Grant started to ask another question, but the line went dead.

NINETEEN

Riley Gates' farm was, now, one of the saddest places on Earth. In its prime, when Gates, a former police detective and Grant's mentor, had been alive, it was a place Grant always looked forward to visiting. When they had both been married, and before Rose became sick, there had been many parties at Riley's place, and even after Riley divorced and Rose died, Grant had still considered Riley Gates' one of the finest men he had ever known.

But now . . .

Driving past the long-closed farm stand on the main road, with its faded sign RILEY'S PICK YOUR OWN PUMPKINS, and then through the broken front gate over the rutted road and up to the blackened, gutted, burned house, Grant felt nothing but hollow. He parked near the barn, its paint peeling, one door off its hinges and the other ajar. He got out of his car and walked toward the rutted field that, in earlier years, would have been filled today with families picking their last minute Halloween pumpkins. This year only a few misshapen rogue fruits had grown, pale-colored, wilting and untended. There was a cool breeze in the late day kicking up dust devils in the fallow plot. The sky was growing blue-purple, and the sun in the west, directly across the field, looked shimmering orange, like a pumpkin hiding behind a veil.

Riley's weigh station—a hand-built square booth that had once held a huge scale, long stolen, with a chair beside it, still, miraculously, in place—stood forlorn at the edge of the field. Grant went to it and sat down in the chair. He faced the lowering sun, shook out a cigarette from its pack, lit it, and waited.

TWENTY

"Hello, Detective Grant."

Grant came awake with a start. For a moment he was disoriented in the darkness, then he remembered where he was. There was something in front of him, moving in and out of vision, a deeper darkness than the night. It had turned colder, and Grant felt a chill. The sky had clouded over, and it felt like it might rain.

Grant sat up, pulled his raincoat closed and shivered. His hand went to his pocket and pulled out the remains of a pint of Dewar's.

"Still imbibing, I see," the shape in front of him said.

"Any reason not to?"

"It's been a while."

"Not long enough for me."

The thing was silent for a moment. Grant felt a deeper chill, catching a glimpse of that white face, that cruel red line of a mouth.

"I hoped I'd never see you again," Grant said.

Samhain's smile widened perceptibly. His surrounding black cloak hung almost lifeless, swirling slightly at the bottom. "I'm sure. But I rather enjoy your company. And it seems we have mutual business—again."

With every ounce of his courage, Grant fought to stay under control in front of this . . . *thing*.

"Oh, come now, you're not afraid of me anymore, are you, Detective?"

"Why shouldn't I be?"

"What is there to fear? You already know who I am, and what I represent. All men face me eventually. Don't you consider it a privilege to . . . shall we say, interact with me now and again, before your time?"

"It's a privilege I could pass up."

Samhain threw back his head and gave something like a laugh. It sounded hollow and cold. "I have been studying your kind for thousands of years, and still you puzzle and interest me."

"What is it you want, Samhain?"

"Ah." The blackness swirled, the Lord of Death came closer. Grant felt the temperature drop, a dry cold that belied the weather.

"I merely want you to leave Marianne Carlin alone."

"Why?"

"Because she has something I'm . . . interested in. Mr. Ganley was going to bother her, so I had to dissuade him."

"I thought so."

Samhain turned back to Grant and came even closer. "I cannot scare you off, Detective, like I did the doctor and the sister. We both know that."

"You tried once before."

"I did. And I failed."

"You'll fail again. I won't let anything happen to Marianne."

"You think I want to *harm* her, Detective? You don't understand at all. That's the last thing I want."

"Then what *do* you want?"

"I'm not ready to tell you, Detective. But I will tell you this. Tomorrow is Halloween. Please leave her alone until the day is over."

"I won't let you near her."

Samhain gave something like a sigh. "We both know that I can only bring direct harm to those who can be influenced. I cannot influence you. You know many of my tricks, but not all of them. I would prefer that we discuss this reasonably."

"I don't think that's possible."

After a pause, the shape said, "I thought we understood each other."

"I doubt it."

The thing swooped up very close, its surrounding black form snapping and moving in the cold breeze. Grant felt the deeper cold of its breath on him, and the white face was very close to his own.

"Don't. Interfere."

Grant held that empty gaze, felt bile rise in the back of his throat, felt a black cold charge run up his back and make his teeth chatter. Samhain reached out a spectral hand, long white vaporous fingers ending in short, sharp silver claws, and held it in check in front of Grant's face.

"Listen to me, Detective."

"I won't let you near her."

The figure receded to its former position. The face was half-hidden again, the shadowy folds of its surrounding darkness part of the night itself.

"We'll see."

All at once the thing was gone, leaving only the cool night and a few stars peeking from behind scattering clouds.

His hand trembling, Grant brought the last of his whiskey up to his mouth and drank it.

TWENTY-ONE

"Wake up, Petee."

Petee Wilkins was having the only good dream he ever had. He had it every once in a while and always enjoyed it. In it he and his best friend Bud were in the house they broke into on Sagett River Road, eating from a huge box of chocolates they had found in the kitchen. Petee had never seen a candy box so big, covered in gold foil and tied with a silky red ribbon. The card had said, "To Bonny, Please, please forgive me! Signed, Paul." They had gotten a good laugh over that.

"Wonder what the old poop did!" Bud laughed, stuffing his face with what turned out to be chocolate-covered cherries. After a moment of bliss he cried, "Ugh!" and spat them out onto the kitchen table, which was huge and marble topped. "I *hate* chocolate-covered cherries!"

Petee laughed and then gagged, spitting out his own mouthful of candy, which he had actually been enjoying.

Bud started laughing, holding his stomach, and then Petee began to laugh, too.

"Funny!" Petee said.

Bud took the box of chocolates and dumped it out on the floor. Then he began to stomp on the candy, making chocolate mud.

After a moment Petee joined in, and then Bud said, "Come on!" and they tramped into the living room, leaving chocolate sneaker prints on the white rug.

There was much more to the dream, trashing the living room, throwing a side chair through the large screen TV—

But now Petee abruptly woke up.

"Oh, no—" he said, looking at the hovering, flapping, black thing above him with the oval white face.

"Now how can you say that, Petee?" Samhain asked.

"I thought you were gone for good," Petee whimpered.

"Didn't I tell you I might need you someday?"

"Sure. But I didn't think . . ."

"That's right, Petee, you didn't think. But you don't have to. I did you that favor back in . . . what was it? Junior high school?"

Petee nodded, wiping the back of his hand across his running nose. He sat up in bed and looked down at the covers, not at the thing.

"That's right," Samhain said, "I kept you from getting into big trouble when you and that idiot Ganley drowned the Manhauser's cat. Oh, your father would have beat you to death if the police had been involved in that one, don't you think?"

Petee would not look up. "Yeah," he said, grudgingly.

"And what did you promise at the time? Didn't you promise to do me a favor if I ever needed one?"

Eyes downcast, Petee nodded.

"Good. And now it's time. Here's what I want you to do, Petee . . ."

TWENTY-TWO

Another Halloween.

The day dawned gray and bloodshot. Grant woke up in his lounge chair in the basement with a sour taste in his mouth. A finger of scotch lay pooled in the bottom of the Dewar's bottle on the table next to the chair. The glass next to it was empty. The television volume was low, the movie on Turner Classic Movies a film noir with too much talking.

Grant got up, walked to the casement window and pushed the partially open short curtain all the way open. A mist of rainwater covered the storm window, and the sky through it was battleship gray–colored and low.

He could just make out a row of pumpkins, already carved into faces, frowns on one end slowly turning into smiles by the other, on the rail of his back neighbor's deck. It was a yearly tradition.

He turned off the television, oddly missing the sound after it was off, and trudged up the stairs to the kitchen. He checked the back door, which was locked and bolted, and then the front.

Back in the kitchen, he made eggs and toast and a pot of coffee, then dialed into work from his cell phone.

"Chip? This is Grant. Captain Farrow knows I'm not coming in today, right? You told him, like I asked?"

The desk sergeant said something, and Grant snapped, "Then tell him now, you dimwit. I won't be in."

Grant pushed the off button on the phone and tossed it onto the kitchen table.

From upstairs there came a sound, and Grant froze in place, listening. Then it came again, bedsprings creaking. The detective relaxed, turning back to his eggs, which were bubbling and snapping in the frying pan now.

After breakfast he cleaned up the kitchen, poured a second cup of coffee and went back down to the basement. A sour rising sun was trying to fight its way through the scudding clouds.

Maybe it would clear after all.

Grant settled himself back in his chair, turned the television back on and watched two westerns back-to-back, muting the sound every once in a while to listen for sounds upstairs.

At eleven A.M. he went back upstairs and pulled a fresh bottle of Dewar's from its bag, which he had placed on the dining room hutch the day before. He brought the bottle downstairs. He emptied the last finger of scotch from the old bottle into the glass, twisted open the new bottle and added another finger.

A sound from upstairs, a moan, and Grant set the bottle of scotch on the TV table, took his glass, and went up to the kitchen.

"Shit."

Another moan followed, and Grant slowly trudged up the stairs to the second floor of the house. There was a short hallway with two bedrooms and a bath off it. He passed the bath and his own bedroom and stood in the doorway of the other, sipping scotch.

Marianne Carlin lay on her back on the guest bed, the covers kicked aside, half-asleep.

Her belly under her nightgown was huge.

As Grant watched, she moved her head from side to side, eyes closed, and moaned again.

Grant went to the bed, put his glass down on the bedside table and picked up the washcloth that lay folded on the edge of the water bowl there and dipped it into the water. He wrung it out and patted the young woman's forehead with the cloth.

Marianne mumbled something in her sleep, the name, "Jack," then wrenched herself over onto her side away from him and began to softly snore.

Grant rearranged the covers over her, folded the washcloth back on the edge of the bowl, retrieved his alcohol and left.

Another movie brought him to lunchtime—a grilled cheese sandwich—and then two more short old westerns got him to four o'clock in the afternoon. The schools were out by now, and the younger trick-or-treaters would start soon. He went upstairs to check his candy bowl by the front door, and for good measure added another bag to it, which made it overflow. He picked up the fallen Snickers bars and put them in his pocket.

He glanced outside and saw that the sun had lost its all-day fight with the gray clouds and was dropping, a pallid orange ball, toward the western horizon.

A porch light flicked on at the house across the street, which seemed to trigger a relay—two more houses lit up, one of them with tiny pumpkin lights strung across its gutter from end to end, the other with a huge spotlight next to the drive illuminating a motor-driven, wriggling spider in a rope web arranged in the lower branches of a white birch.

Back in the basement, Grant noted that the pumpkins on his back neighbor's deck railing were now lit, flickering frowns to smiles.

He tried to watch another movie, but his palms had begun to sweat.

Upstairs, the doorbell rang. He went up to answer it. Two diminutive sailors, one with a pirate's eye patch, looked up at him and shouted, "Trick or treat!" They thrust their near-empty bags up in a no-nonsense manner, glaring balefully at him.

He gave them each two candy bars, and they turned immediately and fled sideways across his lawn to the next house. Grant was closing the door as a mother, parked watchfully in a Dodge Caravan at the curb, began to shout, "Use the sidewalk, Douglas . . . !"

The van crept up the street, following Douglas and his fellow pirate.

As Grant was stepping back downstairs the doorbell rang again, and soon he was sitting in the living room with the lights out, smoking his second cigarette, waiting for the bell to ring.

It did, again and again: hobos, men from Mars, ballerinas followed by more hobos.

There was a lull, and Grant went into the kitchen, made another grilled cheese sandwich for dinner.

The doorbell rang again.

Abandoning the grilled cheese sandwich, Grant grabbed a handful of candy bars, yanked open the door—

Petee Wilkins was standing there, snuffling, looking at the ground. There was something in his right hand, which he jerked up—

Instinctively, Grant twisted aside as Petee's eyes briefly

met his and the gun went off. It sounded very far away
and not very loud. But it must have been a better handgun than Grant assumed, because the slug hit him in the
side like a hard punch. As Grant kept twisting, falling
into the candy basket and to the ground, he heard Petee
hitch a sob and cry, "I'm sorry!"

Then Petee was gone.

Grant lay stunned, and waited for pain to follow the
burning sensation of the bullet.

It came, but it wasn't as bad as he feared.

As he sat up, a lone trick-or-treater, dressed in some indeterminate costume that may have represented Mr.
Moneybags from the board game Monopoly, stood in the
doorway looking down at him. He said the required words
and Grant fumbled on the ground around him and threw
a handful of candy bars his way.

"Gee, thanks, mister!" Mr. Moneybags said, and ran off.

Grant scooped as much of the candy around him as
possible out through the doorway, then stood up with an
"Oooof" and, holding his side, kicked closed the door.

He limped into the kitchen and had a look.

There was blood on his hand, which was not a good
sign, but there wasn't a lot soaked into his shirt, which
was. He pulled his shirt out of his pants, took a deep
breath, and studied the wound.

Just under the skin, left side, in and out, looking clean.
He knew he would find the slug somewhere in the front
hallway.

"Thank you, Petee, you incompetent asshole," he
whispered, and cleaned the wound at the kitchen sink as
best he could. He tied three clean dish towels together
and girded his middle.

The blood flow had nearly stopped already.

The front doorbell rang, but he ignored it.

He called the police dispatcher, whose name was Maggie Pheifer, identified himself, told her to have a patrol car visit Petee Wilkins' father's house, where they would probably find Petee Wilkins hiding under his own bed. "Consider him armed and dangerous, just in case. I'll call back in later."

From upstairs came a moan, louder than the others.

"Shit," Grant said and, taking a deep, painful breath, hobbled to the stairs and limped his way up.

TWENTY-THREE

Marianne Carlin's eyes were wide open. She lay pushed back on the bed, knees apart. She was breathing in short little gasps.

"Hello, Detective," Samhain said calmly from the foot of the bed, where he floated like a wraith. "I see Petee didn't do his job, which is just as well. I really didn't want you dead, only . . . incapacitated."

Grant felt suddenly short of breath, leaned against the doorjamb. He slid down to the floor, staring at Samhain.

"My, my," Samhain said, "Petee seems to have done a fine job at that."

"What do you want, Samhain?" Grant said, gasping. There was a growing pain in his left side, which wasn't going to go away.

Samhain said nothing, staring at Marianne Carlin, who gave a moan and arched her back.

"You want the baby," Grant said.

"Yes," Samhain said simply.

"Why?"

Again the wraith was silent as Marianne threw her head

back in pain. Grant wanted to help her but felt as if his body was filled with lead. He could barely lift his left arm.

"Do you know what ghosts are, Detective?" Samhain said, quietly. "It happens now and then that someone on the way to my realm from yours gets . . . caught in the middle. These are usually very strong personalities. Often, there is something very important that they are leaving behind. Unfinished business, if you will.

"Jack Carlin got . . . away from me, you might say. At the moment he was to be mine, he broke away and reached his wife. This has never happened quite like this before. He was neither of this Earth when this happened, nor completely in my own place. He was dead, Detective. And yet . . ."

Samhain stood silent vigil at the foot of the bed, staring at Marianne Carlin in a kind of wonder.

Grant said, "The baby is from your world."

"Yes. The child is of . . . death. It is mine, in a way. Do you understand now? It is . . . life from death. This . . . has never happened."

Grant gasped, gathered his strength. "You sound almost proud."

Samhain turned a mild, almost fond, look on Grant. "You give me too much credit for cruelty, Detective. I serve, nothing more. And after eons of death, to see something born from it like this . . ."

His attention was brought back to Marianne, whose cries were coming more closely together. Her stomach was taut with effort, her legs spread impossibly wide.

"It will not be long now . . ." Samhain said, in wonder. He moved up over the foot of the bed to hover above the birthing woman.

Grant took a deep breath and pushed himself back against the doorjamb. With a supreme effort he stood.

For a moment the world went black, but he held his position and when his sight cleared he urged himself forward.

"Don't try to interfere, Detective," Samhain snapped.

"That thing could bring death into this world. I can't let that happen."

"I said don't interfere . . ."

Grant took two halting steps forward and then the pain in his left side flared to broiling heat. He stumbled, reaching out to clutch at the side of the bed as he fell to his knees. He pulled himself up, fighting for breath, to see the crown of a baby's head appear between Marianne Carlin's legs.

"Good, Marianne—good!" Samhain urged, as the young woman screamed and arched and pushed.

Grant took a long shuddering breath, put his right hand into his coat pocket, resting it on the butt of his 9mm handgun.

Samhain moved up and closer over the woman, almost alive with excitement.

"Push, Marianne! Push!"

Marianne Carlin screamed. The baby's head appeared, a gray wrinkled thing with closed eyes and a puckered mouth.

It was followed in a rush of blood by the rest of the body, tiny hands and skinny legs and tiny feet.

Samhain moved over the baby, straightened, his head thrown back, his red mouth opened wide.

"*Mine!*" he cried.

The thing on the bed kicked, and then its tiny mouth opened and then its eyes.

It looked up at the thing hovering overhead.

Grant tightened his grip on the 9mm.

The baby wailed, a hollow, long, hoarse shriek.

It held its tiny hands out to Samhain, and opened its mouth again.

As Samhain tentatively reached out to touch it, the baby turned to dust, head to foot, the blood surrounding it and the umbilical cord also.

Its dying empty moan echoed to silence.

"*Noooooooooo!*" Samhain wailed, throwing his clawed hands down to the empty spot on the bed where the baby had been. "*Noooooooooo!*"

Grant's grip loosened on the handgun, and he saw black, and fell to the floor . . .

TWENTY-FOUR

Sunlight made Bill Grant wince. He opened his eyes, feeling a hot sharp pain in his right side, which abruptly tapered and subsided. He was in a hospital bed, a white sheet pulled up to his chin, a lightly curtained closed window to his right. It was broad daylight, the sun high in a sapphire blue cloudless sky over the rooftops outside.

"Welcome to November," a sarcastic voice said.

He pushed himself up as Marianne Carlin's sister Janet appeared at the foot of his bed, hands on hips.

"You . . ." Grant said.

Her cheeks colored slightly. "Let's just say I felt guilty as hell over being such a chickenshit," she said. "I started for home right after I talked to you on the phone. Said my last good-byes to Chuck and Baby Charlie and got to Marianne's house just in time to find it crawling with police. I followed one of them to your house. It seems some trick-or-treater found a handgun on your front lawn and put it in his bag. When the police got there they found you and my sister both half-dead in your guest bedroom."

"How—" Grant began.

"Marianne's fine. She doesn't remember anything that happened the last few weeks. But what everyone wants to know is, what happened to the baby?"

"The—" Grant said, but was again cut off, this time by Doc Williams, who appeared next to Janet. He looked no better than the last time Grant had seen him.

"There was no baby," Williams said. "It was an hysterical pregnancy after all." He glanced at Grant briefly, his eyes hooded, and cut off Janet Larson when she tried to speak.

"The investigation is complete, Mrs. Larson. There was no fetus, no placenta, no cord, no blood."

For a moment their eyes met, and then Janet said, "Oh. So you had a little visit from our friend in the black cape, too."

"He won't bother you anymore," Grant said.

They both looked at him, with a mixture of hope and dread on their faces.

"It's over. Forget about it," Grant added.

"Is it?" Janet asked.

"For you two, it is. He's got plenty else to keep him busy. And Halloween is over."

Later, much later, after they all had gone, and the sun was sinking into the purple west toward another dark night, Grant thought, just before he slept a blessedly dreamless sleep, "Until next year."

SIMON CLARK

THIS RAGE OF ECHOES

The future looked good for Mason until the night he was attacked…by someone who looked exactly like him. Soon he will understand that something monstrous is happening—something that transforms ordinary people into replicas of him, duplicates driven by irresistible bloodlust.

As the body count rises, Mason fights to keep one step ahead of the Echomen, the duplicates who hunt not only him but also his family and friends, and who perform gruesome experiments on their own kind. But the attacks are not as mindless as they seem. The killers have an unimaginable agenda, one straight from a fevered nightmare.

ISBN 10: 0-8439-5494-9
ISBN 13: 978-0-8439-5494-4